Books by Sharon Duncan

The Scotia MacKinnon Novels

Death on a Casual Friday

A Deep Blue Farewell

The Dead Wives Society

The Lavender Butterfly Murders

Quantum of Evidence

The Officer St. Claire Novels

Going Dark

Our Agent in Mayfair

sharon duncan

going dark

an officer st. claire novel

Western Isles Press
Gig Harbor, Washington

westernislespress@gmail.com

Going Dark

Copyright © 2017 by Sharon Duncan

ISBN 978-0-9993949-6-0

Cover photograph and logo by Getty Images
Interior and eBook design by W. Bruce Conway

First published in the United States by Iona Press
Second edition published by Western Isles Press

Digital Edition August 2017
ISBN: 978-0-9993949-0-8

Print Version October, 2018
ISBN 978-0-9993949-7-7

Distributed in the United States by Kindle Direct Pubishing

Dedication

For Nan Droz
1934 - 2017

*Cherished friend, first reader,
purveyor of style and grace.*

Part One

The owls of Minera fly only at dusk.

—Georg Wilhelm, Friedrich Hegel

Chapter 1

Deborah Mackenzie, Deputy Director of MI5, did not believe in coincidences. The early morning incident in Mayfair following the Friday murder of St. Claire's asset in Tavistock Square was no exception.

On Saturday Deborah awoke at half-past seven in the bedroom she shared with her husband Ian and a Havana Brown named Cat. Careful not to wake Ian, she crept into the bathroom. While trying to make sense of the murder, she'd been pulled into a late-night kerfuffle with Ian about why he needed to spend the weekend in Paris following the biological sciences conference. The fact was, she knew why he was staying on.

After showering she toweled off, dried her long blonde hair and arranged it in a smooth French twist. Mentally preparing for the hastily-arranged meeting with the new Deputy Director of Ebony 13 and then the debriefing with St. Claire, she chose the black pantsuit, a crisp white shirt open at the throat, the gold omega. Shoes in hand, she tiptoed down the long spiral staircase and into the kitchen. She checked her personal mobile she'd left charging on the breakfast bar, found the text message light blinking. She unlocked it, stared at the text from Black Irish. *Available Saturday or Monday. U*?

If only she'd never attended that bloody hen party.

She deleted the text, opened a can of chunky tuna for Cat, then brewed a cup of green tea. She carried the cup of tea into the drawing room, opened the drapes covering the floor-to-ceiling glass sliders. All was misty on the flagstone terrace. Across the barberry hedge she caught a glimpse of their neighbor prowling in her own garden. The neighbor was mad for gardening and the plot between the two houses was dense with tall grasses and row upon row of exotic herbs.

She collapsed onto the sofa, groped for the TV remote, listened to the red-haired anchor deliver the morning news. Whenever she turned on the telly it was with the lurking fear that some new horrific catastrophe had befallen the planet. Or worse, her own patch of the United Kingdom.

Today the local news was about par for a weekend. An East London constable had died in a high-speed car chase. An irate passenger on the Underground was going about shooting out CCTV cameras. Flooding continued in the north as a result of the weeks of constant spring rains. The international scene was more disturbing: 10 foreign tourists being held at gunpoint by masked terrorists in Kuala Lumpur and 14 people shot at a casino in Las Vegas. Searching for more details on either event, Deborah began to surf channels, stopped suddenly by the image of a news reporter standing in a blackened cobblestoned street beside the charred, mangled remains of a small vehicle. With indrawn breath, she listened.

. . . an explosion at 6:18 a.m. this morning in Mayfair . . . victims are the Honorable Earl of Axmoorland, Lord Jonathan St. Claire, his wife, the former ballerina Carmela Aragon, and an unidentified woman who was asleep in the upper floor of the residence on Canterbury Mews when the vehicle exploded. All three were transported to St. Thomas hospital. Responsibility for the bombing has been claimed by an unnamed pro-ISIS splinter group.

Sod all. Deborah put the cup of tea on the side table with a shaking hand, staring at the blue and white panda cars.

"What are you doing up and about so early on a Saturday?" It was Ian, standing behind the sofa. He laid one hand on her shoulder which she resisted shrugging off.

She continued staring at the chaos on the screen. An unnamed ISIS splinter cell? *God knew, they would claim responsibility for any atrocity. Was the attack related to St. Claire's Syrian asset? Some connection to the surveillance that Officer Johar was doing?*

"I said, Debs," Ian repeated with an edge to his voice. "You're up early. Bloody hell, isn't St. Claire one of yours?"

CHAPTER 2

Kate St. Claire, MI5 surveillance officer, found the long white florist box on her doorstep when she returned home to Canterbury Mews from Thames House on Friday afternoon.

It had been a day of endless rain and endless frustrations.

Her early morning workout at the dojo cancelled because of some kind of electrical problem.

A morning staff meeting dominated by the usual internecine politics of "G" Branch and a petulant secretary seconded from MI6 across the river.

Then the maddening wait for her informant, Jamila Fakhouri, code name Sheherazade, the wife of a Syrian physicist allegedly working for the Iranians. Seated at the wrought iron table under the orange canopy at the café on Clifton Street, she'd sipped the white coffee, scanned the passing pedestrians for a glimpse of Fakhouri, and considered the recent poll that three out of four U.K. women were spying on their men. Kate also reminded herself that running a confidential informant could be a double-edged sword. That many of them were criminals and loaded down with a lot of psychological baggage. Fakhouri wasn't a criminal; she'd been a walk-in at Thames

House, which didn't mean that she didn't have her own agenda.

After an hour, Kate gave up and left the café, hoping for some word that Fakhouri was safe, that her husband hadn't discovered her clandestine meetings with an MI5 officer.

Back at Thames House there were no messages. Her superior, Deborah MacKenzie, was closeted with the Counterterrorism Task Force. Her associates' cubicles were empty and she'd headed out into the April downpour. She'd searched in vain for a taxi, wondered if God was punishing her for some unknown transgression by removing all the taxis from the streets of London, finally put her head down and bolted for the Underground.

Kate shook the raindrops off the white box, unlocked the red door. Inside, she nudged the door closed with one boot-clad foot, put the box and her shoulder bag on the hall table. She entered the disarm code into the security system, turned back to the box. Before she could open it, her private mobile rang. It was her father. She moved into the kitchen where the mobile reception was better.

"There's a carburetor problem with the Bentley, sweetheart. The mechanic can't see to it 'till Monday. Neighbors are making a bloody ruckus about the new survey and I've got an early tee-time tomorrow. Nothing I couldn't miss, but if you plan to stay in town for the weekend, could we borrow the Spider? Hate to inconvenience you."

Kate did plan to stay in London for the weekend and seldom drove the Alfa Romeo in the city. Knowing Lord Jonathan hadn't willingly missed a Saturday round at the Royal North Devon in a decade, she agreed to leave the Spider out before she went to bed.

"Splendid. I've got the duplicate key. We'll get a cab, pick it up early tomorrow and be off for Millview before you get your eyes open." He chuckled. "Especially if you're seeing that banker friend of yours tonight. Say hullo for me."

Kate pressed the End key, left a reminder sticky note on the kitchen door. Moving back into the entry hall she was nagged by what could have happened to her The antique longcase clock began chiming and she returned to the white florist box. Inside she found a cellophane-wrapped bouquet of long-stemmed dark red roses. So dark that in the dim light of the hallway they almost appeared black. She removed the bouquet, spied a smaller packet of petals on the bottom of the box and a small card. The handwriting on the card was familiar: *Imagining you by candle-light among the petals. Pick you up at 8. Dinner at The Greenhouse. T.*

Friday night dinner was a standing date with Tariq Kassar. Wondering at the roses' significance, she returned to the kitchen, filled a vase with water. She arranged the elegant blossoms in the vase, remembering the winter day she met the Lebanese banker. Snow had been falling all day on London. Big fat flakes that settled softly on your hair and tangled your eyelashes. Christmas carols spilled from loudspeakers. From Carnaby Street to Camden Hill Square to the upscale boutiques of Bond Street, the city on the Thames was in holiday attire. Kate's father, Lord Jonathan, gave a heated speech that day in Parliament, exhorting his fellow peers not to confuse murderous extremists with true followers of Islam. Her mother had a head cold and was staying in with a hot toddy, so at her father's behest, Kate accompanied him to the reception in the House of Lords honoring a delegation from the Muslim World League. It was Lord Jonathan himself who introduced her to the tall investment advisor. That was 16 months ago.

Now, after a muddled day, dinner at The Greenhouse, an oasis of tranquility in central London. Kate smiled, retrieved her shoulder bag and headed for the curving staircase.

Perhaps the day could be saved after all.

Chapter 3

Westminster, London

In the dark wood-paneled dining room of the gentleman's club once known as Mrs. White's Chocolate House, the Friends of the Prince finished the roasted grouse by two o'clock. The serving dishes were removed and the porter discreetly disappeared beyond the closed doors. Peter Szabo, founder and CEO of Juno Capital Management, shifted in the carved wooden chair and scanned the faces of the Friends. Two Dukes, one Earl, two bankers, one Duchess, one high-tech billionaire. And Sir David Chaucer, chief of MI6. Szabo inwardly smiled at the thought of the machinations that must have taken place to allow the presence of two females in the ancient establishment.

All eyes were riveted on the Prince who was seated before the curtained bow window. Outside the room, heavy rain sheeted against leaded window panes.

"Their civilization goes back to 6500 B.C. They've suffered indescribable atrocities. Saddam gassed thousands, then straffed the survivors when they attempted to escape. They're a people without a country. They're being obliterated, their women sold into slavery, and the Western world just yawns. Something has to be done. If we don't do it, no one will. If we don't do it now, it will be too late."

Peter Szabo shot a quick glance at Sir David who was laconically silent during the Prince's quiet tirade. The two men's friendship extended back to student days at Cambridge, a connection reinforced by their marriages to two sisters. "I thought the P.M. wouldn't get involved because of blowback," Szabo offered. "Are you suggesting we launch The Blessed Invasion, your highness?"

"No. No. Last thing we want is to play into the prophesy. It's not a question of manpower. They have that. And womanpower. What they lack are weapons."

"And nobody dares help because they're so bloody afraid of offending the Turks." This from the Duke of Waverley.

"Ignorance is bliss, especially on the Bosphorus." An interjection from the 8th Baronet of Blackvale.

"May I ask, your highness, specifically what weapons you have in mind?"

"Assault weapons. Small arms. Ammo. RPG's. They need everything." He nodded to the 5th Earl of Westmoreland. "Geoffrey has the list."

The Earl pulled one sheet of white paper from a thin leather portfolio and passed it to Szabo who scanned the neatly printed enumeration of weaponry. "We're talking about several hundred million pounds sterling. Are you suggesting that Juno fund this venture philanthropically?"

"No, Peter, not at all." The Prince fingered his pale blue silk tie. "We know how generous JCM has been in combating altruistic evil, but funds are available. Three hundred million."

"Have you approached our own aeronautical and armaments vendors?"

The Prince frowned and shook his head. "We can't. Because of the connection with the Saudis."

"Ah, yes, there is that." Szabo lifted his glass of 50-year-old Scotch, sipped the peaty liquid, replaced the glass on the table top, glanced again at the list. "You think anything can be accomplished without boots on the ground? Or wings in the air?"

The Prince shrugged and glanced around the table. "We think weapons are better than nothing. Unless Section 10 is available." He let the statement hang in the air for several long moments. "If they are, then I know the Cousins would be willing to make a monetary contribution."

Szabo quirked his left eyebrow. "And my role would be what, your highness? Procurer? Expediter? Money launderer?" Waiting for the answer, he considered how the op would involve Gingerman.

The Prince spoke quickly. "We want a hundred 'chutes blossoming in the skies over Erbil. As if by magic. No footprints that can be traced back to the U.K. through loose lipped armaments dealers. No financial tracks. You are the deniable conduit." He paused, then added, "We understand you have a cargo plane."

"Two, actually."

"Excellent. We know you have the connections. What you did in Nigeria and Sudan, nothing short of a miracle." The Prince twirled the amber liquid in his glass. "There will, of course, be a reasonable commission. For you and your agents."

"What financial institution will the Friends be using?"

The Prince glanced across the table to the one Scot among the group. "Julian?"

"Riggs, your highness. The funds were deposited ten days ago."

Peter Szabo's left eyebrow quirked again. "In spite of their ostensible link to the CIA?"

"Not in spite of, Peter. Because of. Time is of the essence, of course."

"Right. Operation White Blossoms begins today, your highness."

Half an hour later, Peter Szabo and Sir David Chaucer proceeded down the stone steps to where Sir David's black Mercedes S550 was idling on the opposite side of the street. Inside the vehicle, Sir David directed the burley black driver to their destination, then closed the sliding privacy partition. "You didn't exactly answer the question about Section 10, Peter," Sir David murmured once the men were buckled into the back seat. "Are they a possible?"

Section 10 was the hand-picked unit of battle-wise, multinational, private military force that had turned the tide in Niger the previous year.

"I'll see what Koslov thinks."

Both men were quiet with their thoughts. As the Mercedes turned off St. James Street onto The Mall, Sir David broke the silence. "About the family thing we discussed last week, Peter. Can we extricate Kate from the tangle?"

Peter Szabo smiled. "White Blossoms will kill two birds with one stone."

"So Gingerman will be the liaison?"

Szabo smiled. "I gave The Fox a heads-up. They're meeting as we speak."

CHAPTER 4

The bearded man known as The Fox leafed idly through the pages of The Gentlemen's Journal, one eye on the faded blue door of The Cabbage Leaf.

The café was a cliché. From the trays of cold *meze* on the wooden bar top to the flaky baklava and the faded brick facade fronted with tall pots of red geraniums. Not the sort of place Graham Greene would have chosen. The Fox hadn't chosen the venue for the tucked-away entrance in an alley nor for the iconic menu. He chose it because Mustafa Talal, the Cabbage Leaf's owner, also owned a sister café in Dubai. He chose it because a portion of his childhood had been spent in Istanbul and the café felt like home.

He checked his watch. Gingerman was late. He took a sip of the pomegranate juice and stared across the lounge at the framed portrait of the fierce mustachioed warrior in khaki and gun belt, dagger at the ready. "My George Washington," Mustafa had proclaimed proudly.

Inside The Gentleman's Journal a thin thumb drive rested in a cut-out pocket along with the passports. The Fox would have preferred to handle the assignment electronically with no personal contact, but Szabo had been adamant. "Do it in person. Look him in the eye. You've been handling him for five years, but Gingerman is still an unknown with a bloody lot of baggage." And then the final admonition a hour ago: "White Blossoms has zero margin for error. Be sure to mention the fatwa."

The Fox had no idea how both he and the asset he was waiting for had been extricated from MI6 and now reported to the CEO of one of the world's largest private military contractors masquerading as a hedge fund. Gingerman had been a coup for The Fox, a long recruitment that paralleled the asset's slow disillusion with the murderous extremes of Islam and the simultaneous disenchantment with Fatima.

The blue door opened. A slender dark-haired woman in a black Mackintosh and grey beret entered, shook the water from her hat, took a seat across the lounge. After shedding her coat she settled onto the settee, pulled a mobile phone from her orange leather bag, began thumbing a text. Feeling The Fox's gaze, she looked up, looked past him, went back to her texting. A fit bird, he noted, with beautiful eyes and a rose tattoo on the inside of her left wrist. She wore black leather boots and the short black skirt revealed several inches of well-toned thigh. Finding nothing amiss, he continued leafing through the Journal, scanning the article on What a Gentleman Wears to Bed, considering operational alternatives if Gingerman proved uncooperative.

The door opened again with a gust of wind. A wiry, black-haired, olive-skinned man wearing faded jeans and dark green hooded windcheater stepped inside. The man closed the door, quickly scanned the windows across the lounge that faced on the alley. He removed the windcheater and took a seat in the chair across from The Fox. "Sorry to be late," he murmured, picking up a menu. "A bit of diversionary backtracking."

Across the lounge the waiter served a small cup of Turkish coffee to the woman with the orange bag, then headed toward the two men. "*Merhaba*, gentlemen. What may I bring you?"

"*Merhaba*, Murat. I'll have the tarama salata."

"Excellent. And for you, *effendi*?"

Gingerman put down the menu. "An ale. Dark Star."

"Why the diversion?" The Fox asked, watching the waiter move back toward the swinging doors to the kitchen.

"Just a feeling. Turned out to be nothing." Gingerman glanced toward the woman who was sipping coffee, mobile to one ear. "What's up?"

"You need to leave London."

The two men exchanged a long glance. "I've been compromised?" Gingerman asked."

"A fatwa has been issued. And there is a new assignment. Operation White Blossoms."

"A fatwa. Wonder what took so long. How much time do I have?"

"48 hours."

A raised eyebrow and a frown. "The itinerary?"

"For now, Geneva and Dubai."

"What is my legend?"

The Fox tapped one finger lightly on The Gentleman's Journal and moved it toward the center of the table. "Mehmet Celik. Dubai investment banker. I.D., passports and itinerary. Details are on the thumb drive. Get a new phone. I'll use Rumi for the coded comms."

Gingerman smiled. "Always the poet."

"You know the protocol. Go directly to the bank in Geneva." The Fox glanced toward the swinging door to the kitchen. "When you land in Dubai, Mustafa's brother will meet you. He has a house for you. The servant is vetted."

"Ah." Gingerman glanced around the room. "The Baklava Connection," he said drily.

" We've set up an office for you."

"In the Burge Khalifa, I presume."

"Close."

An indecipherable shadow passed over Gingerman's face. "I have to tie up a few loose ends."

"One last shag?"

Gingerman's dark eyes were unfathomable. He did not answer.

"Make it fast." The Fox glanced across at the woman with the tattoo, sipping her coffee, still immersed in conversation with her mobile. "When you leave, go by way of the kitchen."

CHAPTER 5

Tower Hamlets, London

Nadia Sultan, dressed in her favorite blue abaya, emerged from the Shoreditch tube station. On Brick Lane, she joined the crush of pedestrians, detouring around three giggling teenaged girls in hijab and skinny jeans. She walked briskly, taking deep breaths. A cool, damp wind swept the street. Nadia adjusted the hijab around her face and thought about the role fate had played in discovering the slut her husband was sleeping with.

Fate and a facial recognition program.

It all began at the British Museum. One of the women she recognized from the mosque was talking to the tall woman with long chestnut hair. They were standing in front of the exhibit of Arabic calligraphy and from nowhere came the impulse to snap a photo of the two. A photo that her flatmate identified and Dervish ran through the facial rec program.

Dervish was good, a Checken hacker who'd been generous in transferring the dark fruits of cybercrime into the Sisters' bride fund. He'd also helped numerous times with passports. She knew him only through encrypted emails and she had the impression he fancied himself some sort of religious Robin

Hood, abetting an uprising of true believers against infidels. For a price, of course.

She poured over the photos Dervish turned up. High fashion poses of a younger version of the woman. A newspaper photograph of the same woman standing next to a man in mufti beside a small airplane. Thanks to the cybersleuthing, now she knew the slut's name and she knew where the slut lived and where she worked.

Nadia pulled the scarf tighter about her face, pausing at the news vendor to scan the black headline in the *Sentinel* that proclaimed PUSHBACK ON MUSLIM PATROLS ENFORCING SHARIAH LAW IN E. LONDON. On the corner of Brushfield Street three dark-skinned young men in white shirts and faded blue jeans lounged around a scarred wooden table on the sidewalk. Smoke from their cigarettes drifted overhead. They eyed her boldly. One made a comment to his companion. She twisted the ring she wore on a gold chain and pulled the hijab tighter about her face. She needed to get back to the flat, finish preparations for the evening.

She reached into her leather bag to check the time on her mobile. It wasn't there. Puzzled, she stopped and searched carefully, running her hand all the way to the bottom of the bag, checking the small inside pockets and the large outside one. Not there. She'd had lunch at the curry house with Salima, her flatmate. She remembered checking for texts. She must have left it behind. She would ring the restaurant, pick it up later.

It was Salima, seconded from her job at the Home Office to assist in translations at "G" Branch who had supplied the missing details on the slut. From the beginning, she mused as she turned into the Old Market, it was as if someone had been dropping bread crumbs in the darkness of the forest.

Kismet.

CHAPTER 6

Black Raven Wharf, London

In the 15th floor office of Juno Capital Management, Peter Szabo lifted the cup of black Kenyan coffee, sniffed the rich fragrance, and scanned the daily update on the activities of JCM's projects and interests around the globe. The offshore hedge fund. A report on the latest suicide bombing in Istanbul. A watch list of natural gas stocks.

Surprisingly, given the current global financial climate, the hedge fund continued to be healthy. Szabo penciled a note to give the fund manager a bonus. He leaned back in the chair and watched the late afternoon rain inundating the docks, then picked up the Qatar folder and read to the end of page one when his private phone rang. It was Dominic Koslov. "Yes, Dom."

"It's Beatriz. She was killed this morning."

"Killed? I thought she was on holiday with her sister. What happened?" Beatriz was Koslov's former security partner when both were working with Section 10 in the Sudan, a striking ebony- skinned Brazilian who had been trained in police work in her native country before fleeing a jealous husband. Dom had soothed her broken heart and trained her in hostage retrieval.

"She cancelled to help a family whose daughter was abducted in Thailand on a birdwatching expedition. When she went in to get the girl, she underestimated the kidnappers' firepower. The girl is still hostage."

Szabo took a deep breath. "Dom, I am so sorry."

"Just wanted you to know. Life stinks."

The line went dead. The intercom on his desk buzzed. "Count Misha on line 7, sir."

Szabo pressed the button for the encrypted line. "What news, my friend?"

"I have found your man."

"Do I know him?"

"Dmitri Semchov."

"Russian?"

"Russian and currently domiciled in Morocco. His company is PanAsia Agricultural Enterprises. He was a protégé of Viktor Bout. He has found vendors for nearly all the items on your list except for the AK-47's."

"What's the problem?"

"The order says 'source directly from Kalishnikov.'"

"Yes, we want the best, unused, in the box."

"Kalishnikov says they need three months to fill the order."

"That's unacceptable." Peter Szabo listened to the silence on the line. "I will make a phone call."

"We can go to the Bulgarians for the ammo," the count said.

Szabo considered. The Bulgarians had furnished the ammo for the Section 10 op in Nigeria. "Yes, no problem. What about the export licenses and end user certificates?"

"Semchov will arrange them."

"Semchov is trustworthy?"

"Trustworthy is relative. Of all of those who fly below the radar, he's the best. Viktor taught him well. After you make your phone call, he will place the orders. Please do not go around him on this."

"Understood." Szabo pressed his lips together and stared out the window where heavy rain obscured the River.

"Semchov suggests the items be shipped to Algeria or Morocco. Your planes should meet the cargo there and ferry it on to the final destination. You will need to arrange for the flyover permissions. I know you do not wage war, Peter, but neither Semchov nor I want to know where the cargo is going."

"I will talk to my pilots and get back to you. Where will my man meet Semchov for the transfer of funds?"

"Geneva. Banc Privat de Geneve. On the 14th, at ten a.m. If your agent approves of all the documentation, the funds should be transferred per Semchov's instructions, with a 2% commission to me and 2% to Semchov, as we agreed. I will courier Semchov's identity today. I will need the same from you for your agent to my Vienna address. Are we on the same page, my friend?"

"We are on the same page, Misha. Well done. I will get back to you on the Kalishnikovs."

Szabo pressed the End Call button, replaced the handset and reached for his encrypted mobile. He

scrolled through the contact list, found his man, dialed the number.

A man answered in Russian-accented English.
"Peter. Good to hear your voice."

"And yours, Mr. President. Congratulations on
your successes in the Levant."

"One does what one must do. How may I help
you?"

"We have a new op, assisting the enemy of your
enemy. We need AK-47's but we are told they are not
available for three months."

"How many?"

"Ten thousand."

A soft whistle, then, "Well done, Peter. I will
make a phone call. My assistant will call you. Consider it done."

"Spasiba, Mr. President."

Szabo pressed the End Call button and turned
to the laptop computer, opened the White Blossoms
folder. He scanned what Count Misha called his
shopping list.

AK-47 assault rifles (10,000), acceptable only if pur-
chased directly from Kalishnikov
AK-47 ammunition (22 million rounds)
Rocket propelled grenades (5000)
Anti-tank missiles (5000)
G3/G6 Assault rifles (16,000 + 6 million rounds)
Hand Grenades (10,000)

He stared at the first item on the list for several
long minutes, the most widely used weapon in the

world. By some estimates, as many as 500 million in circulation on five continents. Weapon of choice for child soldiers, invented by Mikhail Kalishnikov who had been exiled to Siberia and survived the turbulent times under Stalin, Khrushchev, and their successors.

He swivelled in his chair to gaze out at the darkening, rain-drenched city. A lot was resting on The Fox and Gingerman. Much would be lost if one of them fucked up. Semchov was a total unknown, but Misha had never failed before.

He turned back to the computer, smiled, and added two additional items which would come out of JCM's percentage.

SUGV Bomb hunting robots (25)
MQ-1 Predator drones (10)

CHAPTER 7

Westminster, London

At half nine on Friday evening, Nadia Sultan exited the tube station and joined the crush of humanity spilling out onto Piccadilly Circus. A quarter moon struggled for presence behind roiling clouds. The temperature was dropping.

She had memorized the map of the area, walked it numerous times. There was a sense of familiarity in the act of crossing the busy thoroughfare and hurrying down Boulton Street, pausing twice as if to window shop. Then a right turn onto Curzon to Audley. Stopping briefly near a pub with its bright boxes of red geraniums and tumbling ivy, she let a group of boisterous German tourists pass her by.

Fifteen minutes later she rounded the corner of Canterbury Mews where a portion of the sidewalk was blocked by a construction site. She moved around the obstruction into the evening shadows of the archway across from the residence at Number 14 where the street light illuminated the red entry door with its brass knocker and small window. No interior lights were visible. Nadia pulled the niqab away from her face and scanned the dark cobblestone street. All was silent. Nothing moved. She located two CCTV cameras, one at each end of the mews. She'd heard that as many as a million cameras were installed in London, most of which were maintained by private companies. She smiled behind the niqab.

Half an hour passed. The moon rose and deeper shadows draped the street. As the skies cleared and the temperature dropped, she was glad for the wool sweater and blue jeans under the abaya.

A pair of headlights turned down the street and a dark sedan halted before Number 8, a two-storey mews house that long ago had been a stable. The headlights illuminated the white sign on the garage door that said, No Parking at Any Time. A man and a woman exited from the back of the vehicle, the man handed something to the driver, and the couple walked to the entry door. The vehicle did a U-turn and drove away. At Number 14 rays of moonlight spilled over the slate roof and silvered the climbing roses on the stone wall beside the garage door. There had been climbing roses in the garden in Damascus. On summer mornings her father would bring in a fresh rose for her mother. After he was killed in Rmeilleh by the infidels, she had wanted to continue the morning ritual, but her mother could only shake her head and wipe away the tears, and six months later she was diagnosed with the cancer.

Nadia moved one shoulder then the other to relax the muscles stressed by the burden of the canvas bag of tools. *C4. Wire for the ignition. Needle-nosed pliers. Detonator. Tilt fuse. Torch.*

She glanced at the Casio, the F91W that had been her graduation gift in Peshawar. Half ten already. She wished she had her mobile. She'd called the curry house, but they hadn't found it. Three times she'd rung her number and three times the calls went directly to VoiceMail. A gust of wind swept through the street. She shivered as another set of sodium vapor headlights turned the corner. The vehicle, with a three-pointed star on the hood, halted in front of the mews house with the red door. The motor stilled, the driver's side door opened, the interior light came on.

Nadia took a deep breath.

The woman brushed her long hair away from her face. She was laughing. Nadia moved further back into the doorway. Replacing the niqab over her face, she was absorbed into the shadows. Her eyes narrowed. She drew a long painful breath. For a minute or so she felt a paralysis so sharp her lungs ached. She forced herself to exhale, watched the man step out of the car and walk around to open the passenger side door. The woman climbed out, he locked the car with his remote. His arm around her waist, the couple climbed the steps and disappeared behind the red door. An inside light came on. The outside light was extinguished. *Breathe*, Nadia reminded herself. *Keep breathing.*

Three minutes passed, or perhaps four. A light appeared in the second-storey mullioned window. Then a tall figure opened the window and pulled the drapes over the opaque curtains. Nadia checked the Casio one more time. 10:45. Exactly on schedule, she watched the two CCTV cameras pan away from Number 14. Nadia took another deep breath and leaned back against the archway to wait, eyes on the upstairs window.

Chapter 8

Mayfair, London

Kate St. Claire stepped out of the black skirt with the handkerchief hem, the phone conversation with Deborah MacKenzie still playing in an endless loop in her head.

The call had come in during dinner at The Greenhouse. Their table overlooked the exotic outdoor plantings and the Scottish langoustines had just been served when Kate picked up the distinctive tones of her encrypted mobile. The caller was Guinevere, Deborah MacKenzie's code name. She felt Tariq's eyes follow her as she headed to the foyer. The call had gone to VM and she redialed. She was the first to speak. "Leopard here."

"You took your time about that."

"Sorry. I'm at dinner."

"Some bad news from the Met. A woman matching Sheherazade's description was found dead in Tavistock Square this afternoon. Throat slashed."

Kate shivered, suddenly chilled. "Who found her?"

"A French tourist."

"Bloody hell. I should have gotten her protection for our meetings."

"She knew the risks," Deborah said. There was brief silence. "Where are you?"

"The Greenhouse."

"Nice choice. Watch your six on the way home. We'll talk tomorrow. My office at ten." The connection went dead. Returning to the table, unable to share her informant's murder with Tariq, Kate had chattered about her parent's plans for the weekend, tried to focus on what Tariq was saying about the Sufi Council for Peace, and ultimately drank too much red wine.

She stared blankly into the mirror above the bathroom vanity as she removed the ivory satin camisole. *Sheherazade had two small children. What would become of them? Had her husband followed her? Did he know about the previous meetings? Did he have any idea who his wife was meeting with?* From the adjoining room she heard the breathy notes of a Japanese flute. She removed the ivory lace thong, pulled the black lace gown over her head, and padded into the bedroom. Tariq was in bed. Large candles flickered on both bedside tables. Dark red petals spilled over the pillows and sheets. She hesitated by the bed for several seconds, willing the tones of the flute to erase the horror of the phone call.

Shaking her head to clear the image of Sheherazade's lifeless body, she slid into bed. He embraced her, kissed her shoulder, pulled her down onto the petaled sheets. "I have an early morning flight, *habibi*," he said, bending over her, smoothing her hair against the pillow. "I will not be able to spend all night. We must make it memorable."

* * *

Below, from the archway, Nadia watched the thin sliver of flickering light behind the drapes.

Her body quivered. Ten minutes or so passed. The sliver of light disappeared. With a patience nearly supernatural, she waited, inhaling and exhaling. Control was everything.

An hour passed. There was neither light nor movement behind the drapes. Nothing stirred on the street. Clouds scuttled across the moon, darkening the mews.

It was time.

Studying the dark residence draped in moon shadow, she adjusted the niqab, moved out of the inky depths of the archway, and was about to cross the cobblestoned street when the moonlit silence was broken by the harsh sound of a garage door grinding upward on its track. Retreating, she strained to see in the darkness. A light came on inside the garage at Number 14, a small light-colored vehicle slowly backed out and parked parallel to the building in front of the garage. She watched the familiar figure emerge from the vehicle, close the car door, hang the key on a hook in the lighted garage. As he strode to the Mercedes, the garage door came down, the light went out. Tariq opened the door of the vehicle, stared up at the upper floor of the mews house for perhaps three seconds, then quickly climbed inside.

Nadia heard the Mercedes start up, watched it do a U-turn, stared after the red tail lights disappearing around the corner of the mews. All around was silence and the blackness of darkness. Clutching the canvas bag, she approached the small roadster. Sometimes things were easier than expected.

Allah helps those who help themselves.

Part Two
Three months later

When the past no longer illuminates the future,
The spirit walks in darkness.

—Alexis de Tocqueville

CHAPTER 9

Warwickshire, the Cotswolds

At half past seven on the second Monday morning in June, Kate St. Claire reread the handwritten letter with the Provence postmark, tucked it into her travel bag, then refilled her cup from the carafe of coffee on the sideboard. She'd slept badly, awakened by the pain in her right shoulder and 4:00 a.m. dark thoughts of what it would mean to return to London and Thames House and three unsolved murders. Wondering if she was ready to pick up the pieces of a new assignment and soldier on as if she hadn't lost the last vestiges of anything resembling family.

She went to stand at the open French doors overlooking the lush garden of tall lavender. The morning was misty. The pergola surrounding the antique stone urn overflowed with white roses. On the east side of the garden, a sturdy squarish man emerged from the stable leading a large dark horse across the stable yard.

The stable and the Cotswold cottage house where Kate had spent the last six weeks belonged to her cousin, Gwendolyn DeLuca, a London barrister, who at that moment strode into the dining room. Gwen was wearing tailored black trousers and a black-and-white-checked jacket over a white shirt.

She was followed by a white Borzoi named Gorby. Gorby came to nudge Kate's hand as her mobile announced an incoming text. She removed the mobile from the pocket of her jeans. The sender and its content were a surprise: *Some developments WRT Sheherazade. Discuss b4 you meet with the DD? Meet 2day? Carnation*

Carnation was Sara Johar, a "G" Branch intelligence analyst. Kate absently patted Gorby's head and frowned, staring at the text, puzzling out why Johar was contacting her directly and why before her meeting with Deborah MacKenzie. Two weeks earlier, Kate had reached out to Deborah's P.A., asked for an update on the bombing that had killed both her parents, and was abruptly put off. Now the request for a meeting from Johar. What had changed?

"Everything okay?"

Kate nodded. "Sorry, Gwennie. Good morning. Yes, everything's okay." Kate shrugged. "Relatively speaking, of course."

Gwen served herself from the sideboard and returned to the table. "Are you one hundred percent certain you're ready to go back? You can stay on another fortnight. Gorby would much prefer staying here."

"Absolutely sure. I'm going mad."

Gwen gave Kate a speculative glance and tucked into the eggs and sausage. "Five won't fall apart without you."

"My leave is up this week. Meeting with my superior next Monday. I need a few days to get organized."

"They're not going to let you get involved in the investigation."

"I'll find a way. I will find answers."

"You don't have to solve the case yourself."

"Actually, I do. How was your canter?"

"Not much of a canter. Molly's lame. I called the ferrier. You've already eaten?"

"Sorry, I didn't wait. Did an early run and came back ravenous. The eggs are delicious. Likewise the cinnamon buns. You should take Miranda back to Montague with you."

"Ha. Don't think I haven't tried. I'll never lure her away from her Cotswold hills. Or the stable manager."

"You're in full Silk attire. Court today?"

Gwen cut a piece of sausage and nodded. "A Scottish client whose Egyptian husband is intent on taking their son back to Cairo. None of the outcomes will be good. I saw your bags in the hall. Leave in half an hour?"

The drive from Warwickshire to London was usually a matter of two hours or less. On a Monday morning in June tourists admiring the dreamy country estates and stone-built villages clogged the M40. Neither Kate nor Gwen were given to small talk. Gorby watched the passing landscape from the back seat of Gwen's vintage Jaguar. Gwen broke the silence only when they passed the turn-off to Oxford. "I'm worried about Maddy."

"Because?"

"She's gone Goth. Acquired multiple piercings and a shock of blue hair. Become an activist about women's rights in Myanmar. She and a classmate are making a film on human trafficking."

"Important topic."

"She's been interviewing some rather shady characters. I don't like it."

"Have you talked to her about it?"

"We never talk. We only text."

"Better than nothing."

"She's acting out. She was furious when I starting seeing Peter. Went on a hunger strike, became anorexic. She says I was so into becoming a Silk I never had time for her."

"Does she know all the hard work that's behind the right to wear that silk robe and the black rosette?"

"She thinks it's pretentious. Peter and I always made time for her but apparently it wasn't enough."

Peter Szabo, the Hungarian property developer and hedge fund manager who developed Black Raven Wharf on the site of London's old cargo docks, had appeared in Gwen's life six months after her husband died of a heart attack while playing golf.

"Don't beat yourself up," Kate said. "My mother was a full-time mother. I'm sure you remember the stuff I dabbled in before I grew some brains."

Gwen chuckled. "Yeah, your Soho years. I was *so* envious when I heard you were doing nude modeling. And that artist you were living with, René what's his name. Oh, my God, he was gorgeous." She gave Kate a long glance. "Whatever happened to him?"

"When I came back from Milan, he'd packed up and left. Never heard from him again."

"Was Milan worth it?"

"Milan was roses and white wine and cocaine. Not my scene."

Another long glance from Gwen. "You think you'll ever have children?"

"Nappies don't fit very well in the intelligence world." *And apparently neither did parents. Or boy friends.*

Gwen gave her a quick look, exited the M40 and headed downtown. "You ever hear from Tariq?"

Kate shook her head. Where the bloody hell had Tariq disappeared to? He'd left at midnight before the bombing, pleading an early morning flight. A flight to where? Did he say? Had she asked? Not a word when she'd been in hospital, nothing when she was recovering at Gwen's flat in Montague Square. Not one call, not one text. She tried to swallow over the lump in her throat and it all rushed back.

The exploding glass.

Hurled onto the floor, shards of glass in her forehead, her arms, her shoulders.

Blood, dark and red, staining the white silk duvet.

Searing pain followed by shock.

She hadn't been back to the mews house since the bombing. Or what was left of it. She shook her head, momentarily nauseous, never able to erase the image of her asset murdered in Tavistock Square. She pulled her mobile from her bag and texted back to Johar: *4 p.m. @ The Rose.*

"I'll help you sort out your parents' flat when you're ready to sell it," Gwen said. "That is, if you're going to rebuild the mews house."

"I don't know. Have to talk with the adjusters."

"I took the liberty of installing a security system for you."

"At my parents flat? It's not exactly a high crime area."

"Neither is Mayfair. That didn't stop the bomber."
Kate shrugged.

"Peter had one of his geeks vet the new system"
Gwen said. "Totally state of the art. You can check it
on your mobile from anywhere on the planet. Arm it,
disarm it, check the video in real time."

Kate was silent.

"That bomb was meant for you, Kate. It's a miracle you're alive. And if someone wanted to murder
Lord Jonathan, they would have targeted the Bentley,
not the Alfa."

Kate sighed and nodded. "Ergo, the bomber had
to be connected to one of my assignments." *Ergo, the
murder of Sheherazade.*

"I want you to stay with me at Montague until
the Met or MI5 or whoever's working on it clear the
case."

"Appreciate the offer, Gwennie, but I've been
hiding out too long. I'm ready as I'll ever be. I'll take
the tube from Holborn."

"Don't be daft." Gwen checked the time on the
digital display on the console. "15 minutes to spare.
I'll drop you at the flat. Ring me tonight. We're doing a drinks party on Thursday. Will you come? Peter
wants to have a word with you."

"About?"

"He has a contact at the Met who might be able
to get you some info on the bombing. You can't do it
on your own."

Kate was silent for several miles, then asked,
"What exactly is Peter Szabo into? Are the stories in
the press true? That he meddles in foreign govern-

ments and has his own private army? What's the press call it? Section 10?"

Gwen was silent for a few moments, then said, "Peter's spent millions fighting tyranny around the world. He believes it was criminal that half a million Iraqis had to die to get rid of one murderous dictator. That a private force could have done it and the price would have only been a few Republican Guards. But that's ancient history. Right now? He thinks the entire Middle East is tottering and that the African nations will fall one by one and the people who could do something about it are in denial."

"Denial about what?"

"That the jihad is about politics and conquest." Gwen was silent for several minutes, then said, "He sees Section 10 as his small contribution to keeping the barbarians outside the walls. Right now, I think something big is about to come down."

"Any idea what it is?"

Gwen shook her head. "He'll tell me when he's ready. Or not."

Gorby whined softly from the back seat. Kate turned and scratched him behind his ears. "I'm going to miss you, Gorby."

"As for Peter meddling in foreign politics," Gwen continued."Who knows? He tolerates Maddy's shenanigans, treats me like royalty, and the sex is fantastic. So . . . drinks party on Thursday at the penthouse. Sixish. Put it in your diary. By the by, Peter thinks you should leave Five."

Chapter 10

Denchworth, Southmoor

Secrets remain what they are only so long as they are not shared. Not ever, not with anyone. The problem with secrets is that they are a two-sided coin and the dark side of the coin is lies.

In the bar at the Fox and Hounds Inn, Connor O'Connor watched the blond-haired barmaid place the foaming glass of ale on the scarred wooden table. He automatically returned her flirtatious smile and considered how to eliminate the possibility of his secret coming to light.

Until now, Connor never cared a rat's ass what people thought of him. He was a rising star in the exploding cybersecurity galaxy. His work at 5th Domaine took him to Oslo and Frankfurt and Barcelona, building firewalls to protect clients from internet marauders or investigating the latest government cyberattack. Breaching supposedly unbreachable systems. What he did on evenings or weekends with women who called themselves Emma or Danielle or Catarina was nobody's business. Or what he did with what he learned about them.

The double life had begun when he'd agreed to stand in for a friend as a gentleman host on a high-end Mediterranean cruise, whereupon one of the ship guests hired him as an escort for a wedding, which in turn led to the guest's sister hiring him to do a strip act for her hen party where he met a wealthy Parisian whose husband was in the President's cabinet. The Parisian affair was the first of a string of lucrative liaisons with what he thought of as "highly placed women," whose contributions had provided the down payment for the stone cottage in Southmoor he was sharing with "Z," a colleague at 5th Domain. It was the perfect location to live with Ada, the Harris hawk that was the second most important thing in his life.

After the Parisian Affair there had been the Spanish Interlude with Amelia that lasted six months until he received a threatening phone call that he'd traced to the Ministerio de Defensa. The intrigues he'd set up with Emma Whyte were like the rest: He did what he did because he could. Because it was fun. Because the sex was good and *he* got paid for it. Despite her little subterfuges, he knew Emma Whyte worked for the Secret Service. It was just a matter of time before he figured out exactly what she did and what she might be worth.

It was brilliant.

At the end of the day, Connor didn't need extra money. 5th Domaine paid him well. His little trysts were like the hacking: he did them because he could. And until now, he didn't give swag who knew about his double life.

Now he had to be more discreet. The one person who must never learn his secret would be arriving in fifteen minutes, assuming the traffic from Oxford was reasonable, which it seldom was. Unlike Emma and

Danielle and Cataria, Jenny Wen was not a paying client. He intended to marry her.

The door to the pub swung inward. Connor stood and moved to greet the porcelain-skinned, dark-eyed young woman whose uncle was the Chinese Commercial Attache to the United Kingdom.

CHAPTER 11

Once part of a large forest, Knightsbridge is now a mix of red brick gabled mansion blocks, early Victorian terraces and mews houses. The St. Claire pied-a-terre overlooked Garden Square near Walton and Beauchamp Streets, a few minutes walk from Hyde Park and Harrods.

Kate waved as the white Jag pulled away, glanced at the tiny card with the security code Gwen had given her, then turned up the flagstone walk. Sun broke through the dark clouds and the smell of something fresh from the oven wafted from the French bakery across the street. As promised, the porter supplied the key to the flat and insisted on carrying her bags to the second floor and waiting while she entered the code. "The wi-fi password is Churchill 1945, Lady Kathryn," he said. "Here is my card. Ring or text if you need anything. And be sure to try the croissants at Patisserie Bleu."

The door closed with a discreet click. She put the chain on and stood for a minute in the silent hallway. It was the first time she'd been in her parents' flat since before the bombing.

She kicked off her shoes and headed down the hall, pausing at the archway to the sitting room with its gas fireplace and French doors that opened onto a small balcony overlooking the square. An Elena Ferrante novel lay face down on the leather sofa. Beyond the separate formal dining room was the well-appointed kitchen with white granite counter tops.

The flat had two bedrooms, each with en suite bathroom. Both doors were closed. Kate hesitated at her parents' bedroom, then slowly opened the door and scanned the silent room with its king-sized bed and the walk-in closet. Her mother's white toweling robe lay across the back of the vanity chair. The bed was neatly made. A framed portrait of Kate and her twin brother Kincaid sat on the tall bureau. It was taken at Millview the summer before she left for Kenya. Her father's favorite tweed jacket lay across the bed as if he'd intended to take it to Devon and then changed his mind. The door to her father's adjoining office was open, a stack of files and books on the desk, no doubt left there to peruse on the Monday morning he never returned to.

Kate backed out of the room, softly closed the door and moved into the second bedroom. The adjoining bathroom had been under renovation in the spring. She admired the artisan Italian tiles on the walls and floor, let her eyes linger on the oversized jetted tub, returned to the entry hall for her luggage. Half an hour later her meager wardrobe was unpacked, her laptop connected to the wi-fi. Still nagged by the ache in her right shoulder, the one that had taken the brunt of the trauma when she'd been hurled from the bed, she checked the time on her mobile. Three hours until her meeting with Johar.

She glanced at the oversized tub and began peeling off her clothes.

Submerged up to her neck in the warm water and herbal salts, Kate leaned into the jets of water and pondered possible assignments she might face at Thames House the following Monday. Gwen was dead on that Deborah would never allow her to participate in the bombing investigation and she wondered what Sara Johar had discovered about Sheherazade. Johar was a Senior Intelligence Analyst in "G," smart, beautiful, and remote. Born in Mumbai, she grew up in Oxford where her father taught mathematics.

Kate slid deeper into the warm water to let the jets massage her shoulder. Despite the two months of therapy, the muscles never seemed to relax. Propping her feet on the wall at the end of the tub, she contemplated the sad state of her pedicure and dozed. She was awakened by the ringing of a phone. The ringing stopped, followed by a man's muffled voice. She turned off the jets, pulled the stopper on the tub and stepped out. Wrapped in a thick, cream-colored toweling sheet she padded into her father's office. The light on the answer phone was blinking, the call was from Emerson James, the caretaker at Millview. She hit redial. He answered on the first ring.

"Hullo, Emerson."

"M'lady. You're back in London."

"Just returned. Have to get back to work. How is everything?"

"Not so good," Emerson replied. "We missed ye. Lorna don't ken as to why ye went to yr cousins and didn't come home to get well."

"It's a security thing, Emerson. I'll explain when I see you."

"Sooner than later, we hope. There's a problem with the neighbors again."

"The Australians?"

"Ay, and they've been doing more surveying."

"How did that go?"

Emerson sighed. "Had another call today from their solicitor. Unpleasant chap. Said if ye don't see to the 'irregularities,' that's what 'e calls them, with the property lines, 'e's going to the magistrate. Wanted your phone number, but I didna give it to him."

"Didn't my father order a survey last spring?"

"Ay, just afore the accident and the fencing contractor installed the new fence on the boundaries. Now the neighbors are fightin' mad. Something about a 'bloody GPS.'" He sighed again.

"GPS determines a location by triangulation from a satellite. It's more accurate than the old way of measuring line-of-sight distances."

"I don't know about satellites," he muttered.

"Give me the name and number of the solicitor, please, Emerson."

She took down the information, then inquired about the livestock. Two Welch ponies, three Black Angus, and a herd of Suffolk sheep. The ponies were being exercised by Emerson's granddaughters who lived in the village, he told her. The cows had been sold. The sheep, Millview's main source of revenue, were doing fine, whatever that meant. Emerson told her the Bentley was ready for her. Kate promised to deal with the unpleasant solicitor and to ring Emerson back. She put the phone back into the handset, stared out the long window into the walled garden below where a short, brown-skinned man in a gray cap was trimming a tall stand of blue hydrangeas, and began dressing for her appointment with Sara Johar.

CHAPTER 12

Lambeth, London

Walking briskly from the Vauxhall station in the light drizzle under leaden skies, Kate St. Claire arrived fifteen minutes early at The Rose on Glasshouse Walk. Sara Johar was earlier, ensconced at a heavy wooden table in the back corner facing the door, an orange leather bag and coffee mug on the table in front of her. She was wearing large, tortoiseshell dark glasses and a red silk tunic with faded blue jeans and multicolored trainers. Her sleek black hair was styled in a trendy wedge cut. She removed the dark glasses, extended a hand to Kate. "Welcome back, St. Claire."

Kate felt a small metal object slip into her hand. She closed her fingers over it and slipped the thumb drive into her coat pocket. "How goes it at Box 500?"

Johar produced a small smile. "The usual. Yesterday it was a delusional idiot who's gone to the press with a story that Five has been ruining his life for ten years. Bugging his house, destroying his job prospects, harassing him when he travels."

"Have you?"

"We've never heard of him, but the tabloid press believes him." She took a sip of the coffee. "And Taramelli is allegedly running phantom agents."

Gianni Taramelli's career in the Secret Service

had paralleled Kate's: linguist in the language unit, intelligence officer, mobile surveillance officer. "A case of 'throw him to the wolves' to distract attention from someone else's worse transgression?"

Johar shrugged. "At Five, one never knows. He was transferred to E-13."

A waitress in a black uniform and white apron hovered.

"Coffee, white," Kate ordered.

Johar glanced around the pub. The only other customers were a seventy-something couple perusing maps and tourist brochures near the entrance. Kate waited.

Johar took a deep breath. "It's about your boyfriend," she said in a low voice. "The one who did a bunk after your car got bombed." She twisted a silver ring on her left hand.

Kate remembered she and Tariq had run into Johar at the theatre, perhaps a year ago. Kate introduced them. *But how did she know Tariq disappeared*?

"I'm doing surveillance for Deborah," Johar continued. "On a female we suspect of recruiting young women to send to Syria and Yemen. Goes by the name of Fatima. We're liaising with E-13. We found information that connects her to your boyfriend. To Kassar."

"When did you go on surveillance? And what the hell is E-13?"

"Right after you went on Leave. With you away, we're stretched thin. E-13, it's a new department, sole focus is Counterterrorism. Did Deborah tell you about Kassar's connection to Hizb ut-Tahir?"

"I haven't spoken to Deborah since I went on Leave." The waitress placed the cup of coffee on the table, then went through a swinging door to the kitchen. "What connection?"

Johar finished her coffee and leaned toward Kate, propping her chin with one hand. Kate wondered if the small rose tattoo on Johar's wrist was new or if it had always been there. "We think Kassar has been laundering money for terrorists," Johar said. "Hamish wanted to call you, but Deborah said she'd handle it. I guess she didn't."

Not trusting herself to speak, Kate felt her throat tighten. She looked at Johar, then at the cup of coffee. Hamish McTeague, alleged heir to a Scottish earldom, was Director General of MI5. A tall, thin, balding man with pale blue eyes behind black-rimmed spectacles, with a penchant for Italian silk suits. And, if one could believe rumor, an appetite for young partners. At the time of Kate's recruitment, he was Deputy Director. A year later, he was elevated to D.G. and Deborah became Deputy.

"No offense," Kate said quietly, "But your intel cannot be accurate. I thought you wanted to talk about Sheherazade?"

"E-13 is liaising with Scotland Yard. There's a video, of course, the night Sheherazade was murdered. In the Square. And I think Fatima's connected to Tariq Kassar. That's what I wanted to tell you."

"Connected how?"

"Maybe his handler."

His handler. Kate felt a quietness inside her head. A silence that seemed to extend to the entire restaurant. The tourist couple left with their stash of brochures, the door closed without a sound. Laughter trickled from the kitchen. "Tariq had nothing to do with my parent's death. I don't know who the hell this Fatima is or what the fuck is going on. What's E-13 to do with Sheherazade? Or Tariq?"

Johar's mobile vibrated. She checked it, read a text, thumbed in a quick response, put it back on the table. "I'm not sure yet how all the pieces fit together. There's a bloke, D. I. Koslov, Scotland Yard, Serious Crimes Section. Taramelli is liaising with him."

Kate recalled that Johar had always struck her as a bit dippy, but today's conversation was over the top. Was she on drugs? Kate lifted the cup to her lips, realizing that, in fact, Johar hadn't connected Tariq to her parent's death. *She had.* Had it always been there? Hidden away in some dusty subterranean passage in her mind?

The coffee was too hot and burned her tongue. Blinking back tears, she replaced the cup in the saucer with an unsteady hand. "Just because Tariq's in international banking doesn't mean he's involved in money laundering. He doesn't have a *handler*. It's sheer fabrication. Or some twisted agenda Deborah or Hamish is working. Surely Five vetted Tariq. They vet all relationships with Five personnel. Why didn't Hamish say something then?"

Johar glanced around the restaurant. "I have to go. I shouldn't be discussing this with you. Read the file. Here's the password." She penned a line of letters and numbers on a paper napkin, handed it to Kate. "Wipe the file after you read it."

Johar stood up, pulled on a knee-length black leather blazer, buttoned it. "Watch out for Koslov. As for the vetting, and why she didn't tell you?" Johar shrugged. "Deborah has her agendas. And her ambitions. Be safe, St. Claire."

CHAPTER 13

Knightsbridge, London

Kate arrived back at the flat at half past five. She'd followed Johar out of the pub and headed blindly in the opposite direction along the Embankment in the downpour, making her way across the river to St. James Station and back to Knightsbridge. She unlocked the heavy wooden door, entered the security code, and hung her dripping coat in the hall. Removing the thumb drive from her pocket, she headed for her father's office where she roused her laptop from its sleep mode. There was one file on the little portable drive: *Kassar*. She entered the password Johar had written on the napkin: *inthedeepmidwinter1914*. Barely breathing, she stared at the one line of bold black type centered on the title page.

Tariq Kassar aka Issam al-Mat.

Kate continued staring at the line of text for what must have been a full minute before her eyes reluctantly moved down to scan the file.

Born in Damascus . . . father an architect, mother a lawyer . . . three siblings . . . family Sunni Muslims. Mother's family immigrated from Palestine . . .

Kate recalled that Tariq was proud of his mother who came from a poor family. She hadn't known the woman was Palestinian. She read on, synthesizing dates and places, fighting back the encroaching wave of unreality . . . *age 15, recruited by the Syrian Muslim Brotherhood movement . . . age 17, expelled from Syria and moved to Beirut. Age 18, joined local branch of Hizb ut-Tahir.*

Hizb ut-Tahir was the radical Islamic political group whose goal, like the plethora of groups that followed it, was to establish a world wide Caliphate. She continued reading, her shoulder muscles tightening. *. . . attended London School of Economics, received degree in finance . . . ten years in Beirut, working for London Bank of Commerce in the foreign currency department. Frequent travel to Western Europe. Began using alias Omar Javid, . . .* Kate left off reading, stood, and moved into the dining room to the oak liquor cabinet in search of her father's bottle of Macallan Single Malt. She stood for several minutes, staring down at the garden, taking small sips from the crystal glass, then returned to the computer and the dossier.

. . . under which he worked to establish offshoots of the Muslim Brotherhood movement in the immigrant populations in Germany and France . . . worked at Dubai branch of London Bank of Commerce . . . transferred to London . . . May have connections to Nadia Sultan aka Fatima. Kassar disappeared from London on or about April 15. No intel on current whereabouts.

It was lies.

Whoever had assembled the file knew about Kate's relationship with Tariq and was trying to smear her. She herself had done a background search on Tariq when they began sleeping together. Found nothing about the Brotherhood. No mention of anybody named Fatima or Sultan. Shortly thereafter, the Home Secretary appointed Tariq to the Race Relations Council. The appointment, Tariq told her, was because of his work trying to reduce racism and unemployment among London's Muslim communities. *"The jihad has to fail," he'd said, "The cells have no contact with one another. There is no leader. You can't lead a religious revolution from a cave in Pakistan. That is why we founded the Sufi Council."*

Who was *we?* Had there been other names but she hadn't been paying attention? What if he never left the Brotherhood? What if the Sufi Council, whatever it was, was a cover for money laundering? Or was connected to this woman Fatima? Supposing everything she knew about him was a lie and she, Lady Kathryn St. Claire, became a piece of his cover? Thinking back over the months of the relationship, she realized the only acquaintance they'd ever socialized with was Tariq's business partner, whose name she had forgotten.

She stood up wearily, was about to head back to the dining room for a refill on the Macallan when her mobile chirped. A text message from sjohar: *Rousseau@Interpol has a file on Kassar. Bonne chance.*

Kate continued on into the dining room, refilled the glass, stood staring down at the rain-drenched garden, sipping the Scotch whiskey. After half an hour or so she returned to her bedroom. She located her travel bag at the foot of the bed and extricated the letter from Provence.

Dear Kate,

We always agreed when the twins were old enough we would tell them the truth. I wanted to delay such a conversation as long as possible. Jacques thinks it should never take place. Last week Angelique did a genealogy project at her school and she asked to see her birth certificate. I didn't know what to do, so I said I must have mislaid it. I know we can't avoid this forever. I'll appreciate your thoughts. Fondly, Maggie.

The decision she'd made in the sterile white room in the maternity clinic in Arles had seemed the right one at the time. No one could ask for better parents for two infants than Maggie and Jacques Rousseau. It was a decision made before Kincaid's plane disappeared. Made before she returned to London and her parents were incinerated in a barbaric act of terrorism. And now the only blood connections that remained in her life lived 456 miles away. 1200 kilometers. How could she or anyone else possibly tell two ten year olds that everything they thought they knew about their life was false?

Kate pulled the blue upholstered chair to the window and sat. Sipping the Macallan, lost in memories of the days and weeks and months of the torrid affair with MI6 officer Michael Farraday, she watched darkness fall on the garden. She'd known from the day they met that he was married. Hence, all that had followed now seemed a morbid path of self destruction.

When the crystal glass was empty, she switched

on the desk lamp, lowered the blind. After re-reading the dossier on Tariq Kassar aka Issam al-mat aka Omar Javid, she donned the still damp Burberry and boots, hurried down the block to the Windmill where she consumed haddock and chips and returned to the silent flat to send an email to Jean Pierre Rousseau at Interpol.

Chapter 14

Morocco, North Africa

I arrived in Meknes four days ago. I am here to attend the circumcision ceremony of my nephew. The chateau is quiet. This area is seldom visited, although the growing fame of the wines of the Celliers Marocs is luring more European tourists. From the open window of the bedroom I look down on the fields of grapevines and beyond to the crests of the Atlas Mountains. They are blazing gold in the reflection of the setting sun. The air is filled with the scent of lemons. After all the aggravations, all the dreary hours in airports, my soul needs this.

Tariq Kassar, a trim man with an angular face and very dark eyebrows, wrote in Arabic. He paused at the foot of the page. Twirling the gold pen with the black lettering that said, "IFS Dubai," he read the journal entry.

In the past months he'd spent way too much time on airplanes. The sudden flight from London to Dubai. The trip to Geneva, then back to Dubai waiting for word that the first package was ready for transfer. And waiting and waiting and flying to Algiers to discover that there was a problem with the end user certificates for the RPG's and the bomb seeking robots. Too many trips and too many legends. The Egyptian passport on the flight to Dubai, the Canadian one to Geneva and Rabat. Covering his tracks had been second nature in the days of the Brotherhood. And for years he'd gotten away with it. But now there was the fatwa. Had Nadia instigated it? Did she hate him so much for leaving her that she'd found the sympathetic ear of a radical iman? Or was someone else behind it?

He watched dusk fall on the vineyards and felt an ugly shadow creep across his shoulder. Raja'a Sultan, a colleague at the bank, had introduced him to the woman he first knew only as Fatima whose father, a Syrian cabinet minister, was killed by a car bomb blamed on the Israelis. Fatima had introduced him to the world of the East London Mosque. To the English Sisters and Hizb ut-Tahir. To Peshawar.

Fatima and two other Sisters were the first women allowed in a training camp. Most of the men thought it undermined everything they were about. To the chagrin of several, it quickly became apparent that while the women took longer to get up to speed on the physical training and endurance, they learned the weapons and explosives quicker than the men. And Fatima became astonishingly good at hand-to-hand combat taught by the instructor from Sudan.

Tariq frowned. The bipolar stuff he didn't learn about until much later. "My sister is the youngest," Raja'a told him. "She always wanted to do everything our male cousins could do. When she wasn't allowed, she would have a tantrum. When she was eleven, she cut our mother with a knife." She'd hesitated, then continued. "She has a phobia about water. I forget what you call it. When she was fifteen, someone pushed her into a pool. She went crazy and attacked one of the servants. The woman lost her eyesight."

It was Raja'a who pointed out that Nadia liked the extremes of the disorder and hated the levelness the lithium created.

The relationship with Nadia deteriorated when he left the bank and partnered with his Turkish friend to provide financial consulting and investments to the Arabs flooding into London from the Gulf states with bags full of petrodollars. And deteriorated even further when he met The Fox and was persuaded to become an asset of MI6.

He stared through the open window at the mountains, recalling in vivid detail the day he overheard Nadia confiding to one of the Sisters that she wanted to become pregnant, wanted a son so that he could die a martyr and ensure her a place in Paradise. And finally, the last tantrum, the screaming, "I will never let you go. Never." The plastic vial of pink tablets flying across the floor as he went out the door.

The only track remaining from what Tariq thought of as the Years of London Madness was the most recent trip to Sierra Leone. He smiled, thinking of how the hawaldar couldn't have cared less that instead of doing the transfer of funds to London, it was to the Council's account in Cairo. It seemed that money in its pure form knew no politics.

Tariq turned a page in the brown leather journal and finished his entry. *Dusk is falling. Tomorrow after the ceremony, I will go to Marrakesh. It will be good to see Pedro again.*

The scent of roasting meat drifted in the window. The red glow of the sun disappeared from the mountains. A golden silence enveloped the pink stucco buildings of the winery. Tariq closed the leather journal, laid the black and gold pen on top, crossed the room to wash in the large porcelain basin on the wooden bureau. He dried his hands and face and feet with a thick white towel, unrolled the hand-knotted prayer rug, a dark red Berber kilim, and placed it on the floor in front of the window. From the tower over the winery, the first recorded notes of the *adhaan* drifted in the window. With a comforting sense of predestination, he murmured the words of his repentance, took a standing posture facing toward Mecca, and let the melodious chant fill his soul.

CHAPTER 15

Oxfordshire, England

Connor O'Connor watched Jenny Wen's trim figure walk away from the car and turn to give him a wave and a smile before entering her quad. The afternoon had gone well, he thought, Until they'd gone for tea.

Earlier they'd taken Ada, the Harris hawk, to a bank on the flanks of the Downs. The area was honeycombed with rabbit holes. Jenny had gone with him to hunt with Ada once before, but this time, after two hours of watching the hawk twist and turn in the air and swoop down on a rabbit with bone-crunching impact there was a wildness in Jenny's eyes that was beginning to mimic the fierceness of the raptor. Connor adored the wildness almost as much as he adored her baby smooth skin and small round breasts. After they'd returned Ada to her cage, they'd driven back to Denchworth, found the cottage empty, and spent the remainder of the warm afternoon naked in Connor's second floor bedroom. Afterwards, watching her step into the red satin thong and pull the matching camisole over her head, Connor felt his breath quicken and knew he couldn't wait any longer. He would die if he lost her.

Later, over the mint tea and pecan tarts, he

posed the question. Jenny reached across the table to touch his hand. He wrapped his fingers around hers. "Please say 'yes', Jenny."

"Yes, Connor. I want to marry you. I want to live in England. Of course, I have to ask my father. "

"Should we meet?"

"My father is still in Shanghai. My uncle investigate you."

"Your uncle investigated me?"

Connor felt bile rising in his throat, imagining the Chinese commercial attaché perusing a background search on Connor O'Connor, formerly of Dublin. Teenage hacker. Son of an alcoholic salesman dead at 55 and a mother who ran away to Copenhagen when he was eight. Two divorces, one arrest, no conviction. The hacker school where he'd met "Z." The recruitment by 5th Dimension.

A small red flag appeared in Connor's mind's eye.

"My uncle is very careful with me," Jenny murmured, lifting the miniature tart to her mouth. Her fingers were long and slender, the nails painted a pale rosebud pink. "He will have many questions because you are *a lao wai*."

"*What is a lao wai?* What questions, Jenny?"

"He will ask how much money you earn. He will ask where we will live and will I continue my education."

"Of course you will continue your education. What is a *lao wai*?"

"A *lao wai* is a foreigner. My father will have difficulty trusting me to a *lao wai*."

Connor inhaled a long breath. "Can you be happy here? With me? Without your family?"

"My cousin Xia is here. We study at Headington together. She married to an Englishman last year. My father will like me to live near her."

"Where does Xia live?"

"In Shiplake on the Thames. Her husband bought property there so Xia can ride her horse. We will live nearby after the wedding, yes? There is a beautiful house for sale." She reached into her black leather bag, pulled out an estate flyer. "I think Ada will like it. And please, Connor, will you let me fly the hawk the next time?"

Connor stared at the brochure, scanning the description of the estate. *Detached house for sale . . . 4 spacious reception rooms, conservatory, French doors leading to rear garden. £1,450,000.*

CHAPTER 16

Lambeth, London

The intelligence agencies of the United Kingdom include MI5, which is charged with domestic security, and the Secret Intelligence Service, variously known as MI6, SIS, or simply Six, which is responsible for the U.K.'s overseas security activities.

Since MI5 was established in 1909 at 124-26 Cromwell Road, it has been housed in half a dozen different locations: the Wormwood Scrubs Prison, Blenheim Palace Oxfordshire, St. James Street, Curzon Street, and Gower Street. Currently back to a refurbished Thames House, Millbank, where it sits across the River from Six.

On Tuesday morning Deborah MacKenzie arrived early at Thames House, leaving Notting Hill to avoid another serious wrangle with Ian. He'd come downstairs in a thunderous mood, charging into the kitchen with a package belonging to their neighbor, waving the packing list in her face. "The cleaner left this on my desk. What's wrong with the mail carrier? How hard can it be to read a mail label? Probably some bloody Irish witchcraft stuff."

"Fiona is an herbalist. She makes essential oils."

"She's mad as a bag of ferrets. Growing a bloody apothecary in that garden of hers. And what's this?"

still waving the packing list. "Burgundy Bunny Grass. Purslane and cowbane seeds. Who besides a witch orders this crap?"

"Fiona was your mother's best friend. She's not a witch."

Scanning the headlines in the Guardian – *Security Service Underestimating the Domestic Terrorism Threat* – had not improved his mood. "For God's sake, Debs, these tangos are getting funds from somewhere. You don't send thousands of disaffected youth to war zones without some backing. Money doesn't grow on trees in the U.K., not that I've noticed. They're not traveling by bloody camel. Who's funding jihadi brides? Where's the money coming from?"

"Terrorism is being funded by drugs, Ian," she'd replied coldly. "Opium, hashish, you name it. A lot of it coming out of North Africa. As you're well aware, it's child's play to make an online recruitment of whatever idiot teenager decides it's time for *hejira*. My people are running as fast as they can! And so that you know, to follow one person twenty-four hours a day, you need twenty people."

Even though it only required one day of surveillance to psych out why Ian needed to spend so much fucking time in Paris and what her name was.

"What, no drones? All it takes is a dozen geeks at a terminal to survey the entire bloody city. What about that poor sod of a soldier that was beheaded? All those victims on the bridge. Right here in London, Debs. They're not invisible. Why can't these thugs be found *before* they pull a massacre? Where's the bloody intel?"

Where's the intel? How to short-circuit the funds? How to stop the lone wolf attacks? How to surveil the 5,000 EU citizens who'd joined the jihadist ranks? And from her private perspective, how the hell to keep them from returning to the U.K.?

The questions haunted her throughout a nearly sleepless night and plagued her while she walked along the Embankment in a light rain. Waiting at the kerb for the traffic light to change, she wondered how much of Five's inability to identify potential suspects early enough could be attributed to the bend-over-backwards politically correct, let's-not-offend-anyone's-civil rights-or religion stance. If only one P.M. had the stones to call the terrorists exactly what they were. Criminals. Thugs. Monsters.

She went up in the security lift and walked down the silent corridor. The door of her office clicked automatically shut behind her. In the small adjoining kitchen, she brewed a cup of Dragonwell green tea, smiled at the hand-lettered sign over the counter.

After tea break staff should empty tea pot and stand upside down on the draining board.

Back in her office, Deborah reviewed the list of appointments for the day and upcoming meetings that her P.A. had placed on the desk before leaving the night before. Sipping the tea, she considered the name Gillian had highlighted, reflecting on what she'd overheard late yesterday. There was some plumbing problem with her own private loo, so she'd stepped down the hall and had been in a stall when she overheard the secretary seconded from Six tell Gillian that Falcon was back at Six.

Falcon was Michael Farraday, a distant cousin of Deborah's husband, Ian, and a Six operative. Staring out at the windblown rain, Deborah remembered vividly it was a day such as this that she'd found him standing on the corner of Millbank and Horseferry, staring vacantly at the bridge in the downpour. He'd looked grey and desolate and Deborah had inquired after his health. He was fine he assured her, but it was his wife: she was terminally ill. Mentally ill. He was overcome with guilt. Because of his work with Six, he'd been away from their home in Cornwall for extensive periods. Deborah had offered to buy him a drink. He said he had to get back to his flat in case his wife's attendant called.

Shortly after that he took on several assignments in Africa, and that's where he met Kate St. Claire and her twin brother Kincaid. Deborah wondered if Farraday had ever told Kate who had orchestrated the 'girlfrend in Jo'burg' and sent Kincaid on his last mission.

Officer St. Claire was a problem. She'd refused Deborah's offer to extend the Compassionate Leave. The woman was like a bulldog when she got her teeth into something and there was no way in hell Deborah would let her sniff around either the Mayfair bombing case or the murder of the Syrian asset. Not with the new intel from Officer Johar.

Sounds of her P.A.'s arrival leaked through the adjoining door. Deborah turned to her computer and began speed-reading files of memos and reports.

Midway through she found the latest report from Johar. She frowned, clicked through her saved files to the Editorial from the 15 March edition of *The Sentinel* that she'd passed on to Johar with the directive to follow up on the columnist's allegations.

The English Sisters: Quilting Society or Mujaidaats?

A group of local women variously calling themselves the English Sisters, Angels of Allah, and the Sisterhood, may comprise a local sleeper cell with ties to the Islamic State (ISIS). The Sisterhood is thought to be headed up by a 30-something Syrian immigrant, who reportedly attended a training camp, possibly in Peshawar, and became instrumental in forming classes for local females in consciousness raising, target practice, hand-to-hand combat, and explosives. She is also thought to be actively recruiting local women as brides for holy warriors fighting for the establishment of a world-wide Caliphate.

Deborah took a sip of tea, put the clipping aside, and began reading Johar's latest surveillance report. It was five pages in length. It detailed her undercover forays to the East London and Brick Road mosques, to the women's gallery, to Wednesday Tafseer, to the Saturday Halaqa. She had hung out, alternately in hijab and western clothes, at the cafes and shops of Brick Road and Edgeware Road and Chicksand Street. Finally, Johar had been invited to a meeting of the Sisterhood and met its founder, the woman known as Fatima.

Johar had taken the Sisters' classes in firearms and explosives. She was planning to take a class in hand-to-hand combat. She had, she believed, discovered a possible link between the Sisters and the slaying of St. Claire's asset, Jamila Fakhouri, and hypothesized that St. Claire's boyfriend, Tariq Kassar, had a connection to Fatima and also to an MI6 asset known as The Fox. Could Deborah confirm the Six connection?

Deborah's personal mobile chirped an incoming multimedia text. She pulled the phone from her handbag, unlocked it. She recognized the number, even without the name ident. *Missing you. Mon. Nite?* She clicked on the attached photo and gasped. And stared and stared and shook her head, remembering.

It had been the second glass of wine. And the one after that, and way had led on to way.

Chapter 17

It was the last Monday night in May, when Ian was consulting in Stockholm. Or said he was. The third of the trysts with Black Irish. Twice more than she'd sworn would ever happen.

She'd stopped at the wine shop on the way to the MI5 safe house, a nondescript flat in Bayswater that had been compromised and was for sale. She'd arrived early, poured a glass of the Reisling, put the bottle to chill in an ice bucket someone must have added to the inventory to entertain the Ukrainian defector who'd turned out to be a triple agent. Before changing into the silk negligee tucked into the bottom of her attache case, she placed the fee – mentally she referred to it as an honorarium – in the plain white envelope.

The scenario was a repeat of the previous meetings. Trysts, Irish called them. Opportunities for ecstasy. Whatever she wanted, however she wanted it. When they'd finished, she'd watched him rise gracefully from the bed, cross over to the bureau where he'd arranged the wine bucket, pour each of them a glass. She'd let her eyes linger on the long naked muscular line of his back so beautifully downed in dark hair, the perfectly toned glutes. Visually drinking in his maleness, she felt some chemical change occurring in her brain. Dopamine? Norepinephrine? Who knew? Returning to the bed with the box of chocolate truffles, he'd tucked two pillows behind her shoulders. "You should know I'm a chocaholic, " he said, then asked casually, "What do you know about helium-3, luv?"

She'd taken a long sip of the chilled wine. They'd never exchanged personal information. The name on his business card was Dylan Chandler. He called himself Black Irish. He'd hinted that he did something with computer security, that he traveled internationally. That he'd been a teenage hacker. "I never stole anything. Just did it because I could."

He knew her as Emma Whyte. He couldn't know what her job was. Not unless another of the women at the drunken hen party where he'd been the *piece de resistance* had called the number on the business card he'd given each of them. And then engaged in pillow talk. Hamish McTeague was the only one she'd ever discussed helium-3 with. And its top secret connection to Ardnamurchan.

Collecting her scattered thoughts, she'd taken yet another sip of the wine, replied with a chuckle she thought there was a mad scientist somewhere up on the moors who thought the world could be powered by helium, and then had gotten up to shower.

One more time she read Irish's text and studied the photo. When the bloody hell had he taken it? Where had he hidden the camera? How many more had he snapped? And why had he asked about HE3? Security on HE3 was handed over to Five personally by the Home Secretary, who, according to Hamish, made the assignment at the request of the Prime Minister.

None of her searches had turned up any background on a security consultant named Dylan Chandler. Deborah sat for a long time, staring sightlessly at the River below, recalling the sex-and-wine muzzy chitchat, considering the implications of ignoring the latest Monday night invitation.

What a bloody sodding mess.

She buzzed Gillian's intercom twice. Immediately there was a knock on the door that led to her P.A.'s office. Deborah pressed the button near her right knee and the door opened with a buzz. She covered the mobile with one hand and responded to her assistant's cheery greeting with a nod and a request. "Gilly, please forward me St. Claire's CV."

Three minutes later the surveillance officer's photo popped up on her computer screen. Deborah scanned the Registry file. Born and raised in County Devon near Dartmouth. Education was at the Stowe School and Oxford, where she read languages. Spanish, Arabic and Russian. Mother a former dancer with the Spanish National Ballet. Father a barrister. Early work history included fashion modeling and a stint as an art gallery clerk in a Whitechapel gallery. Following graduation from Oxford, she worked as Personal Assistant to Sir David Chaucer at Six's Nairobi station. Deborah paused, wondering about a personal connection between St. Claire and Sir David, who, after the posting in Istanbul, had returned to Whitehall as chief of Six.

St. Claire's Nairobi posting was followed by five years as intelligence analyst at Interpol. Then her return to the U.K. and her recruitment at Five. Brother and parents deceased. No marriages, no children. She wondered why St. Claire had transferred to Five instead of following Sir David to Vauxhall Cross.

Deborah read the Black Irish text one more time and smiled. St. Claire would be the perfect goat, sacrificial or otherwise. She buzzed Gillian one more time. "Gilly, have St. Claire come in soonest."

Chapter 18

"I called you in early because we have a sensitive case." Deborah MacKenzie settled back into her black executive chair and fingered the green file folder on her otherwise naked desktop. "I'm assigning it to you because I know how discreet you are. We're having some upgrading done on the cubicles in CT, should be completed in a fortnight, so feel free to work at home."

Deborah had gotten right to it, following perfunctory inquiries as to Kate's health and well-being, had she a safe place to stay, and the not-so-subtle avoidance of anything leading to a discussion of her parents' murder.

Deborah opened the green file. "We have a person of interest. His name is Dylan Chandler. He hasn't committed any crimes yet, that we know of, but he's making threats. I'd like you to track him down. Put together a dossier soonest. Photos, work history, current residence, known associates, romantic involvements."

"What sort of threats is he making?"

Deborah clicked her computer to life. The movie-star-handsome face of a dark-haired man with intense blue eyes appeared on the flat screen. "Dylan

Chandler is most likely an alias. Perhaps a code name. We think he drives a vintage MG, but we don't have a license tag. We think he works in IT for a firm probably within driving distance of London."

"Is he a security risk?"

"Yes. He may travel for his work, on the continent, even to Asia."

"Can you be more specific about the threats? What am I looking for?"

Deborah frowned. "He may hack into our files or Hamish's files or he may come after the Director."

"You mean come after Hamish personally?"

"Possibly."

"What's the evidence he can do this?"

Deborah took a deep breath, tucked up two wayward strands of blond hair into the French twist. "That's what we need you to find out." She frowned. "I'm not privy to the details, but he's made threats. We have reason to believe he would have no trouble hacking into every file we have."

"What about Ebony 13? Aren't they tasked with domestic cybersecurity?"

Deborah blinked. "How do you know about E-13? I was going to brief you, of course, but it's not been made public."

"One of my parents' neighbors is a free lance journalist," Kate lied. "She asked me. She thinks I work for the Home Office."

"Bloody hell." Deborah tapped the green file, bit her bottom lip. "E-13 is top secret. A shadow branch of GCHQ. The Home Secretary created it because the sodding tabloid press has muddied GCHC to the point where it is totally impotent. What did you tell the reporter?"

"I told the truth. Said I knew nothing."

"And now you want to know why I'm assigning you to Dylan Chandler rather than turning him over to E-13?"

"Yes."

Deborah took a deep breath and realigned the file with the edges of her desk. "Because Hamish refuses to bring E-13 into this. We need you to track down Chandler and find out what leverage we can create against him. Hamish is not to be mentioned. Never. May I count on you?"

"By leverage you mean . . . ?"

"I want to know who Chandler really is and where he lives and works and anything we can use to stop him from blackmailing us or Hamish or blowing the HE3 Project. This is a background and surveilling task, St. Claire. Don't approach or confront."

"HE3? The fantasy of mining helium-3 on the moon?"

"Maybe not a fantasy, St. Claire. Russia and China have already signed an agreement to share the mining. Read the file. It's Eyes Only."

"Right. I'll do my best."

"One more thing. Dylan Chandler moonlights as a male escort named Black Irish. When you're ready to leave, Gillian will walk you out through security with the file."

Kate blinked once and took the green file Deborah handed across the desk. A rent boy. So Hamish's little indiscretions had caught up with him. All mixed up with a pet project of the Prime Minister. What a jolly assignment Deborah had manufactured to keep her out of her parents' murder file. And to keep her out of the office. What was it Johar said? Deborah has her agendas.

CHAPTER 19

Tower Hamlets, East London

My dear sisters: Salaam aleikum!

I salute you from my heart with wishes for love and peace. For the past fifty-two weeks we have discussed the weighty challenges facing Muslim women around the world. I hope your lives have been stimulated by my words.

A special thanks to Anika in London and to Um Lamees in Cairo. You two have been my moral compass during a year of personal and spiritual struggle. I hope my thoughts and the comments posted by you and your sisters have clarified your roles as 21st century Islamist women who voluntarily and devoutly follow the teachings of the holy Qur'an.

In answer to Aisha's question, Is suicide bombing justified under Islam? My answer is based on Surah 4:74 – "Let those fight in the way of Allah who sell the life of this world for the other. Whoso fighteth in the way of Allah, be he slain or be he victorious, on him he shall bestow a vast reward."

In this surah, and in others, it is clear to me that while suicide is against Islam, martyrdom is not. "Suicide bomber" is a term invented by nonbelievers to describe what we in Islam know as a Fedayeen or

Shahid. A martyr. To conclude, I call your attention to the event that occurred in Islamabad whereby 3000 Islamist women gathered and vowed to raise their children for Holy Jihad. Truly, for these women who are willing to sacrifice their own children for Allah, there is no greater devotion or honor. My dear sisters, let them be your inspiration. Please check the sidebar for information on local meetings. If you are planning a hejira, don't hesitate to contact me directly if I can be of help.

Ma'a salama.

Nadia Sultan logged off, checked for new email, then pushed back the chair and began to pace her bedroom. Three months had passed since the fiasco in Mayfair. The failure nagged her daily, along with the memory of the long black hours while she'd kept the vigil below the drawn curtains in the upstairs bedroom in Canterbuy Mews.

The hour was late. She still had to prepare lesson plans for the following day. She moved over to her bureau, opened the top drawer, looked inside. She smiled, picked up the white Qur'an. It fell open to Surah 24. She knew it by heart, except flogging was too good for *el sharmuta*, the slut. She closed the bureau drawer and returned to the computer.

The woman had dropped out of sight. There was no activity at the burned out mews house. No sign of her in the afternoon crowds around Lambeth Bridge or along the Embankment. Nadia needed help. Specifically, she needed Dervish. She typed an encrypted message. *Need updated information and location of Kathryn St. Claire. Also need intel on location of Tariq*

Kassar aka Issam al-mat aka Omar Javid.

About to log off, she spotted a new email. *Dear Fatima, Thank you for your blogs. They help me a lot because my family are not true believers and I feel alone. I want to help with the Caliphate and to help our brave warriors. Please tell me how to help. Alone in Manchester.*

Nadia smiled, hit the Reply key, and began typing.

Chapter 20

Black Raven Wharf, London

Kate St. Claire turned her back on the rising decibels of Peter Szabo's cocktail gathering, took a sip of the Prosecco from the crystal flute, and stared down at the winding River. On a long ago school holiday, Kate and Kincaid must have been nine or ten, their mother declared it was time for an adventure and they had set off to discover the source of the River Thames. They'd followed the waterway from its rising in the Cotswolds some two hundred miles to the North Sea. They'd passed through Oxfordshire and Windsor, floating giddily under the three bridges of Westminster, Lambeth and Vauxhall, ending the adventure at Galleons Reach.

Looking down at the meandering waterway from the wall-of-glass residence, Kate mused that in the right frame of mind, the serpentine waterway could be mistaken for a moat, protecting certain boroughs of the City from dragons and marauding sea monsters. And other areas, not so much.

Across the room Peter Szabo stood beside the polished ebony piano talking to a tall man in blue jeans and light-colored blazer over a black shirt. The man's face was the color of café au lait, craggy, the kind of cragginess that's the product of a lot of mileage at high speeds. His dark hair, cut military style, was grey at the temples. Twice he glanced in her direction. From the opposite end of the long salon Gwendolyn DeLuca wended her way through the guests, nodding and kissing cheeks, elegant in a white satin shirt and dark-blue silk trousers, her toffee-colored long mane upswept in a tousled bun. She carried a frosty martini glass.

Kate heard a male voice behind her back. "In case you're wondering about the bloke talking to Peter, it's Dominic Koslov."

She turned with a smile. It was Sir David Chaucer, OBE, head of MI6, Kate's former superior when she was at the Nairobi station where she'd worked first as his personal assistant, then later as unofficial surveillance officer. He was semi-bald with a fringe of steel gray hair above his ears. He wore a houndstooth jacket over white shirt and flannel trousers. She hadn't seen him since the memorial service for her parents, when he'd appeared without his wife. There were more vertical lines in his face and something about his eyes behind the rimless glasses bothered her.

"Sir David, what a wonderful surprise."

"My dear Kathryn." He pulled her into a quick embrace. "I heard you were back in town."

"How is Ann?" Kate asked. "Is she here or in Devon?"

"Ann left me."

"Sorry?"

"She left me. We'll chat about it later. Tell me about you." His eyes searched her face. "You look quite wonderful, by the way, given what you've been through. Sodding awful experience."

Kate took a deep breath. "Yes, it was sodding awful. Still is, most days. I won't rest until whoever set that bomb is found."

"We were to play a round that morning in April." Sir David twirled the brown liquid in his cut glass tumbler. "Your father and I."

"I knew he was keen to get back for golf. I didn't know it was with you." She hesitated, then continued. "The thing is, Sir David, I can't get any information. Apparently no one has been arrested."

"When are you returning to Five?"

"Next Monday."

"There's someone I'd like you to meet before you go back. He's talking to Peter just now. Name is Koslov."

Kate frowned, recalling the conversation with Officer Johar. "Scotland Yard?"

"Yes." Sir David gave her a quick look, but didn't ask how she knew. "We seconded him from Six specifically to work on your murder case. You should also know that Peter has a couple of super smart geeks he'll make available to you on the Q.T."

"That's good to know." Kate drained the last drops from the crystal flute. "Why is Koslov here?"

"Dom and Peter have a history. Before he joined us at Six, Dom was with Special Forces in Libya and he did training in Afghanistan. Private contract. I think he and Peter met there. Or it might have been another hot spot involving some hostages and Navy Seals."

"I should think the Met would be a bit tame for a former commando."

"It is. He's doing it for me."

Kate eyed the man across the room, taking in the trim physique and well-tailored blazer. "What's his ethnicity?"

"Mother was Cuban, father a Russian engineer. As I understand it, when the Russians finished their Cuban project, his mother refused to move to Russia. I think some of the family got out in the Mariel boat lift. A younger sister and an aunt. For some reason Dom ended up here with an uncle from St. Petersburg." Sir David lifted the tumbler of brown liquid, took a sip, eying her over the rim. "He's in Serious Crimes Section."

Kate grimaced and finished off the Prosecco. "I'm not supposed to talk to anyone about the bombing."

"'Not supposed to' has never stopped you before. Heads up, they're coming over. Be patient with Koslov. He just lost his girlfriend. He's a bit of an arse, rough round the edges. There might or might not be a diamond underneath."

Kate turned to greet her host who gave her a brisk kiss on one cheek.

"Welcome home, Kate. Meet Detective Inspector Dominic Koslov."

"Lady Kathryn. A pleasure." Koslov's tone was borderline insolent, the handshake was brief. His smile didn't quite reach the dark eyes. He gave her a thorough once-over, from her white poet's shirt to her short black pinstripe skirt and sling-back stiletto sandals.

"Detective Inspector. Nice to meet you." *He really is an arse, even though the black silk shirt looks like it might have come from Kilgour.*

Sir David beckoned a waiter.

"Peter was telling me you've just returned to London," Koslov said.

Kate watched the waiter refill the flute, wondered what else Peter Szabo might have shared. "Then I assume you know why I was away."

He nodded. "My deepest condolences on the loss of your parents."

Sir David laid a hand on Szabo's arm, his attention focused on a couple entering the foyer. "The Corbetts are here, Peter," he said softly. "I think Gwen is signaling us for assistance."

Szabo nodded. "Kate, Dom, we'll leave you two to get acquainted. Kate, call me directly if you need help." He pulled a white card from his blazer pocket, handed it to her. "Any kind of help. Please excuse us while we play host."

Sir David touched Kate's arm. "Come by and see me soon," he said, "I'm in Cheyne Walk now." With a cryptic backward glance, he followed Szabo across the room. Kate watched them move away, slipped Szabo's card into her bag, took a sip of the Prosecco. She met Koslov's dark eyes over the rim of the flute.

"I know you're not supposed to talk to me," Koslov said. "When would you like to not talk to me?"

Chapter 21

Awake at 6:00 a.m., Kate went mindlessly through her yoga routine, then blended up a strawberry smoothie, furious at Deborah MacKenzie for the make-work assignment of tracking down a rent boy who might or might not be blackmailing Hamish McTeague, replaying the brief conversation she'd had with Dominic Koslov at Szabo's drinks party. "I know we're not supposed to speak, but Szabo says you might need some under the table assistance and I've got something you could help me with. Might be connected to your asset's murder. Maybe your parents. I'll ring you." That was two days ago.

After a 7:00 a.m. run followed by a take-away fresh orange juice, almond croissant and café au lait from La Patisserie, Kate settled at the kitchen table to work on the green file labeled *Chandler*. The first page contained Deborah's notes on the male escort known as Black Irish, followed by several pages on helium-3. Nowhere in the notes was Hamish McTeague's name mentioned.

Kate found the website for *5starcompanions. com*. The photo and abbreviated profile for BlackIrish4U was halfway down the first page of male escorts. It was a standout for being one of the few that didn't display a semi-naked male torso or specific body parts. What was displayed were classy photos of an urbane man about town: Lounging in the driver's seat of a white sports coupe. Seated at a bistro table against a background of pricey yachts. Leaning against an old stone wall with a river in the background, a small hawk on his outstretched wrist.

Black Irish presented as the ideal companion. *My name is Dylan . . . a young 42, 6' 2" tall, slim build, blue eyes, black hair . . . always smartly dressed . . . confident, articulate, charming . . . with old-fashioned manners . . . your ideal companion for corporate functions in or around London, cocktail parties, a day at the races, a cruise, or whatever you require.* He listed his location as London and Southmoor. Contact info included a telephone number and his escort identifier code.

Exactly the sort of gentleman you would kill to spend an evening with.

There was no indication in the profile as to sexuality and Black Irish was a man of eclectic tastes – *I enjoy theatre, cinema, fine dining and dancing . . . a nonsmoker . . . prepared to travel with a minimum of 2 hours notice . . . my rates are £100 per hour plus expenses . . .*

A tad pricey for a cruise in the Greek Islands, perfect for your cousin's wedding party. All too good to be true, as Hamish McTeague had apparently discovered. Kate wondered if the rent boy was a casual encounter or if Hamish had been targeted.

Four search engines and multiple social media sites produced a list of 18 Dylan Chandlers around the world, complete with photos, three of them in the U.K. None resembled Black Irish. Absent biometric data like fingerprints or an iris scan, the remaining possibility was a facial recognition system. MI5 had a state of the art system. Which couldn't be used because Hamish was terrified that a whiff of his sexual predilections would become public knowledge. Facial rec might produce a searchable name for a vehicle registration, which in turn might produce a residence address. Then surveillance.

Kate wandered into the kitchen, fixed a plate with tuna salad on flaxseed crackers, found a bottle of lemonade and went to sit at the dining table. For several minutes she stared down into the walled garden, nibbled at the crackers, and reviewed her options. Gianni Taramelli was a genius at facial rec. Johar said he'd been transferred to E-13. Wouldn't take him more than ten minutes to find a match if it existed. If it got back to Deborah, the shite would be flying in all directions. If. The other alternative was to follow up on Szabo's offer and see what his IT geek could come up with. But 'going outside' would be even more unforgivable.

She returned to the laptop, copied the best head shot of Black Irish onto her hard drive, typed the email address from memory.

To: gianni.taramelli@fivebranchg.co.uk
From: kathryn.stclaire@fivebranchg.co.uk
Subject: Need Facial Rec. Help?
Can you run the attached photo through your system? Vehicle registration if possible. EyesOnly task for the D.D.G. Much obliged.

Kate's mobile announced an incoming call. An un-known number. She hesitated, then answered it.

"Dom Koslov here. Are you available to continue our non-conversation? In person?

"Yes. When?"

"Two o'clock. West Side Station. 3rd floor."

CHAPTER 22

It was a six-minute walk from the Oxford Tube Station to the West End Police Station. The officer at the front reception confirmed her identity and she found Koslov in a semi-private cubicle on the third floor, Homicide and Serious Crimes section. Papers covered his metal desk. A tablet lay atop a stack of colored file folders, alongside a thin laptop computer attached to a large flat screen monitor. On the wall next to the window, where the only view was of the neighboring red brick building, Kate spotted a framed poster of two tango dancers. The caption read *Tango Para Piano, Café Buenos Aires.*

"Lady Kathryn. Or is it just St. Claire?" Koslov stood up, made a feeble attempt at organizing the loose papers, motioned her to a chair.

"St. Claire will be fine."

"Have a seat. Thanks for stopping by. I need you to look at something."

The insolent tone from the drinks party was gone, but Dominic Koslov did not waste time on small talk. The black silk shirt he wore to the drinks party was replaced by an oxford blue with sleeves rolled up to the elbows, untucked over black denim jeans.

He swivelled the flat screen monitor so she could view it. "CCTV from Tavistock Square Park seven minutes before Jamila Fakhouri's approximate time of death at 1430 hours. Do you know recognize any faces?"

Kate stared at the black and white video that ran for three minutes: first a woman in a white head scarf and long dark skirt or dress entered the square from the right. Her head was partly bent but the face was easily recognizable. It was the Syrian asset, code named Sheherazade, who'd been murdered the day before Kate's parents perished in the bombing. As the woman in the white scarf disappeared to the left out of camera range, a second figure entered the park, wearing dark pants, dark jacket, and a printed head scarf. She – assuming it was a female – was lifting a mobile phone to her head. Her hair was totally covered, only dark brows, dark lashes, and one gloved hand were visible. Half a minute later, a wiry, dark-haired bearded man in white shirt and blue jeans entered the park and followed the two women off-camera to the left. "Play it again, please." Kate watched the mini-scene a second time, stared at the second woman and shook her head. "The first woman is Jamila Fakhouri. Her code name was Sheherazade. I don't recognize either the second woman or the man."

"The man, Emile Giscard, is the one who found Fakhouri's body, lying under a park bench. Name Giscard mean anything?"

Kate shook her head. "Who is he?"

"A school teacher from Marseille. He claims he was in London to visit a woman he met online.

A nurse. Giscard has no criminal record here or in France."

"What do you know about the nurse?"

Koslov scrolled through several pages of his tablet. "Twenty-one year old female from Glasgow. No record."

"Who is the second woman?"

"That's what I hoped you could tell me. I'm calling her Madame X."

"No facial recognition matches?"

"Not yet. Still working on it."

"Are you handling both cases? Fakhouri's and my parents?"

"I have your parents' case. Fakhouri's is being handled by D.I. Grover down the hall. She's not been forthcoming with progress. Talk to me about Jamila Fakhouri. How did she get mixed up with Five?"

"She was a walk-in. She's Syrian, as is her husband."

"Age?"

"Twenty-eight, I think."

"Immigrant?"

"From Damascus, five or six years ago. Arranged marriage. Two young children."

"Why did she come to Five?"

"She lost all of her family. Killed by a rocket in Darayya. She hated the regime and she thought Hassan, her husband, had become a spy for the regime and she was worried he was sending sensitive material to the Iranians."

"What do you know about Hassan?"

"Old Syrian family. Been here since the 19th

century. Made their money in cotton. They own factories in Leeds. Hassan has an engineering degree from U.C. Berkeley. He teaches mechanical engineering at Imperial College. Jamila found some robotic schematics in their FAX machine. She thought he sent them to a cousin in Tehran. We turned them over to GCHQ."

"How many times did you meet with her?"

"Only three. I wanted to get protection for her until we knew what was going on, but she was terrified he would find out."

"How did the two of you communicate?"

"Texting. She refused a burner phone, insisted on using her own mobile. I met her in different places. The last time when she didn't show it was a café in Bloomsbury. Was Hassan arrested?"

He shook his head, shuffled a few papers and peered at a handwritten note. "At the time of Jamila's death, he was teaching a class to 23 students in Thermodynamics. No other suspects. Case still open."

"Were you with the SOCO team at my parents' murder scene?"

"I was not. I was seconded three days later. But believe me, St. Claire, once it was known one of the victims was a member of the House of Lords and another worked for the Secret Service, no bomb fragment went unturned."

"Do you have photos?" Kate asked. For months she had deliberately kept herself from imaging the state of the two bodies after the bombing. Death – natural death after some seven or eight or nine decades of life lived – was difficult. But accepting that on Friday evening both parents were alive, breathing, enjoying a cocktail before dinner, planning a round of golf or a walk with Hawkeye . . . that only produced shock and dislocation. Somewhere in the dark reaches of her mind she had convinced herself that those two emotions would only ever go away when the perpetrator of the untimely deaths had been found.

"Yes. You don't want to see them. Trust me."

Kate was silent, then asked, "Tell me about the bomb."

"That's an interesting question." Koslov riffled through the file of manila folders, pulled out the thickest one, opened it. "There were two bombs actually. An old-fashioned vehicle type wired into the ignition and a second bomb fixed magnetically to the underside of the carriage. A little device called a tilt fuse. The latter explodes when the vehicle moves suddenly or bumps over rough terrain. Both of them detonated. Your bomber wasn't taking any chances."

"Any trace evidence?"

"The entire mews was swept. Except for what belonged to your parents, nothing. No fibers, no hairs, no fingerprints that we can match to any known perps or terrorists. All your neighbors were questioned. No one saw anything. Or saw anything they would talk about. This wasn't an amateur." Koslov closed the file.

"What about CCTV? There are at least two cameras in the mews."

"Yes, interesting, that. One was partially blocked by a construction site and it turns out there is no footage on the other one from . . ." he opened the file, consulted handwritten notes. ". . .from 9:45 p.m. to

1:00 a.m. Cameras came back on at 1:01 a.m. exactly. Great footage of the actual explosion." He closed the file again. "I've been meaning to ask: why did you leave the Alfa Romeo outside the garage that night? Do you usually do that?"

"My father wanted to pick it up early in the morning."

"So you put it out before you went to bed?"

"Yes."

"What time was it when you put the Spider outside?"

"I think it was around 2:00 a.m."

"You always stay up that late?"

"I had insomnia."

Koslov stretched his arms above his head and yawned. "The world is not a nice place, St. Claire, as you and I both know. I wanted to talk to you earlier, a month ago. Your barrister cousin is somewhat protective, y'know. A bit of a dragon lady. She also didn't want me anywhere near your father's associates, which I dutifully ignored."

"Did you learn anything?"

"Only one who would talk was your father's P.A. She seemed quite broken up."

"She's been with him a long time. What did you learn?"

"Your father had a few enemies. I've tracked down most of them. Nothing that would lead to a bombing."

"The bomb was intended for me."

"Why are you so certain?"

"If the carburetor on my parents' Bentley hadn't

been on the fritz, I would have been the first person to turn the ignition on the Spider. My father rang on Friday afternoon. He's collected his share of enemies, but no one except my mother knew they were borrowing the car."

"You can't know that. Who else besides Fakhouri's husband hates you enough to want you dead? Who've you pissed off, St. Claire?"

Kate shook her head. "I'm just a lowly surveillance officer. Before Jamila Fakhouri my assignments were mundane. Several of our officers have more high-profile cases. None has been killed."

"Did you have a domestic security system?"

"Yes."

"Was it set the night of the bombing?"

Kate stared past Koslov's left shoulder, out the window to the roof of the adjoining annex. Had she set the alarm before they went upstairs? She couldn't remember. If she had, how did Tariq get out without setting it off? Did he know the code? And then she remembered. *An incident that had been all but obliterated by what had followed in the early morning. The security system alarm that had gone off a few minutes after she heard Tariq put the Spider out.*

Foggy from the wine and sex, she'd stumbled downstairs, entered the abort code, checked the doors and windows, reset the code, made her way back upstairs to fall into the tumbled bed.

"Well?"

"Yes, it was set."

"Do you carry a gun?"

"No."

"Do you own a gun?"

"Negative. MI5 doesn't kill people. This is London, not Detroit."

Koslov produced a lopsided grin. "More like Detroit every day. The Met has just increased the number of armed officers to 3000."

"May I see a copy of the forensics report?"

"Only person who can release that report is my superior, whose office is upstairs. Assuming the request were to arrive through the proper channels, it is possible that he might share the report with your superior. Who might share with you. But I suspect not." The insolent tone was back. "Have a good think for the rest of the day, St. Claire. If you think of any old enemies with grudges or Fakhouri's husband turns up —" His mobile phone rang. The ring tone was *Yesterday*. "Koslov." Pause. "Are you shitting me? A *virga* over the Heath? On my way."

CHAPTER 23

"Kate, you have to tell him." Gwendolyn DeLuca slid out of her navy blue linen jacket and laid it across her lap. The bartender placed a glass of red wine on the bar in front of her.

"Tell him what? That I wasn't the one who put the Spider outside? Or that the alarm went off when Tariq was leaving?"

"Both. Even if Tariq had nothing to do with the bombing--"

"Tariq had nothing to do with the bombing, Gwen." Kate took a sip of the Macallum she'd been sipping while waiting for her cousin. It was half five on a Friday and the Yorkshire Grey was filled with local solicitors and their friends and nemeses. Golden light bounced off the dark wood paneling behind the bar. Beyond Gwen's shoulder a blond-haired man with a goatee oggled both of them and raised his glass in salute.

"Koslov still needs to know that you weren't the one to put the vehicle out," Gwen said. "If the alarm went off after Tariq left, then it's possible someone tried to get into the house. Might be the someone who set the bomb. Would opening the garage door set off the alarm?"

Kate shook her head. "No. The door into the house would have to be opened. But it might have been the garage door coming down that set off the alarm. Or if I set it before we went upstairs, the delay might have been enough for Tariq to leave and open the garage door."

"Who besides Tariq knew that your parents were borrowing the Spider?"

"I'm not bringing Tariq into this, Gwen."

"Why?"

"He dumped me. I hate him and I don't ever want to see him again, but if he'd wanted to kill me he had a thousand opportunities to do so. As for murdering my parents, he and my dad were friends."

"Did you ever, well, enquire at his office? Or talk to his landlord?"

"Yes, to both. The office space is now occupied by an aid group."

"What about his flat? Did you go there?"

"I went there the day before I left for the Cotswolds, back in May. I rang the bell twenty times. The porter came out, said he hadn't seen Mr. Kassar since April, and would I please go away. Except he didn't say please."

"So Tariq didn't give up the flat. He'll be back."

Kate shrugged and stared into the wine glass. "When I called his mobile, the service had been disconnected."

"Don't you find it even a mite suspicious that he disappears just hours before the bombing?"

Kate clenched her jaw. Her mobile rang, an incoming text. It was from Emerson James. Chagrined,

Kate read it, remembering she promised to call the solicitor in Devon. *Neighbors r tearing down the fence behind the stable. What did solicitor say? When r ye coming down?*

"Bad news?"

Kate handed the mobile to Gwen. "Trouble at Millview."

Gwen read the text, handed the mobile back. "Are you going down?"

"Looks like I'll have to. Can you get away? Come with me?"

"I'd love to, Katie, but Peter has some people in from St. Petersburg and I promised to help entertain the wives."

"Hedge fund people or Section 10 connections?"

Gwen shrugged. "Not sure. Do you have to deal with it yourself? Didn't your father have a solicitor? Cameron somebody?"

Kate nodded. "Andy Cameron. It's more than just the fence. Emerson and Lorna are at loose ends. Don't know what's going to happen to them." She signed. "It's my problem. I'll call Andy, see if he can fix it. But eventually I'll have to go down." She drained her glass, nodded to the hovering bartender. "What's going on with Maddy?"

"I can only guess. She's sending noncommital texts. Nothing about the human trafficking assignment. She's got a new boyfriend."

"And?"

"He's with Police Scotland."

"That's good, no?"

"I haven't the slightest idea. He's 35."

"Better than a fuzzy cheeked teenager. Maybe take her mind off trafficking. Anything I can do?"

"Probably not. I don't want her knowing I'm talking about her." Gwen drained her wine glass, and waved to a ruddy-faced balding man in a wrinkled flax-coloured blazer seated at the far end of the bar.

"Your admirer is approaching," Kate said softly, watching the man in the blazer vacate his seat and make his way across the crowded pub.

"That bloke is not an admirer. He hates my guts and he wants to gloat because my client failed to show for a hearing and he got a judgment."

Kate glanced at the empty wine glass. "Refill or shall we depart?"

"Let's depart. My white knight awaits in his tower. By the way, I asked Peter about the 'virga over the heath'?"

"And?"

"Koslov is a cloud freak. A virga is a cloud that looks like a jellyfish."

It was a few minutes past eight when Kate got back to the Knightsbridge flat. Too late for a conversation with Andrew Cameron of Cameron and Foxhill, but a voice message would be a start. Kate rang the number in Dartmouth that she'd found in her father's brown leather address book in the study, listened to the ringing three times. A recording invited her to leave a message, which she did in as succinct a manner as possible.

Returning home from The Yorkshire, she'd stopped for Thai take-away. She ladled the Crying Tiger and Jasmine Rice into her mother's small white dishes, settled down at the dining room table to continue reading Deborah's notes in the green file on Black Irish.

Half an hour later she'd learned that helium-3 was a stable isotope of the element helium composed of two protons and one neutron, from which, through a process of fusion reaction, vast amounts of energy could be generated. Energy to power the whole of the U.K. The problem was that helium-3 existed in only minuscule quantities on the planet earth, while, according to government calculations, over one hundred million tons of helium-3 were buried nine feet beneath the moon's surface. Enough unlimited energy to power the earth for a thousand years.

At the bottom of the last page Kate found Deborah's handwritten note: *According to MI6 agents in Beijing and Moscow, China and Russia have signed an agreement to mine helium-3 on the moon. If they are successful before the U.K., the U.S. and European powers, they will hold a monopoly on helium. Find out what Chandler knows about this.*

Reading on, Kate realized that Project HE3 involved more than mining the moon. Project HE3 was a plan to develop space-cargo landing sites, where the gas would be unloaded and conveyed to fusion reactors around the U.K. According to Deborah's notes, the P.M. had specifically tasked Hamish McTeague to secure the cyber defenses at the new plant.

Mining on the moon. Kate turned over the last page and closed the file feeling like she'd wandered into a science fiction plot. A small window on her computer announced a message from Gianni Tara-melli.

Welcome back. This was an easy one. See attached. BTW, I dug into the dark net where Umarova has quite a rep. Alias Dervish, hacker for hire, trained at Veronezh, Available for further help if you need me to dig. Sending you link to best facial rec program. PSWD is tuscany.

Kate clicked up the attached page and learned that Hamish's rent boy was Connor O'Connor. Place of birth, Belfast Northern Ireland. Parents deceased. No siblings. O'Connor's higher education included the IT Institute in Belfast and one year at Cambridge University. A 6-week session at The Hacker School in Virginia. Currently employed in the IT International Divison, 5th Domaine Security, Malvern. Vehicle registration: 1961 white MG MGA, registered to an address on Briar Lane in Southmoor. The property was titled in the name of Connor O'Connor. The address was also the residence of Zulema Umarova.

After sending a reply of gratitude to Gianni and a query on Veronezh, she placed the white dishes in the dishwasher and left a VM for Deborah MacKenzie's P.A., requesting a hire car for the following morning.

CHAPTER 24

The M40 was clogged with Saturday escapees from the heat in the city. The A420 from Oxford was little better. It was nearly noon when Kate motored down Circuit Street in Denchworth and into Hyde Road and found the property address from the vehicle registration for Connor O'Connor alias Dylan Chandler. A semi-detached two-storey white stone cottage, the property backed up to acres of grassy fields separated by a fenced lane. A low slung classic white MG with the top down was parked in front of the house beside a late model black Hyundai.

Kate's drove past the house to a turn around, reversed and returned to park the hire car, a Fiat Mini, up the road in front of a smaller cottage where several vehicles were clustered for what appeared to be a convivial neighborhood gathering. A 30-ish blond-haired couple carrying a wicker basket passed by the car with two small children in tow. They gave her a wave and she returned the greeting, lifting her mobile phone to her ear for cover.

She had an unobstructed view of the ivy-covered white stone walls of the O'Connor residence, including the long wooden door at the end of the house. Mindful of Deborah's admonition to surveil but not approach, she had just focused her mobile's camera app on the cottage when the wooden door opened. A petite Asian female emerged. Several seconds later she was followed by a tall dark-haired man carrying a cage with a bird inside. The man was recognizable as Devon Chandler aka Black Irish, but the female, twenty something, wearing skinny black jeans and a sleeveless white top, did not look like an Umarova. A legitimate girl friend or a client?

Kate slid down in the seat and began snapping photos. The couple walked to the white MG, the man put the cage carefully in the back seat, and both got into the car. The engine started up, the man leaned over to kiss the woman, then reversed out of the driveway and they motored up Briar Lane and disappeared around the corner toward Hyde Road.

Kate stared after them, snapped a photo of the license plate on the Hyundai, and considered her options. She glanced back at the cottage, scanned for video surveillance but saw no cameras. She got out of the car, inventing a cover story in the event the cottage was inhabited. The day was still heating up and she wished she'd worn something more practical than the long sleeved black shirt and blue jeans.

Three taps on the wooden door produced only silence. The ivy had grown thickly above the door and was reaching for the second-storey window. Thick bushes with white blossoms screened the lower windows. She knocked again, waited, then moved to her left and stared down a long tree-sheltered gravel path along the side of the cottage. The path led her past a kitchen window, through which she glimpsed an Aga and a pine table with two chairs, and on into a rear garden with a red-tile roofed shed. Beyond the garden lay a tilled field and beyond that a fenced green pasture with two black horses grazing.

Half expecting someone, anyone, to come bursting out of the house to demand she immediately quit the property, she walked to the closed stable door at the back of the house and peered into the window at one side. The salon was empty, furnished with a hodgepodge of red leather and blue fabric furniture, the walls hung with a variety of framed art of no particular style. Through the wide window on the left side of the door, she could see an unmade four-poster bed with a white coverlet covered in large cabbage roses. Not what she would have expected a debonair man about town to choose. She stepped away from the house and just finished snapping half dozen more photos when her mobile announced a text.

The text was from Jean Pierre Rousseau, her Interpol connection. Then, too late, she heard the crunch of quick footsteps on the gravel path and was confronted with a scantily attired dark-haired female of probably some thirty years. A purple-scaled dragon wound its way round her right bicep. A black sea monster coiled about her bare left thigh below the brief denim shorts. And in a two-hand pose she held what looked like a Glock G42.

"Who the hell are you and what the fuck are you doing on my property?"

CHAPTER 25

The Downs, Southmoor

Connor O'Connor watched Jenny Wen straighten her back and extend her left arm. He placed the hawk on her glove and adjusted her fingers to hold the jesses, the thin leather tether he put on Ada in unfamiliar situations. The hawk settled onto the glove, never taking her black eyes from Connor. Looking from the eyes of the hawk to the eyes of the human female, Connor knew, like a splinter of ice on the back of his neck, that some part of him would cease to exist if he lost either of them. "I'm going behind you and I'm going to walk away so she can't see me. When I signal you, turn to your right, stretch out your arm and open your hand."

Half a minute later, he gave a shout. Jenny turned, stretched her arm a fraction of an inch and the hawk burst toward Connor, flying low over the grass, wings wide, her eyes fixed on Connor's glove. Jenny let out as cry as Ada brought her feet up as if to strike and hit squarely on Connor's glove.

"Did I do it right, Connor? Can I fly her free one day?"

"When both of you are ready, Jenny." Connor extricated the hawk from his glove and put her in the cage. "Shall we go back to the house? I have a Picpoul de Pinet chilling for us."

"I have to get back to university today. Big examination tomorrow."

She watched him place the cage in the back seat of the MG, then she climbed into the black leather passenger seat. As he settled into the seat beside her, she touched his thigh. "Connor, I have a favor to ask of you."

"Anything, my love."

"It is for my father."

"He's okay with our getting married?"

"My uncle told him you do very important work. He needs your help."

Now it comes, he thought. The bride price. "How can I help your father, Jenny?"

"You remember we talk about helium-3? When we read the newspaper article."

"Yes."

"We know that the U.K. and the U.S. will join China in mining helium-3, yes?"

Not bloody likely. "I saw the *Guardian* article, Jenny. I think some of that's just wishful political thinking."

"My father has a scientific company, in Shanghai. After the wedding," she paused and caressed his thigh, "After the wedding when my father returns to China, there is some research he must take back with him. I hope you can help him." She pulled a piece of paper from her leather pouch. "He has been trying to contact this company, but they do not return his communications."

Connor read the precise black hand-lettered

name on the scrap of paper. "Ardramurchan Con-struction Ltd." Who are these people?"

"They are contractors to build a space port in Scotland."

"Jenny, there's not going to be a space port in Scotland."

"My father says there is."

"What precisely does your father he need my help with?"

"He would like access to engineering drawings for the space port."

CHAPTER 26

Denchworth, Southmoor

Connor fully expected Zulema Umarova to be late. He was not disappointed. She was late exactly the time it took him to quaff one and half pints of the Fox's Cask Conditioned ale and consume one Black and Blue Burger. It gave him ample time to study the scrap of paper with the hand-lettered black print. *Ardnamurchan*. Which in turn led to calculating the probability of his housemate's willingness to help.

He estimated the probability at about 50-50 and might turn on what her price would be. Much as he hated to admit it, Zulema was a better hacker than he was, especially when it came to covering footprints. When they'd met at The Hacker School, she was full-on Black Hat, outstanding for her talent to turn a computer into a weapon. For sale to the highest bidder. When she was recruited to work at The Doughnut, the local moniker for the Cheltenham headquarters of GCHQ, she'd chortled that it was because she was one of The Naughty Ones. And with her secondment to the Cyber Security Ops Center, he'd bet money she'd returned to moonlighting in the Dark. Or that she had never left it.

Eyes on the tall wooden door, he played with the small faux vehicle fob on a key chain that was actually a mini PVR spycam with micro SD card, microphone and USB port. He purchased it in Paris, first used it with Danielle, wife of the French cabinet minister. It had been almost too easy.

The pub's wooden door opened with a gust of hot wind. Zulema's tats and form fitting white t-shirt garnered her the glances of appreciation from several pub customers. She had no tender greetings for her housemate. "We had a visit today from some bloody fucking reporter. Or a bloody fucking photographer. Roaming about the estate as if she owned it."

"What're you talking about?"

"Blethering about being lost, thought she was attending some sodding family picnic in my garden. Lost my ass." She folded her arms and leaned over the table. Her silver link bracelet jangled against the table. One of the charms was a whirling dervish dancer, Connor noted. *Mevlevi* the Turks called them. "She was snapping *photos*, dude."

"Of what?"

"Of the bloody *house*."

"And?"

"I sent her packing."

"So, no harm."

"Sodding tourist. I'm putting up the wireless cameras tomorrow. " She scanned the room, spotted the waitress, signaled. "What's so bloody important that it couldn't wait till tomorrow?"

"I need a favor."

"What manner of favor?" The barmaid approached the table, gave Connor a wink which he did not return. Zulema ordered a red wine. The waitress glanced at Connor's empty glass and he nodded, then Connor pulled the scrap of paper Jenny had given him and smoothed it out on the table.

"I need access."

Zulema picked up the paper, read it. "Ardnamurchan. Where'd you get this?"

"Can you get inside?"

"It's the space port. High level stuff. All the sodding billionaires are planning to abandon the planet they've ruined. There's not been a public announcement. How d'ya know about it?"

"Can't tell you."

"What d'ya want?"

" I want construction engineering drawings."

Zulema scoffed. "It's for your Chinese shag, isn't it?"

Connor was silent.

"You can't trust her, Connor. Whoever wants these, if they know about the construction award, that I know for a fact hasn't been announced yet, then Ardnamurchan's already been hacked. It's a trap, Connor."

"It's not a trap, "Z."

"You don't want to mess with this, dude. Somebody wants you out of circulation."

Connor considered the possibility for a few seconds, rejected it. "Can you get them?"

"Course I can."

"How much?"

The wine and the ale arrived. Connor paid the tab and the barmaid departed. Zulema took a sip of the wine, wrinkled her nose, regarded Connor over the rim of the wine glass. "Fifty big ones."

Worse than he'd expected. He mentally reviewed the balance in the Swiss account. Something like 250 thousand Swiss francs, thanks to Danielle. Connor shook his head, tasted the froth on the ale. "Can't do it. Twenty."

"Worth at least half a million to whatever bloke yer selling to."

"I'm not selling."

"Then yer daft. Thirty-five."

"Thirty."

She nodded.

" How long?"

"Three days."

Chapter 27

Southmoor to London

Kate St. Claire pulled into the first layby on the A420, pulled her mobile from the rucksack and read the email from Jean Pierre Rousseau. *In the office on Monday. Are you coming down?*

The night she got word that Kincaid's plane had failed to land in Jo'Burg, Jean Pierre had stayed with her the entire night, using every resource he knew to figure out what could have happened to the small plane Kincaid was piloting. His last known location was over Zimbabwe, then nothing. No weather problems, no reported mechanical difficulties. And not one trace of the plane was ever discovered.

She stripped down to her tank top, thinking about all that had happened in the interim. Her return to London and County Devon to spend time with her grieving parents, the recruitment by Five and her explanation to Sir David about not following him to Six because she needed to stay in the U.K. The recent year of almost normal life, then the bombing and the stay in hospital, the recuperation in the Cotswolds.

So now, a quick visit to Lyon and Interpol might be the chance to prove or disprove the garbage in the file Johar had given her. And to visit the twins. She texted a reply to Jean Pierre. *Monday afternoon. A bi-entot.* Before she could return the mobile to the ruck-sack, it rang for an incoming call. It was a Dartmouth number.

"Katie. Andy Cameron here. Nice to hear from you. You have neighbor problems?"

"According to our caretaker at Millview, big time neighbor problems. As in they're disputing the boundary lines and tearing down fences."

"Emerson still the caretaker?"

"Yes. He's a bit rattled."

"I saw him in town. Your dad had me arrange for the surveyor last spring. How are you? Still in London?"

"Yes, still in London. I was planning to come to Devon, Andy. Just found out I have to go to Lyon on Monday. Won't be away long. Can you look into the matter?"

"My pleasure, Katie. Travel safely. Ring me when you return."

Andy Cameron had grown up with Kate and Kincaid. He'd been one of the tots in her mother's dirty dancing class.

As she pressed the End button on Andy's call, an email from Gianni Taramelli popped up. *Verone-zh: Allegedly a private hacker school run out of "small grungy Moscow apartment." Entrance exam required. Funded by private donations from anonymous sources. Teaches self-defensive tactics in cyberspace. Allegedly."*

So Umarova was trained in Moscow. Having a housemate with that kind of background would give Black Irish a leg up on hacking into MI5, should he be so inclined. But what was his end game? Money? Political influence? Was someone else calling the shots? If it wasn't a matter of national security, wouldn't a simple threat to reveal a homosexual indiscretion be enough to produce a lovely monetary bonus? What was Deborah MacKenzie not telling?

Back at the Knightsbridge flat, Kate installed herself in her father's study and transferred the photos of the Denchworth cottage, the snaps of Connor O'Connor and his companion and the two vehicles to her computer. Traipsing into the back garden in Denchworth wasn't one of her better moves. Given O'Connor's cybersecurity background, chances were good there were surveillance cameras about the cottage. She knew without a doubt the tattooed female hadn't believed her story and the only thing that prevented her from pursuing Kate down Briar Lane was the arrival of the bus at the cottage. A purple-haired Goth female had descended from the bus. The last glimpse Kate had of the two women was of a passionate embrace and a liplock as the bus lumbered away. There hadn't been any opportunity for a snap of the Goth, and strolling back to the hire car, Kate had mused on what it would be like to kiss someone with a nose ring.

It was nearly six o'clock when she finished summarizing the information she'd assembled on Hamish McTeague's rent boy. She'd run the photo of the Asian female through Taramelli's facial rec program and retrieved a passport photo of a 24-year-old female named Wen Hulan from Shanghai on a student visa to the U.K. There didn't seem to be an expiration on the visa. A further search on the name Wen produced a link to the Embassy of the People's Republic of China in the U.K. where Larry Wen was commercial attache. No further background information regarding family *connections* for Wen Hulan or Larry Wen in Shanghai was available, presumably because China was better at protecting the privacy of its citizens than Western counterparts.

The Hyundai license tag revealed the vehicle was owned by Zulema Umarova, whose operator's license black and white photo showed the dark-haired, dark-eyed female who had accosted Kate in the back garden. Umarova was born in Chechnya 34 years ago and the permanent address shown was that of the Southmoor cottage.

Kate added the information on Umarova and the hacker school and transmitted the report and photos in an encrypted email to Deborah MacKenzie. She'd not discovered anything about either O'Connor or Umarova that connected to mining helium-3 on the room. As she brushed her teeth, she recalled Deborah's parting admonition. "Find something we can use for leverage."

Deborah would not be happy.

Chapter 28

"You don't have an anger gene, Debs. Missing from your DNA." It was her father's voice and it echoed now in the kitchen of the house Ian had inherited from his mother. "When you get angry, you get cold. Colder than ice."

Seated on the teal blue leather chair at the counter, Deborah MacKenzie studied the latest multimedia text from Black Irish. A full frontal pose this time. Thank God she didn't have any belly fat. And her boobs were still pert. More or less. How had he done it? Where did he hide the camera? Where were her brains? The text was explicit. *We need 2 meet, Emma darling. Monday? Same place? 7ish?*

The gloves had come off.

After all the years as a lowly clerk, the years scrambling to be outstanding, to become an officer, tolerating the still existent old-boys sexism, making it almost to the top despite her lack of an Oxbridge education, it had come to this. Being blackmailed by a male escort, a vindictive cybersecurity expert who not only might be able to hack into the top secret space cargo project he'd alluded to, but could, in one click of a mouse, send either or both photos to one of the tabloids.

Deborah could see the headlines. *Security Services Deputy Director snared in tryst with male escort. Wife of prominent London scientist in flagrante delicto.* The exposé would be followed by a summons to the fifth floor, then to the Home Secretary's office. There could be no good outcome.

She took a deep breath and considered her options. She would have to keep the Monday night date to find out his price. She stared out the window at the darkening sky, heard a small chirp from her laptop announcing the arrival of an email. It was the encrypted report from St. Claire. As she read through the report, her brain searched frantically for a solution. There had to be something she could use for leverage. Something more about the Checken housemate. Or the Asian girlfriend. Anything to prevent her entire life from crumbling into tiny bits. For a long time she stared out at her neighbor's garden, and then, impossibly, the image of the S & W .38 that Ian insisted on keeping in the locked drawer of his desk hovered in the background.

Chapter 29

Tower Hamlets, London

Driving back into the city under a darkening sky tinged with green, Nadia Sultan listened to her friend chatter on about her new boyfriend, a Jordanian named Hani, a Harvard Law School grad working for a firm of solicitors in London. Nadia and Salima were returning from a Sisters class. Salima had been blethering on for thirty minutes while Nadia wanted to talk about important things. About the Muslim family that had been denied boarding at Heathrow on a flight to Disneyland. About the two young women from Birmingham about to set off on the first leg of their *hejira*.

Without taking her eyes from the road, Salima said, "You seem a bit edgy. Did you forget your meds today?"

"I don't like the side effects."

"Lithium evens out your moods."

"I am *not* moody."

Several minutes of silence filled the car.

"Are you coming to the meeting tonight after prayers?" Nadia asked.

"I read the bulletin. But really, I'm tired of hearing about female circumcision. Anyone who's idiotic enough to allow their daughters to be mutilated, isn't going to be there anyway. Are you still recruiting?"

"I am doing whatever I can for the Caliphate."

"It's illegal. You're going to get arrested. You're going to get all of us arrested."

After another interval of silence, Salima returned to enumerating the praises of the handsome Jordanian. "He's a Rhodes scholar, Nadia. He's arranging dancing lessons for us. I'm going to meet his parents next month."

"You know music and dancing is *haram*, Salima."

Salima flicked the left turn indicator, downshifted and turned onto Bishopsgate Road. Nadia twisted sideways in the passenger seat and eyed her roommate's western dress and long uncovered hair. "You're not wearing hijab, Salima. Don't you care that the men in the next car are staring at you? Have you no shame?"

Salima glanced at the black BMW and Nadia watched a flush cover her friend's face. "Hani doesn't like hijab," she said quietly. "His mother thinks it's, well, medieval."

Nadia felt a spurt of rage. *Medieval.* That's what Tariq had called it. She clenched her fists and stared through the windshield for several minutes of uncomfortable silence.

Salima said carefully, "Nadia, I've been thinking about our last conversation. About, you know, how you want to get revenge."

"It is my *duty* to get revenge."

"Please don't go there. Maybe you should, just,

you know, forget about him and move on. Hani has a nice friend from Amman. I could introduce you."

"I don't *want* to meet Hani's friend." Nadia clenched her teeth, felt a familiar heaviness forming in the pit of her belly. "I will *never* divorce him. If the whore wasn't around, he would forget her. She bewitched him, she stole him from me. A filthy Jew. You know what the punishment for thieves is. She is an adulterous thief. You know the penalty for adultery. If she wasn't alive –"

Salima came to an abrupt stop in front the building on Fournier Street. "I'll drop you here. I'm meeting Hani for dinner." She turned toward Nadia. "What do you mean, she's a Jew? They were Church of England. I read it in the newspaper after the–" She stared at Nadia with widening eyes. "Oh, my God. You didn't."

"I will tear her into pieces with my own two hands." Nadia got out of the car, rearranged her dark blue abaya, then leaned into the car. "I don't care if her baba is the King of England," she said. "I want her dead." She eyed Salima's long uncovered hair again. "You are a disgrace to Islam. No man is worth that."

"Murder is *haram*, Nadia. Even of an infidel."

For a long moment the women stared at each other, then Nadia broke the heavy silence. "Nothing is *haram*, Salima. Everything is *halal*."

Chapter 30

Tower Hamlets, London

Salima has a new boyfriend, Nadia thought bitterly, making her way along the covered stone passageway. *She has a new boyfriend and she doesn't want to wear hijab. His mother thinks it's medieval. She doesn't believe in hejira. Salima is a traitor, exactly like Tariq.* Above, a long streak of lightning forked the dark sky. She shivered. Salima was going to be dangerous.

She flung open the door of the two-bedroom flat and stood for a minute, listening to the silence, drained of energy. Replaying her parting words with Salima, Nadia though about *el sariqa.* The thief. Until Tariq met her, there was hope he would come back, there was the hope of having a child. The slut had stolen all of that. A thief and an adulterer. She deserved to be whipped. She deserved to be stoned.

Nauseous and cold, Nadia headed for her bedroom, turned up the heat thermostat. Her room was the smaller of the two bedrooms, but still comfortable with a view out over the large terrace. The flat occupied the first floor of the old house in the heart of Spitalfields. It had a fully-fitted kitchen painted a vibrant red, a small laundry room, a spacious bathroom and access to a flagstone terrace. It was convenient to Brick Lane and the Liverpool Street Station, and she could walk to the Academy where she had been teaching since their return from Peshawar.

Still enervated, still focused on Salima's betrayal, Nadia removed her abaya and head scarf, shook out her hair, checked her image in the long mirror. She was wearing the pink satin brassiere and the matching pink lace thong. Gifts from Tariq, from the days when he couldn't wait to peel her out of her street clothes, run his fingers through her long hair. She turned away from the mirror, unpacked her suitcase. After brewing a cup of mint tea, she headed to her laptop computer in the bedroom alcove to check email and for comments on her last blog, on the joys awaiting brides in Syria.

There were ten comments of praise, three of condemnation. She shrugged. She couldn't please everyone. She could only write what she believed. The email inbox contained the usual allotment of spam, a message from her sister Raja'a, a message from Dervish, and an anxious epistle from Alone in Manchester who couldn't stop dithering and was terrified of what her father would do to her if she accepted Fatima's assistance with the flight to Istanbul.

About to open the message from Dervish, she read the name in the Sender line of the last message. With trembling fingers, she opened the message.

Please do not write to me any more. I no longer consider myself your husband. I have moved on.

Sitting outside her own body, watching herself react to the words on the screen, Nadia felt the iciness in her fingers traveling up her arm, up her spine and across her shoulders and neck, creeping up into her head. From outside, a long low rumble of thunder. A sharp pain attacked her left temple. As she jerked up from the chair, it crashed over on its side. The pain in her temple shot across her head. She grabbed the chair and hurled it against the wall, then stumbled over to the bed. Throwing herself down on the rose-colored duvet, she beat her hands against the coverlet. *I no longer consider myself your husband.* The words drummed in her brain like a horrible mantra, a death knell. *I no longer consider myself your husband.* She continued to pummel the bed and the sharp pains in her head became a dull throbbing counterpoint to the ever closer bursts of thunder.

It was the loud crash of thunder that woke her. Then she heard voices. A man and a woman. Salima called her name. Nadia did not reply. Turning on her side she drew her knees up to her chest and stared sightlessly out the window to the terrace. More sharp thunder followed by hard rain against the window.

As the rain increased, Nadia remembered how Tariq had been after they returned from Peshawar. Caring, romantic. Bringing her flowers, talking late into the night, sharing their hope for the Caliphate. She tried to remember when he started to change, but it all seemed a blur. Thinking about how Salima was changing her lifestyle for Hani, Nadia was now certain Tariq had changed because of the slut. The filthy spook.

She would hunt her down, obliterate her. This time, *inshallah*, she would not fail.

She yawned, stretched, got up from the bed and

righted the chair, ruefully noting the dent in the wall. She sat down before the laptop, knowing she would not be deterred until she found her quarry. She clicked up her email, found Dervish's latest contribution with two attachments. The first was a copy of a request for Compassionate Leave from "G" Branch for Officer Kathryn St. Claire, dated the previous May. It could only have come from the MI5 network. Dervish was good. More than good. Nadia smiled and continued reading. The second document contained four pages downloaded from the Internet and three pages of OCR-scanned text from *The Sentinel* and the *Devon Gazette*. The focus of the news clippings, also from the previous May, was the 'shocking and tragic death' of the 5th Earl of Axmoorland and his wife Lady Carmela Aragon in the London terrorist bombing attributed to the IRA. The *Gazette* article included photos of the couple's Postbridge farm.

The message from Dervish was brief. *Subject 1 traveled Eurostar Monday to Paris. Subject 2 whereabouts unknown, search continues.*

Nadia's reply to Dervish was brief. *Need address and security code for Subject 1 family residence addresses in London and Postbridge (Devon.)*

Dervish's reply arrived half an hour later. *Subject 1 is living in Knightsbridge, see attached map. Security system vulnerable. Advise. Still searching for Postbridge residence.*

Part Three

This is the hour of pride and power,
Talon and tush and claw.
Oh, hear the call! Good hunting all,

That keep the Jungle Law!

-Rudyard Kipling

CHAPTER 31

Lyon, Provence, France

Kate St. Claire checked her face in the small mirror on the pull-down visor of the hired Renault. Too many lines around her eyes. Vertical lines on each side of her mouth that hadn't been there six months ago. She applied a touch of lip gloss, donned the tan leather jacket, locked the car and headed toward the concrete-and-glass monolith that housed the entity called Interpol, the clearinghouse for international crime where she spent five years as an Intelligence Analyst. She strode toward the entrance, fiercely determined to find answers from the one person who wouldn't lie to her.

The temperature was cool, the skies blue and sunny. Walking toward the tall green iron fence and the unmarked gate, she mused that with the exception of savvy international criminals or the high-level law enforcement officials of the member countries, the only image many people had of Interpol was based on the fictitious agent of the U.K.'s long-running TV series. Even fewer knew how the Interpol concept came about: A seed planted in Monte Carlo in 1914 when Prince Albert of Monaco, desperate to stop the European swindlers and con men who were operating in his lucrative casinos, convened police officers from twenty countries around the world.

In front of the security gate Kate paused and listened to a disembodied voice address her in French through the speaker. She identified herself, waited for the heavy gate to allow her entry, and stepped into the small security building. She nodded to the uniformed guard studying her from behind the bulletproof glass. After sliding her passport through the metal tray, she was admitted into the slender glass tube to be scanned for weapons. She had been through the security procedure many times. Despite the extent to which she applauded the procedure, she still felt the cold, damp frisson of claustrophobia. She also felt a tug of anxiety. She had not seen Jean Pierre Rousseau since the evening at the small bar in Lyons where, when she told him she was leaving Interpol and why, he proposed marriage.

The weapons scan completed, the door opened. A security escort appeared whose biometric print was sufficient for entry to subsequent doors and the elevator to the seventh floor where she was passed off to a chic brown-eyed blonde in a trendy black knit mini-dress. The chic blonde's ID tag identified her as Genevieve Mersault. Genevieve's desk sat in an alcove whose dark wood panel designated the area as *Seccion des analysts d'intelligence*. Genevieve welcomed Kate in precise British English, offered her a cup of coffee she declined, and in turn escorted her into Jean Pierre's office.

The door closed noiselessly behind Genevieve. The solid, slightly balding man stood up from the black leather chair and came round the desk. His smile was welcoming. "Kate. *Bienvenue*. What a plea-sure to see you. " They embraced and after a light kiss on the cheek, he held her a second longer, his eyes scanning her face, pausing at the long white scar above her left eyebrow.

Unlike his more casual attire from the past, Jean Pierre wore a pale blue shirt with a dark blue and red striped tie, perfectly creased dark trousers. And, Kate noted with some amusement, his cufflinks displayed the official Interpol seal: the blue glove, the vertical sword, and the scales of justice. Jean Pierre's desktop was clean. A flat screen monitor, a black glass key-board and a thin brown file folder were the only items on the desk. The window behind the desk overlooked the greenery of the Parc de la Tete d'Or.

"Sit," he said, indicating the armchair in front of the desk. He waved toward the window behind. "And enjoy the view. It's better than what we used to have downstairs." His eyes continued searching her face. "It's good to see you. I cannot tell you how sorry I was to hear about your parents. I heard you left London."

Jean Pierre looked thinner. His remaining dark hair had turned silver at the temples. New lines ra-diated from the kindly brown eyes. Along with his attire, he had acquired a more serious demeanor. But then, the world had become a more serious and dangerous place. Interpol was reorganized, and the agency rooted in tradition – where Wanted-persons Notices were once delivered by third class mail – had reinvented itself.

"I've been on Compassionate Leave from Five since May," she said. "Recuperating at my cousin's house in Warwickshire. With six horses, a white Borzoi and a rose garden. How normal is that?"

"A perfect cover for something clandestine. Seriously, Kate, how are you? I've thought about you often. I thought you might call. I would have come to London. It must have been bloody awful."

Kate took a deep breath. "I'm . . . okay. It was bloody awful. Still is. Still no arrests."

He laid one hand on the brown file folder on his desk. "And Tariq Kassar? Where does he fit in? This is a case you are working for Five?"

She hesitated, then lied smoothly. "Deborah MacKenzie, my boss at Five, has information that Tariq Kassar . . . is involved with a woman Five has under surveillance. A female jihadi. We wanted to confirm that."

"I believe the term is *mujaidaat*," he said carefully. "But why is MacKenzie involving you, if you're on Leave? I didn't get any heads up from her. How did you know we're working this?"

"According to the file, Tariq Kassar had connections with the Muslim Brotherhood. That he was, or is, involved in money laundering and funding for terrorists." She paused, then said in a rush, "Sara Johar, one of the other "G" branch officers, suspects Tariq Kassar or his . . . handler had something to do with the death of a Syrian. My asset. She was murdered the night my parents died."

"And?"

"Johar said you've been investigating Tariq Kassar and Nadia Sultan."

He tapped the glass keyboard. Within seconds a

black and white photo and a text file filled the screen. The photo was Tariq. "I have files on Nadia Sultan and Tariq Kassar aka Sheik Issam al-Mat."

Kate watched the screen and waited without speaking. Jean Pierre scrolled down one page in the file and frowned.

"Is Kassar a suspect in your parents' murder? Or just your asset? I was surprised your request did not come through regular channels. Should you even be here?"

Kate shifted in her chair, swallowed, moistened her upper lip with her tongue. "Right. The thing is, I dated . . . I was involved with Tariq Kassar in London before my parents were killed. We discussed politics a lot. I know he's not a terrorist. He thought . . . " she paused, then said in a rush, "He thought Bin Laden was insane, that he was doing more harm to Islam than anyone in the Middle East. He applauded when the SEALS took him out."

"Again, what does Tariq Kassar have to do with your parents' murder? Or your asset?"

"I don't know. That's why I'm here."

"Deborah MacKenzie knew about your relationship with Kassar?"

Kate nodded. "I never tried to keep it a secret."

"Does she know you're here?"

Kate shook her head.

"Lady Kathryn going rogue. Who would have thought?" Jean Pierre's eyebrows lifted. "When did you last see Kassar?"

She took a deep breath. "The night my car was bombed. The night my parents died."

"I see," he said dryly. "Your informant is murdered, your car is blown up, your parents are killed, and your boyfriend coincidentally happens to do a runner that very night."

She leaned forward, pounding her fists on the desk. "*Stop it, Jean Pierre.* Stop it. No, you don't see. There's no connection. Tariq was leaving for . . . a business conference. He left at midnight. The car exploded the following morning when my parents picked it up. I know how it sounds, but there's no connection."

Jean Pierre's eyes locked on hers. There was silence for several seconds, then he asked, "Did he contact you after the bombing?"

"I was in hospital. I had no phone for several weeks. He wouldn't have known where to find me. He . . ." She stopped, hearing her own words. "Okay. He dumped me. But he wouldn't have . . ." She stared at him. "He wouldn't. He didn't know anything about my Syrian informant."

But he did know your parents were going to borrow the car. He was the one who moved it out of the garage. No one else knew about it.

He returned her gaze for several long moments, then said, "For your sake, Kate, I hope you're right." Another pause, then he said softly, "But you're not quite sure, are you?"

"I want to know what happened, I want to . . ." She hesitated and inhaled a deep breath.

"Close the chapter?" he offered.

She nodded. "I want to know what's true."

"What's always true, Kate, is what someone wants you to believe on any particular day." He tapped the keyboard and another page of text appeared. "Tariq Kassar, aka Sheik Issam-al Mat, aka Omar Javid, has been on our radar screen for some time. First in West Africa."

"He was in charge of African branches for London Bank of Commerce."

Jean Pierre shook his head. "LBC sold all their shares in Sierra Leone over ten years ago. Kassar made two trips after that. When we combine our intel with Five's, the picture is he was laundering money and funneling it back to Hizb ut-Tahrir in London."

"Was? Past tense?"

Jean Pierre nodded. "And perhaps to the Brotherhood in Egypt, as well." He shuffled the papers in the folder. "Today I received a heads-up on a recent transfer of funds from Geneva by Mehmet Celik. Six has connected this to Kassar. They said something strange."

If MI6 was tracking Tariq, why hadn't Sir David ever mentioned it to her? "Which was?"

"They said, hands off, he's ours."

Kate digested the information and frowned. "Where did the initial funds come from? Narcotics?"

Jean Pierre shook his head. "A bit more exotic than that. It goes back a ways. Five tracked down a *hawaladar* in Birmingham, a travel agent with a sideline import-export business. The agent had made a payment to two men with ties to extremist groups in London. The funds were used to buy arms and explosives. These two men, as you know, along with others, were found guilty of plotting to blow up two airplanes."

Kate nodded. *Hawala*, the alternative remittance

system used for transferring money from one country to another, bypassing traditional banking channels and monetary laws, was devised in India. Now it had become the preferred mode of sending money to their home countries for Asian immigrants in the U.S. and the U.S. And before Bitcoin, it was used by terrorist groups who wanted to avoid the scrutiny of the international intelligence community.

"Who initiated the *hawala* funds that were disbursed in Birmingham?" Kate asked.

"It took two years before Five deigned to ask us for help and told us that the Birmingham *hawaladar* claimed he was responding to a request from his business partner in Johannesburg. The Jo'burg police seized the man's records, but there was nothing written down. So the trail went cold until the brother-in-law of the Jo'burg *hawaladar* was arrested for receiving smuggled diamonds from Sierra Leone. With persuasion from the local gendarmerie, the brother-in-law came up with a short list of people he had paid for illegal diamonds. One of the names, Omar Javid, led to your Tariq Kassar."

Kate felt her jaw muscles clench. "People will say *anything* under torture. Everything you've got is circumstantial. Just the fact that he made trips to Sierra Leone and some clerk in Jo'burg fingered him?"

Even as she protested, Kate could hear her grandfather murmuring, *Where there's smoke, there's usually fire, lass. If it walks like a duck and quacks like a duck, it's probably a duck.*

Right.

So there it was.

The handsome, well-dressed, accomplished, multilingual bloke she'd had been sleeping with was a criminal. Consorting with shady characters in the underworld, funding terrorists. The very terrorists she, Kate St. Claire, and her associates at Five, were dedicated to apprehending. For all her training, all her supposed great intuitions, she had been as naive as a newborn babe.

CHAPTER 32

"It began long before you met him, Kate," Jean Pierre said gently. "Issam al-Mat was recruited into the Muslim Brotherhood when he was 14. In Damascus. That got him expelled from Syria and . . . " He hesitated, tapping the Page Down key.

"He was raised by his grandparents in Beirut," she finished. "His grandmother taught him French and English. His grandfather was a banker. His grandfather sent him to LSE. He graduated with a degree in accounting and finance."

"All correct. Somewhere along the way he began using the grandfather's name. The degree from LSE, along with the languages, provided the perfect background to land a job with a major bank in their international department. It appears that he was doing nothing but banking until he met Raja'a Sultan."

"Raja'a Sultan?" Kate frowned, tried to remember where she had heard or seen the name. "Who is she?"

"A fellow student at LSE. She went on to work in the same division at the bank. But it wasn't Raja'a that got him in trouble. She's lily white. Currently works at an LBC branch in Brussels. Married to a respectable Belgian attorney. The problem was Raja'a's little sister. Nadia Sultan also known as Fatima. Kassar and Sultan both attended a training camp in Pakistan. They were married a year or so later. In Damascus, apparently, before the war began. There's no record of a divorce in the U.K."

Jean Pierre met Kate's level gaze. She was the first to look away, out the big window. The tops of the hardwood trees in the park swayed in the wind. Beyond the trees, sun sparkles glinted off the blue waters of the lake. In the corridor outside the office, a door closed. A telephone rang once, then again. Kate returned her gaze to meet Jean Pierre's. "I was an idiot."

"You didn't know he was married."

She shook her head. "Not a clue. I did my due diligence."

"*Bien, mon amie.* It is possible your M. Kassar may have had a change of heart at some point. Except for the brief report we received this week from Six, which may or may not be based on a fiction of some lackey's imagination in Jo'Burg, currently Tariq Kassar, now known as Mehmet Celik, appears to be running an investment firm in Dubai that helps wealthy Gulf Arabs invest what's left of their petrodollars. But *la femme*, she is another story. Take a look at this." He clicked up a file with a photograph against a blue background, swivelled the monitor so Kate could better view it. She stared at the photo of a round-faced, brown-eyed woman in hijab and read the accompanying text.

Born and raised in Damascus.
Father was government minister.

Attended private school in Damascus, read history at Oxford. In her first year at Oxford, Sultan's father made a trip to Israel and was killed when a remote-controlled bomb detonated in Rmeilleh near his car. Mother died the following year.

Currently teaching at The Academy, a madrassa in London.

One sibling, Raja'a Sultan
Aliases: Fatima; Sister Miryam.

"It appears that Sultan is *passionelle* about Islamic women's rights." Jean Pierre said, glancing away from the screen. "So passionate that she and two other London women were the first females to be allowed at a jihadi training camp in Peshawar. She's something of a legend among the Muslim women in London. She writes a blog. Bits about the rights of women and traveling safely and reporting domestic abuse mixed in with where to buy fashionable hijabs and how to find a class in self defense. Recently she's been . . ."

Kate listened to Jean Pierre's words as from a great distance and then they faded completely until there was only the voice in her head: *You shared intimacies you have never shared with anyone else. Remember what he told you when you met? "I am a bachelor," he said. But isn't the supreme irony that you, who worked intelligence for nearly fifteen years, never found out what now Five and Six and Interpol know. What were you thinking, Kate?*

It was rumored that all liaisons with employees of Five were automatically vetted. Why hadn't Deborah shared the results with Kate? She remembered the antagonism that had arisen her first day at Five. Johar hinted later that Deborah was jealous of Kate's facility with languages and her experience with Interpol and her father's political connections, ergo immediately assumed that Kate would be a competitor for position as head of Counter-Terrorism. Had Deborah feared her so much she hadn't shared the damning intel on Tariq's background? Hoped that she would be compromised and dismissed?

". . .they call themselves the English Sisters and sometimes the Angels of Allah." Jean Pierre's voice pulled her back. " If we can believe Five's intel," he continued, "Sultan teaches classes in weapons and explosives to selected females she recruits at her neighborhood mosque. She's now suspected of recruiting young women in the West for jihadi brides."

He closed the file. "That's all we know. And the evidence against Javid, --sorry, Tariq Kassar, is, as you pointed out, circumstantial." Jean Pierre leaned back in his chair, steepled his fingers. He gazed at Kate for several silent moments, a small smile on his face. "You should have married me," he said suddenly, in a quiet voice. "Provence is a lovely place to live. And to raise children."

Kate felt a lump in her throat and shook her head violently. "Please don't go there. *Je te prie.*"

He shrugged. "*D'accord. C'est l'histoire ancienne. Bon*, what is it you want? Do you want to find Kassar or whatever he's calling himself this week? To inform him that he broke your heart? To kill him, perhaps?"

To kill Tariq? Oh, my God! Kate blinked her eyes and felt her chest constrict. "Is – Tariq Kassar on an Interpol wanted list?"

Jean Pierre glanced back at the computer screen, bit one side of his lower lip. "He is, if I may use the popular law enforcement euphemism, a person of interest. So, yes, we are watching him. He left Dubai two weeks ago traveling to Paris as Mehmet Celik on an Egyptian passport, then disappeared from our radar. He surfaced in Rabat with a Canadian passport. The man has good back-up."

"You think the Six report is right. You think he's still money laundering? Still funding terrorism?"

"If I tell you, will you help us?"

'Where do I start? Rabat? Riyadh? Mumbai? What does Interpol want him for, specifically?"

"We suspect he is connected to a group calling themselves the Sufi Council of Ijtihad. That he's funneling money again, this time to the P.K.K. Or maybe the Y.P.G."

"The Kurds?"

"Yes." He chucked. "There was a rumor floating around a while back that the Sufi Council was trying to assassinate bin Laden when the SEALS beat them to it."

"*Assasinate Bin Laden?*" Kate felt hysterical laughter bubbling in her throat.

He nodded. "Did he ever mention any connections in North Africa?"

She nodded slowly. "A brother in Morocco, a vintner." *He promised to take me there.*

"Two days ago an asset we have in Marrakesh reported seeing him in the company of the Spanish expatriate writer, Pedro Salazar. Salazar has known connections to Kurdistan. Do you think you could get close to him?"

"Kassar or Salazar?"

"Kassar. I could hire you as a consultant. And I won't tell MacKenzie."

Kate stood up. "I don't *want* to get close to him, Jean Pierre," she said fiercely. "I don't want to see him. I don't want to *kill him*. I came here because I thought Five might have been lying about his history. I knew you wouldn't lie to me. That's all. I must go."

"I understand." Jean Pierre said graciously. He rose to his feet. "Where are you going from here? Will you go to Aix? Will you see *les enfants*?"

Kate nodded. "Tomorrow morning."

"*Bien, mon amie.* If you change your mind, there is a Ryan Air flight into Marrakesh. I can get you on a flight tomorrow afternoon out of Marseille. If you find Kassar, get access to any of his devices, our IT section can check for data to confirm what we suspect and learn what his plans are. Perhaps," he smiled sardonically, "even to assist him." He smiled. "As in all wars, the enemy of my enemy . . ."

Kate extended her hand. "Thank you for sharing information, Jean Pierre. The chapter is closed."

He held her hand for several seconds, caressed the palm lightly. "I think it will not be closed for you, *chére amie*, until you discover who set the bomb."

CHAPTER 33

Having been handed back to security by the chic Mlle. Mersault and scrutinized to ensure she was not smuggling out classified information, Kate was back in the hired Renault. Her mobile chimed for an incoming text. It was from Deborah MacKenzie. *Report received. Need deep background on Chinese student Wen Hulan and her family and possible connection to Andramurchan soonest. My office tomorrow.*

Kate sat for several minutes, biting her upper lip, then texted a reply. *Urgent family matter to take care of, back in three days. Pursuing Chinese connection.* She replaced the mobile in her bag and maneuvered out of the car park and onto Quai Charles de Gaulle. Her thoughts roiling, driving by reflex and memory, she followed traffic south along the Rhone, crossed over the river at the Pont Gallieni, then was lost for nearly half an hour before finding her way south again and onto the fast traffic of the A7, the Autoroute du Soleil.

So. Everything in the Five dossier Officer Johar had given her was true. Tariq Kassar had belonged to the Muslim Brotherhood. He attended a terrorist training camp and laundered money to support terrorists or one sort or another. And his handler was his wife, a *mujaidaat*.

Where did the lies stop and reality begin? Or were they the same thing? Was he now funding yet another nefarious cabal? Although, if Jean Pierre's 'rumor' was even close, nefarious was not precisely the term for anyone associated with an attempt to eradicate the skinny cave dweller who'd tried to bring down Western civilization.

At Orange, Kate left the A7 and followed the N7 westward – the famous *nationale sept* that once meandered through every small village between Nice and Paris – into Aix-en-Provence, birthplace of Cezanne. Founded in 122 B.C as Aquae Sextiae, a cross-roads watering place for travelers journeying from Italy to Spain, Aix was a city of art, a city of universities. A city replete with memories of the weekend with Michael Farraday at the Villa Angelina, a sprawling Provencal structure of golden stone surrounded by plane trees under a cerulean sky. She left the Renault with the valet and walked to the reception desk. She signed the register, pondering her motivations in revisiting the sumptuous country house hotel where she had lost her heart to the operative from Six who was in Lyon to assist Interpol on a case involving a London-based rock star and her Egyptian drug lord boyfriend.

Her check-in completed, Kate followed the maroon uniformed bellhop to a second floor room decorated with hangings and tapestries and an ivory brocaded bedspread. The bellhop put her bag in the closet, opened the French doors to a small balcony overlooking the walled pool area, reviewed the dinner schedule with her. She nodded and proffered what seemed like an appropriate number of Euros.

The door closed soundlessly behind him. Kate moved over to the balcony from where she could see the blue waters of the pool sparkling in the afternoon sun. The stone terrace around the pool was empty except for two very suntanned women in bright bikinis, one red, one indigo, stretched out on lounge chairs partially shaded by a huge ivory umbrella.

After days and days of London rain, the sunshine and pool called to her. As she sorted her suitcase, she did what she had learned so well. She slotted the conversation with Jean Pierre that had produced more questions than answers into the back of her mind, and mentally changed gears to prepare herself for the next day's visit to the home of Maggie and Jacques Rousseau and their two adopted children, Angelique and Antoine.

CHAPTER 34

Jemaa el-Fna, the Meeting Place of the Dead, is the main square of Marrakesh. Constructed in the eleventh century, edged along one side by the *souk*, the maze-like area of traditional North African markets, and on the other sides by the café terraces, hotels and gardens, it is the entrance and centerpiece of the *medina*, the old quarter. By day, Jemaa el-Fna is inhabited by water sellers in colorful burnooses, by orange juice vendors, snake charmers and witch doctors. By fortune tellers and monkey handlers. At sunset, the square becomes the province of Berber story tellers, Chleuh dancing boys, and open air restaurants.

On the terrace of the Café de France a dark-skinned, bearded man in a white shirt and blue jeans, wearing aviator tinted glasses, leaned back in the black wrought iron chair, folded the Arab language newspaper, laid it atop the leather journal. The sun began its descent behind the solid gold balls on the 12th century Koutubia Mosque. The man checked his watch and glanced across the square towards the Derb al Zitoun, the Street of the Olive. Pedro Salazar was late, as usual. Actually, late was not the right word. The expatriate Spanish playwright simply had a singular concept of time, a concept that allowed it was reasonable to show up anytime within two hours of what had been agreed upon.

The two men had met in Paris at the opening of the exhibition of Arabic art. As they traded political views over endless cups of espresso, Tariq Kassar knew intuitively that Salazar was the link The Fox – and MI6 – was searching for. The common bond was Salazar's belief that Spain had reached its cultural zenith during the seven-hundred year occupation by the Moors – especially during the Caliphate of Cordoba – and that Catholicism ruined the country.

For a long while Tariq imagined that, in all probability, Salazar was an atheist, adopting Muslim traditions as a part of his cultural assimilation in Morocco, viewing Islam as no more than keeping the fast at Ramadan. When Salazar's Cuban wife died, he'd abandoned the City of Lights and taken up residence in the old medina of Marrakesh. He was currently living with an expatriate French designer named Isabelle.

Tariq glanced casually toward the souk that serviced the daily needs of the locals and simultaneously enticed the tourist to spend far more for a copper bowl or a camel blanket than she would for the same item at an import shop in San Francisco or Soho. Restless, he touched his coffee cup where only fine dark grounds remained in the bottom, recalling the mother of his client in Dubai who only a month ago read his coffee grounds and predicted a long trip, a beautiful woman in white, and then, startled, rushed from the room in tears.

He nodded at the hovering *garcon de café* who

retrieved the cup and disappeared into the back of the restaurant. His gaze returned to the square. At the exact instant that the sun slid behind the mosque, food sellers replaced the orange juice vendors. Soft smoke began drifting over the square with its red tinted buildings. Marrakesh really was a red city, he mused, scanning the pinks and corals and reds of the old plastered walls surrounding the square. The scent of roasting kebabs drifted onto the terrace. The waiter reappeared with a small white cup of the very strong coffee and placed it on the table precisely at the moment that a large balding man in a white burnoose strode across the café toward the table.

"*Tariq, amigo mio. Salaam aleikum.* Peace be with you. *Bienvenu. La-bas?*"

"*Aleikum assalam,* Pedro." Tariq stood and embraced his friend, exchanging the requisite multiple kisses on each cheek, smiling at the mélange of languages that were a signature of Pedro Salazar's polyglot existence. "I am well, my friend. Sit."

Salazar lowered his bulk into the chair and gave a sigh of satisfaction. "I was delayed because of the new play. My very best. It is about the *madres* of the young men in Tetuan." Salazar frowned. "The problem is, I don't know how to end it." He sighed. "And you, you will come to dinner, yes? You are lodging with us?"

When Tariq had called from the Celliers Maroc, Salazar was effusive and insistent. "We have three *appartements,* one for me and Isabel, one for *les enfants,* one for good friends such as yourself." Tariq knew that *les enfants* were Isabel's two adult children.

"*Bikheer, M'sieur* Pedro." The waiter paused by the table. "What may I bring you?"

"*Thé, Ahmed, s'il vous plaît.*" Salazar turned to Tariq, continuing in French. "We are expected for dinner in an hour. Isabel is preparing for you a special couscous." He paused and gave Tariq a long, serious glance. "It was good to hear from you. I will help however I can. Tell me, how is your beautiful woman? How is life in Dubai?"

"I am helping wealthy Arabs invest their money wisely," Tariq replied, remembering Kate had been with him the second time he met Salazar in Paris.

"Ah, yes, so that as the world needs less and less oil, they will have something besides sand. *Et la femme*? She is with you in Dubai?"

The waiter placed Salazar's cup of tea on the table and disappeared. Tariq shook his head and reached for his coffee before replying, replaying in his mind the televised shots of the burned out mews. "There was a fatwa."

Pedro's eyes widened. "Against you?"

Tariq nodded.

Pedro took a long sip of the tea. "Who issued it?"

"I have enemies in London. You know the punishment for apostasy."

"*Mon Dieu.* But you are not an apostate."

"To my former brethren I am. And to Nadia Sultan."

"The ex-wife? *Pour quoi?*"

"She is not an ex-. She refuses to divorce me. She is a mujaidaat."

"*Madre de dios.*" Pedro sighed deeply and the

two men sat in silence for several long moments, then Pedro finished off his tea and checked his watch. "We are expected at eight. There is much to discuss." He glanced around the café, lowered his voice. "I have found the contact for The Fox. You will meet tomorrow."

Chapter 35

Marrakesh, Morocco

The house Pedro Salazar shared with Isabelle La Croux was located a few hundred yards from the Jemaa el-Fna. En route from the Café de France, Salazar was accosted numerous times by acquaintances. A somber black man in a blue burnoose whose art work was highly prized by the locals. A laughing French woman who chastised the playwright for not attending her dinner party the previous Saturday. A reed-thin teenage boy who shyly thrust a sheet of paper at Salazar and vanished. "My prodigy," Salazar explained with a small smile. "His mother moved here with him after she lost three older sons in Iraq. He wants to write novels."

Tariq followed Salazar's broad back through a labyrinth of narrow, winding back alleys, through a heavy wooden gate and into a cool, shaded cobblestone patio filled with tall orange trees and clay pots of red geraniums where softly swaying fronds of palm trees were reflected in a small still pool. Inside, the worn furnishings were of dark wood, the floors covered with multicolored rugs and large cushions, the sofas upholstered in some kind of creamy damask fabric. And Isabelle, blonde and dazzling in a flowing caftan that mimicked the violet of her eyes.

Following the evening meal of couscous and chicken with cinnamon and raisins served on a low table in front of the cushioned sofa, Isabelle disappeared up the stairs. Pedro brought out the *arak el masaya* and a pitcher of ice water. "The news today is good. Our boys retook Sinjar. We are making a difference. And the second delivery? It is ready?"

Tariq nodded, sipping the milky liquid. "There is a delay. As soon as I have word I will go to Algiers."

"You will go tomorrow to Chez Madeleine. Noor will have the new code your pilot needs." Tariq nodded.

"Turkey is going to be a problem," Pedro said.

"Some countries forget their history."

The conversation moved on to Pedro's existentialist dilemma of his play's ending, and at half eleven, pleading fatigue from the journey, Tariq retired to the guest quarters on the opposite side of the compound.

The main room of the apartment was simply furnished with a bed, a dark carved table with a large porcelain bowl, a plain wood desk near the window. Colorful framed posters, some Spanish, some French, decorated the rough plaster walls. Beneath the window, a dozen or so books filled a black enameled bookcase. Four novels by Juan Goytisolo, another Spanish expatriate living in Marrakesh. The complete works of Borges. *The Illuminated Rumi*. A small Qur'an bound in worn red leather.

After undressing and washing, Tariq murmured the *salat*, then moved aside the tapestry pillows and crawled between the cool cotton sheets, smooth as proverbial silk from thousands of launderings and dryings in Moroccan sunshine

Later, when he woke suddenly, it was to the sound of wind and angry voices outside the arched window. Shafts of moonlight reflecting through the iron grating on the window cast long shadows on the bed. The wooden blinds clattered against the plaster walls in the rising wind.

Puzzled, addled from the wine and *arak*, Tariq slid from beneath the sheets and walked naked to the window. He peered through the blinds. The voices and their shadows were retreating down the narrow passageway to the left. He stood motionless at the window. Silence returned. He moved back to the bed, feeling the coolness from the window on his naked back. As he slid once more between the sheets, his hand touched the petal-soft skin of a woman facing away from him, toward the wall.

His breath stopped. He frowned, tentatively touched the sleeping figure. Touched her shoulder, then the long silken hair. Slowly he exhaled. As he hesitated, heart racing, trying to process how it could be that she was there, in his bed again, she turned toward him, lifted her head slightly and smiled in the moonlight.

CHAPTER 36

Aix-en-Provence, France

Kate felt the kiss on her shoulder, then the long fingers on her nape under her hair, caressing, promising. She smiled, inhaling the familiar scent of citrus. The fingers moved slowly across her shoulder, traced a slow path around the clavicle. She felt her breath shortening as the hand cupped her left breast and his thumb teased the nipple.

From far away, she heard the whistling moan of the wind. She turned languorously and stretched against him, felt his other arm slide around her waist, his tongue lightly taste her shoulder, the top of each breast, then each nipple. Impatiently her body arched. The whistling of the wind grew louder and the vertical blinds tapped rhythmically against the half open sliding door. Below, something scraped the concrete of the patio.

She turned to face him, touched the hard muscles of his chest, teased his nipples, felt his arousal against her belly, moved her leg over his naked hip, eager for the smooth filling and fitting together. The sudden crash came as she arched her back and the lamp on the bedside table shattered on the tiled floor. Kate's eyes flew open. She sat up, staring into the blackness. Shocked, disbelieving, her hand searched the bed.

Nothing. No one. It was a dream.

She shook her head, her mouth dry, overcome with loss. Still feeling his tangible presence, she sniffed the air, smelled only the tangy dampness of the wind moaning through the half-opened sliding door that led to the balcony. Hating to sleep in a room without fresh air, she'd left the door open a few inches. Now the wind was fighting for entrance.

She climbed out of bed, scanning the tile floor dimly illuminated by the security lights outside. The terra cotta lamp lay in three broken pieces, the light bulb intact in the socket, the white silk shade twisted to one side. Kate walked around it, closed the heavy glass slider and closed the drapes.

She stared at the bed and recalled the dreams of the previous winter. Strange erotic dreams that were mutually shared with Tariq.

"I dreamed about you last night," he said casually one morning. "I dreamed we made love."

Shocked, she'd listened while he described a slightly altered version of her own dream. It had happened several times again, without pattern. Simultaneous dreaming, it was called. And now? Was he somewhere in North Africa dreaming of her? Should she accept Jean Pierre's offer? Or call Deborah and go scuttling back to London to find answers?

Intuition told her the answers she sought – Was Tariq connected to her parents murder? To Sheherezade's murder? Why had he disappeared? –did not lie in London. But Deborah had to be placated until she, Kate, could get back to Thames House. That meant feeding Deborah more intelligence on Connor O'Connor and Jenny Wen and a possible Chinese connection to helium-3.

She glanced around the room for her mobile, located it on the desk, and began scrolling through the gallery of photos she'd taken of the petite Asian woman with Connor O'Connor. Cursing herself for not having snapped any shots of Umarova's Goth girl friend, she awakened her laptop and logged on to the MI5 network.

Ten minutes of internet searching produced a Face book profile of Oxford student Jenny Wen, whose photo appeared to match the recent images she'd shot at the Southmoor cottage. Jenny's Facebook posts alternated between English and a Chinese language that Kate assumed was Shanghainese. All of Jenny Wen's Friends had Chinese names. For a 21-year-old, her posts were surprisingly restrained, at least the ones in English. There was no mention of family back in Shanghai. Kate followed a link to the Oxford Society of Chinese Students and found an announcement of an upcoming presentation on Chinese Growth in the Year of the Monkey. Another link took her to an analysis of China's Space Station Ambitions prepared by the China Policy Institute. Its focus was on China's success at spacecraft docking experiments and the development of technologies 'for the launch and establishment of space stations.'

She forwarded all the research to Deborah, with a note that she would continue to pursue the link on the CPI progress with space stations.

CHAPTER 37

The Girls Academy, London

Nadia Sultan watched the last of the first form girls file out of her classroom, her eyes lingering on the neat beige jumpers, white blouses, and white hijabs. It was her second year at The Academy. After Tariq moved out, she transferred from the Islamic school near the mosque to the better-paid position in a more affluent neighborhood. Here English, French and Arabic were taught and the core curriculum was less traditional, which had frustrated her until she discovered that the headmistress was more concerned with parent relations and networking with the sister madrassas in Cairo and Washington than she was with course content or who was wearing finger nail polish.

Her lesson plan for the next day was done. A teachers' meeting was scheduled in an hour. Enough time to write this week's blog. She knew exactly what the topic would be.

Subject: Your hegira.

My dear sisters:

Your comments on last week's posting – mothers willing to sacrifice their sons to Holy Jihad – provoked many responses. To those who disagree with my opinions, I refer you to the Qur'an, Surah 3:169.

Judging from the messages pouring in this week, there is one amazing topic on your collective minds: your desire to travel to the war zone and provide domestic comfort to our brave freedom fighters. If you need help to arrange your migration, use the information in the sidebar to contact Sister Miryam. She is in communication with an official marriage bureau. She will help you with details and arrangements.

Although many of your countrywomen have made the hegira on their own, I strongly recommend that you connect with other like-minded women to make the trip together. The biggest challenge will be in convincing your parents to support you in your new life. If your father refuses to give his permission for the marriage, one of our emirs may be able to help you. If you cannot find the funds for your migration, please message me privately.

Nadia inserted the Green Bird signature, closed down the posting page and clicked up her encrypted-mail program. There were two new messages in Sister Miryam's Inbox. The first was from Alone in Manchester. *Thank you for the chocolates. I shared them with my friend Zara. She had a big fight with her father. She is ready to make the hegira with me. We need a list of what to pack for the trip. Please tell me how much the trip will cost.*

Nadia uploaded the English Sisters' bank account information. The balance provoked a smile that continued after she logged off and composed the reply to Lonely in Manchester. *We will be glad to help. For future messages, please switch to the message app Lockmessage. You will need to set up an account with a password, then message me your trip plans, tell me what names you will use to travel. Tell Zara not to discuss the trip with anyone. How old are you and Zara? Do you have passports? Can you get to Heathrow Airport? We will arrange to have tickets waiting for you there.*

The second encrypted message was from Dervish. *Subject 1 booked flight to Menara airport. Awaiting assignment.*

Nadia scrolled back through the thread, then typed a reply. *Please forward security code for Knightsbridge residence. Does subject 1 have return reservation to London?*

Chapter 38

Connor O'Connor sat at the booth in the back of the restaurant, hands folded over the brown envelope, watching the students come and go. The entire day had been one mad race, beginning with the arrival of the humongous Ardnamurchan file from "Z" midmorning while he was at 5th Domaine. Furious at his housemate for not waiting until he was back in Denchworth, he didn't try to open the file until his fellow security geeks had wandered off for lunchtime breaks. Whereupon he discovered that the file was passworded.

To retrieve the password, "Z" wanted to see the £30,000 in her account. Connor had managed to accomplish the electronic transfer and then "Z" insisted on giving him the password in person. Another hour racing from Malvern to Denchworth, trapped in a traffic slowdown because of a horrendous collision on the A40 involving a lorry and a mini electric vehicle.

When he'd finally arrived at the cottage and obtained the password from his smugly grinning housemate, he opened the file and found 100 pages of drawings. Blueprints, actually. He could have forwarded the electronic file on to Jenny Wen, but he wanted to physically hand over the thumb drive, what he still thought of as the 'bride price'.

It was half seven when he got to the Falstaff; Jenny was on her way. He took a deep breath, recalling the despair he'd felt as he transferred the £30,000 from his moonlighting account to "Z." He'd have to replace it or he wouldn't be able to make a down payment on the house in Shiplake, or anywhere else. He stared at his mobile, then scrolled through the log of recent texts. Nothing from Emma Whyte since he sent the last picture. Was she going to be difficult?

He heard his name called and saw Jenny emerging from the gaggle of denim-clad youth surging into the café. She was wearing a white silk shirt with red embroidery and a red mini skirt that made his heart start thumping. She was easily the most beautiful female in the café. He couldn't take his eyes off her golden tan legs.

"So nice to see you, Connor. You brought it?" She slid into the booth across from him.

He nodded. "This should make your father very happy." He slid the envelope across the table.

She opened the envelope, smiled, tucked it into her blue rucksack. "You are amazing. I already text my father. He is happy."

"I am glad your father is happy. Do we have a date for the wedding?"

"In December, I think. And, Connor, there is one more little thing that would make him *very* happy."

CHAPTER 39

Fulham, West London

Wrapped in icy cold anger, Deborah MacKenzie took a cab from the Tube Station. She'd agreed to "one more tryst" only to fine tune what she thought of as her elimination plan. She asked the driver to circle the block twice, spied the white MG parked around the corner from the house. The vehicle appeared to be empty. The cab dropped her in front of the house, she paid the driver, and walked up the flagstone walk. The house was a single, detached structure, probably vintage 1980, newly renovated. A light shone from behind curtains in the front window. She hesitated, wondering if she'd read the report wrong. After texting Black Irish in the morning, she'd asked Gillian for an update on all the MI5 safe houses in London. This one was listed as a new acquisition, cleaned and vacant. She opened the door, keyed in the security code, and realized the system had been disarmed.

"Hello, Emma darling." Black Irish aka Dylan Chandler aka Connor O'Connor was lounging against the wall in the foyer. Perfectly tailored white shirt untucked over tailored black trousers, tanned feet in leather thong sandals. Crystal flute in hand, blue eyes amused. "Lovely to see you."

God, what a handsome stud.

She forced a laugh, closing the door. "Clever boy. How did you get in?"

"Child's play, my dear." He approached, gave her a kiss on the cheek. "I wanted to be here to welcome you. Wine's chilling. You look marvelous." He took in the pale yellow linen sheath and cream-colored stilettos. "But of course, with that body, you look marvelous in anything. Or nothing." He put an arm around her shoulders and led her into the salon. "May I pour your wine?"

Deborah took a breath, smile fixed in place. "I'd love that, Dylan."

"I've missed you, Emma. Glad you could find time for me. We could have gone out, you know."

He moved over to the ice bucket, poured the champagne into the second crystal flute of the pair that he must have brought with him, handed it to her with a kiss. Unbidden, fizzy chemicals began circulating in her brain, not unlike the bubbles fizzing in her flute.

So this is how we are going to play it. What the hell, why not?

She returned the kiss, felt his hands go behind her back, the zipper every so gently lowered. She took a sip of the champagne, then another. She knew her dress cascaded to the floor and the kisses were on her neck, trending lower. She was no longer cold. The dress was followed by the lacy peach bra and thong and more sips of champagne and without quite knowing how, she was in the bedroom where the coverlet had already been turned down and Black Irish was suavely earning his honorarium.

The request came later, gently, after more champagne and foil-wrapped truffles. "I have a favor to ask, Emma. My mum is very sick. Cancer, you know. The treatment is going to cost fifty thou. It's experimental. NHS won't cover it. She'll die without it. Do you think you could help? A loan?"

CHAPTER 40

Marrakesh, Morocco

The Ryanair flight from Marseille landed at Menara International Airport at noon, only twenty minutes late. Nothing in Kathryn St. Claire's passport nor her one carry-on bag raised any official Moroccan eyebrows. Her quick scan of arriving and departing passengers revealed no one exhibiting any particular interest in the tall woman in a white shirt and long black skirt. Twenty minutes later she was cleared through immigration, and after a stop at a cash machine for *dirhams*, she was outside in the warm twilight. Staring at the swarm of large and small taxis – the *grands* and the *petits* in local parlance – she was glad she'd accepted Jean Pierre's offer to have the riad arrange her transportation to the hotel.

She searched the crowd and the cluster of small taxis the color of yellow sand. A small thin man with a black beard and an anxious frown, wearing the native white pajamas, emerged from the fourth *petit*. He was holding a sign that said "Brown." She greeted him in Arabic. The frown dissolved into a warm smile and he scurried to open the door for her. Sliding into the backseat of the little Peugeot 205, she took a deep breath and silently acknowledged she was still emotionally ragged from her morning visit in Aix-en-Provence.

After the brioche and café au lait at the hotel, she'd driven out to the compact pink stucco house with the red tile roof where she was first greeted by the Golden Retriever and then by hugs from the twins. After a quick embrace, Jacques disappeared in the family Peugeot to help a cousin move house. Maggie had served her homemade tomato soup with a fresh baguette and a carafe of *vin rouge*.

Seated at the scarred wooden table in the big kitchen, the twins updated her on their school and social activities. Tony was playing soccer. Angelique was trying out for the school track team. Both were learning English. Only half listening to their words, Kate's eyes had searched their faces, their dark hair and brown eyes, marveling at their resemblance to Michael. And their Spanish grandmother . . . neither of whom had ever met them. Taking a deep breath, she realized Angelique was waiting for a response to something she said.

"*Je regrette, Angelique*. What did you say?"

"I said I would like to visit you."

Kate glanced at Maggie who nodded without meeting Kate's eyes. "I told her, perhaps when she is older."

Kate took a deep breath. "I'd love for you to visit me, Angelique. Let's plan something wonderful."

"I want to go to school there. In England. "

Kate glanced at Maggie, who quickly stood up and began clearing away the remains of the lunch. Antoine disappeared outside with a soccer ball.

Angelique's mobile rang, she spoke briefly, then announced that she was invited to a party at her friend's house.

"I'm sorry, Kate," Maggie said quickly, seeing the fleeting disappointment on Kate's face. "I didn't know when you called. It's her friend's birthday . . ."

And so Kate smiled and hugged Angelique and promised they could talk more about a visit to London. For the next half hour she sat across the table from Maggie, the lovely redhead from Cornwall who had spent a year teaching English in Aix and then wed the head of the college foreign language department, who was the brother of Jean Pierre Rousseau. When Maggie and Jacques discovered they were unable to make babies, it seemed fortuitous that they take on the adoption when Kate found herself pregnant by the MI6 agent married to a woman he couldn't divorce.

"You got my letter?" Maggie topped off their wineglasses.

Kate nodded. She took a sip of the pale red wine and stared into the glass. "I don't have any answers, Maggie. It would be easier if her mother were someone you'd never met. Or who lived thousands of miles away. At the end of the day, you must do whatever you're comfortable with."

"Even if we never tell them the truth?"

Kate swirled the wine in the glass. She nodded. "Yes, even that."

"Antoine is easy. But Angelique," she shook her head. "Some days I think she hates me. And she's been in trouble at school. Jacques thinks we should find a school in Switzerland."

"And you?"

" I'm thinking England. Stowe. What do you think?"

Kate felt a jolt of happiness somewhere near her heart. She smiled. "I didn't turn out too badly. Let me know how I can help."

Thirty minutes later, driving back to the Villa Angelina, Kate made the decision to accept Jean Pierre's consultancy. She desperately needed to close the chapter, to put paid to the Tariq story. Although she was clear she would be gathering intelligence for Interpol, it was now an intensely personal challenge to find out the whole truth about the Lebanese Banker with the aliases and wife.

To separate fiction from fact.

To be either sure Tariq did or did not have anything to do with the bombing. Even if it meant becoming a rogue agent in the Red City.

Chapter 41

Because all Kate knew about Marakesh came from an old Hitchcock movie, she had purchased a tourist guide at the airport in Marseille and learned that Marrakesh was the second largest city in Morocco after Casablanca, with an unofficial population of around two million. That the possible origin of the name of the city came from a Tamazight Berber word, meaning Land of God. That the plaza called Djemaa El Fna was the busiest plaza in the entire continent of Africa, and that Djemaa el Fna meant City of the Dead.

"I made arrangements for you to stay at a guest house," Jean Pierre said when he confirmed her flight. "Le Riad du Maroc. The innkeepers, Maurice and Colette are French. Maurice used to be with the Gendarmerie Nationale. Colette teaches cooking classes for foreigners."

"And the asset? "

"It is Maurice. And the riad has a wonderful wine cellar."

The taxi had entered the *medina*, the old walled city, passing through a narrow street lined with buildings of red stucco with doors painted green and blue. A woman in traditional dress flattened herself in a doorway while the taxi passed. Kate stared out the window at the darkening city, recalling the opening scene from the 1956 Hitchcock movie when the young McKenna boy had accidentally pulled off the face veil, the *niqab*, of one of the women on the bus. And the resulting rage of the woman's husband. She'd seen the movie with Tariq. He visited Marrakesh often, he said, because his brother had a winery a few hours away. When they'd met Salazar – Pedro Salazar, the Spanish playwright – in Paris, there had been discussion of the Red City over coffee and pistachio pastry. Pedro was planning to move there, to Marrakesh, he told them, to be with his girl friend, a clothing designer. Then the conversation turned to Salazar's passion for Muslim culture and history, and his interest in Sufi theology.

Remembering the conversation now, Kate wondered if the meeting with Salazar had been as accidental as it seemed. Was the Spaniard a political connection, a link or a cut out in a web of money laundering or worse? Would Tariq be staying at a hotel or a riad in Marrakesh? Or with Salazar in a private residence? If the latter, it might be more difficult to "get near him," as Jean Pierre phrased it.

Le Riad du Maroc, a small masterpiece of Moorish-Spanish architecture, was located only a few meters from Djemaa el Fna. At the end of a narrow patio, the carved wooden entrance door opened onto a tiled courtyard reception area. Through an archway to one side, Kate glimpsed a lighted swimming pool surrounded by whitewashed walls. On the opposite side, an intimate dining room extended to an outside terrace lit with brass lanterns. Six tables covered in white linen were set for dinner.

"*Bienvenue au Riad du Maroc, Mademoiselle*. We have put you in the Jasmine Room. I am Maurice." The short balding man with olive skin and very black eyes handed her a large, orate gold key. "You can log on to the Internet from your room. The security code is your last name plus your room number. We serve hors d'oeuvres and beverages in the *bhou*." He gestured toward the alcove off the reception area where a bearded man in a white shirt man sat alone with a martini. "The pool and the hammam are open until ten o'clock," Maurice continued. "You may dine down here or in your room. We begin serving at eight o'clock. If you need anything at all, please ask. You are *en famille*. Now I will show you to your room."

"Monsieur Kassar stays with Señor Salazar for four days. " Maurice explained after closing the door of the Jasmine Room. "It is a *maison private*, not far from the plaza. It has a courtyard and a small *appartement* within the walls. M. Kassar lodges in the *appartement*. They take coffee in the morning, at ten o'clock, at the Café de France, in the plaza. They sit outside. They read newspapers. They talk, they watch people. They go separately, but meet again in the afternoon at five o'clock, for an aperitif, then they return to the Salazar residence."

"Have you been inside the compound?"

He shook his head. "No, but the woman who cooks for Monsieur Salazar is the cousin of our maid." He smiled. "Marrakesh is a small town."

"When M. Kassar leaves the Café in the morning, where does he go?"

"Sometimes he plays *le touriste*. He goes to the Koutoubia Mosque, to the Menara Basin. Yesterday he wanders for an hour in the souk. He buys a gold bracelet for which he pays too many dirhams," Maurice said with a superior smile. "Two times he goes to the bank on Rue Moulay Ismail. And," Maurice added, "In the evening, he visits Chez Madeleine, for an hour and fifteen minutes each visit."

Kate frowned. "Chez Madeleine?"

Maurice produced a Gallic shrug. "A brothel, *mademoiselle*, very chic, very high-priced."

Kate felt Maurice studying her face. She wondered how much Jean Pierre had told him. "Chez Madeleine," she repeated, and then asked, apropos of nothing, "You have been there?"

"No, mademoiselle. But I am told it is quite splendid. Each room has a separate theme. There is the Geisha Room, the Henry VIII Room, the Proust Room." Another Gallic shrug.

She nodded impassively and asked, "And when M. Kassar leaves Chez Madeleine, he returns immediately to the Salazar compound?"

"Yes." He took a sheet from a small pad of paper on the bedside table, scribbled an address, and handed it to her. "You are thinking to visit the *appartement* of M. Kassar?"

"Possibly. How many people live there, at the residence?"

"M. Salazar and his companion, Isabelle. She owns a boutique on Rue Souriya. The house is hers. In three days, only M. Kassar goes out in the evening."

Maurice paused, then added, "The house is not

far from Jemaa el Fna, but you must go through many small streets. It is not a bad neighborhood, but this is Marrakesh. You must be careful, especially at night. I am happy to accompany you, although I prefer not to enter the Salazar courtyard. My chess friend who is with the Minister of the Interior, would be very sad if I am caught in wrongdoing."

From below, a melodious bell sounded. "I must go, mademoiselle. But please check the armoire. *Ma femme*, Colette, has left you a garment to cover yourself. For disguise, not religion. We are both Catholics, and also *aficionados* of the theater. Should you prefer, we have other costumes."

CHAPTER 42

Marrakesh, Morocco

The garment Kate found folded in the dark wood armoire of the Jasmine Room was not the black burka she dreaded, but a djellaba of a misty gray cotton fabric. A silvery grey and white printed silk hijab lay on top of it. There was a matching niqab, in case Kate wanted to cover her face entirely, which she elected to do at the moment. Seated in the very back of the terrace at the Café de France, sipping mint tea, she watched one of the vendors below in the square attempt to pile a row of plump grapefruit atop an already teetering pyramid of oranges.

Kate had arrived at Jemaa el Fna at 9:30, her stomach full of butterflies. She was more nervous, she realized, than when she was running an asset in London. To her relief she was not the only female in the café; at the next table three voluble French women of a certain age chattered over large white cups of café au lait. At 9:35, Tariq appeared, wearing a white djellaba over a pair of faded blue jeans, carrying a folded newspaper.

From behind the niqab Kate felt her breath shorten painfully. Suddenly her mouth was dry and adrenalin flooded her body. Tariq was accompanied by a tall man with thick graying hair in a worn black suede jacket over a faded red T-shirt and a pair of loose black trousers of mysterious ethnicity. The nearest hovering waiter greeted both men in French, and almost immediately returned with two large steaming white cups, a plate of croissants, a small crock of butter, and a jar of what Kate suspected was *mermélade d'oranges.*

Waving off a vendor of sequined Turkish slippers, secluded behind her own Arabic newspaper, Kate studied the face of the man who had been her lover. His olive skin was deeply tanned. He had grown a beard and his dark hair was longer than she remembered. Rimless dark glasses hid his eyes. Slowly her breathing quieted and she watched the two men impassively, occasionally turning the pages of the newspaper. After an hour, cups drained, newspapers laid aside, the two men watched the activities in the square. Salazar made a call on his mobile, looked pleased, murmured something to Tariq. Tariq nodded to the waiter, paid the bill, and the two stood up.

Signaling the waiter for her own check, Kate watched as the men ambled across the bustling plaza, dodging a group of tourists disembarking from a tour bus, heading toward a curved archway in the stuccoed wall. Dropping the requisite dirhams on the table, she gathered her newspaper and meandered toward the archway. She hesitated as she stepped outside, glanced to the right and left. A few paces away, Salazar stood laughing with a brown-skinned woman in a white hijab. Quickly Kate scanned the crowd, spotted Tariq moving past a stall of leather work into the rabbit warren of passageways that made up the souk. Taking a deep breath, checking that the niqab was securely fastened over her face, she headed after him.

CHAPTER 43

Riad du Maroc to Rue du Moulin Rouge, Marrakesh

In the dining alcove of the Riad du Maroc, Kate moved the gold-rimmed plate with the remains of roasted duck to one side and sipped the Moroccan wine. She thought about the MI5 dossier on Tariq: his early involvement in the Brotherhood, his work with the Islamists at the East London Mosque. About Jean Pierre's suggestion that the Sufi Counsel might have been involved in a plot to assassinate bin Laden.

Staring into the wine goblet, replaying her foray into the souk that morning, her smile disappeared, replaced by a sense of disgust that she was, for all intents, stalking her former lover. For two hours she'd trailed him, deep into the labyrinthine passageways, past the vendors of brass lanterns and copper pots, of gold and silver jewelry and richly colored carpets. Twice he'd stopped to chat with a vendor. Once he turned suddenly and looked full at her. She could not imagine she was recognizable behind the niqab, but her mouth had gone dry and she dropped back, colliding with the driver of a heavily-laden mule cart. When she turned, Tariq had disappeared into the throng of milling shoppers. Thoroughly lost, she'd wandered for another hour through the twisting alleyways without seeing him, finally asking directions of a garrulous vendor of watermelons who drew her a map. It was past three o'clock when she found her way back to the Riad.

After the scrubbing in the eucalyptus-scented chamber of the steam-filled hamman and the exhilarating swim in the pool surrounded by whitewashed walls, she dressed and appeared in the dining room where Maurice was waiting with the Ouled Thaled Syrah.

It was now eight o'clock. She had two hours to prepare for the assignment she had agreed to do for Jean Pierre. And once and for all, to answer the unspeakable question.

Chapter 44

Rue du Moulin Rouge, Marrakesh

At 9:45 that evening, Kate moved silently into the rue du Moulin Rouge, walking as she and Kincaid had walked when they were eight, trying to mimic the long strides of their Scottish grandfather. The narrow winding street was empty, lit only by occasional slivers of light escaping from behind shuttered windows. The rising moon cast long shadows before her.

It was a residential area, each residence surrounded by tall stuccoed walls. Well aware that a woman alone on the streets of Marrakesh after dark would call unwanted attention, Kate had chosen a man's local attire: a *kaffiyya* covering her hair that was pulled into a tight knot at her neck, dark colored *kurta* and cotton trousers. On her feet were her own black Puma trainers. Tucked into the waistband of the trousers was Maurice's 9 mm Beretta Model 92. Also in her possession was the set of lock picks supplied by the innkeeper.

"I am not sure what you will find in the courtyard," Maurice told her. "I know there are tall orange trees. Their branches hang over the wall. Besides the main gate, there is a small door on the back side of the compound. I am told it locks from the inside. I assume there is a private sentry." He shrugged. "I wish I knew more, but I did not want to compromise myself."

The plan was that Maurice would reconnoiter the Salazar compound and advise her by text message as soon as Tariq left for his nightly visit to Chez Madeleine. Then Maurice would follow Tariq, presumably to the bordello. Maurice said it would take Tariq thirty minutes, more or less, to walk back to the compound after his evening's entertainment. In the event that the entertainment should have proved too tiring, Maurice would have an unoccupied taxi idling nearby. Either way, he would text her when Tariq left Chez Madeleine. They would rendezvous back at the Riad. He gave her a quick embrace as they parted and murmured the convoluted Gallic expression for good luck that always made her smile. "*Merde pour toi, mam'selle.*"

Kate turned a corner, checked the number on the stucco wall to her left, stopped before the tall wooden gate in the shadows of the leafy trees whose branches overreached the wall. From within the compound came the distant sounds of Arabic television. Nothing moved on the street.

She reached for the lock picks and turned on the tiny pen light, shielding it with the sleeve of the *kurta*. The procedure with the little tension wrench and the various picks took longer than she would have liked. She felt drops of sweat trickle down the back of her neck. Finally she heard a soft click. Exhaling, she pressed down on the latch and slowly pushed the thick gate a foot or so into the courtyard. There was no alarm, just a soft whine of the hinges, inaudible against the sound of the television program. To the right side of the courtyard she made out a low, flat-roofed one-storey structure, totally dark, and to the left, the main dwelling. A window on the lower floor of the main house and one on the upper floor were lit.

Kate moved sideways through the narrow opening, closed the gate carefully behind her, releasing the latch, scanning the area for any sign of a motion detector. All was quiet; the only light was from the brightening moon. Back pressed against the wall, she checked the time. It was 10:08. If Tariq followed his previous schedule, she had less than an hour. The mobile was set on vibrate.

For several minutes Kate stood motionless, listening for any indication her entry was seen or heard. A light wind moved the branches of the orange trees. Through the large window on the ground floor of the house, she saw a woman in a white caftan stand up and stretch and rub the back of her neck. The sound of the television program ended abruptly. A few seconds later, the lights in the lower floor of the house were extinguished.

Moonlight illuminated a small whitish fountain and reflecting pool in the center of the courtyard. Tall spikey shrubs surrounded the fountain. Meandering from the main house, a flagstone path circled the fountain and disappeared behind tall bushes in front of the smaller single-storey structure at the opposite side of the courtyard. That would be the apartment Maurice described. As she moved away from the wall, the door of the main house opened.

She froze. *Sod all!* If she was discovered, she

would be trapped in the courtyard. Heart thudding, she pressed back against the wall, reached for the Beretta. A white figure appeared at the door and she heard the sound of a female voice calling "*Kitte, kitte, kitte,*" Smiling in nervous relief, Kate watched as a dark feline shadow jumped from the top of the stuccoed wall to her right and streaked past her feet. The cat leaped into the lighted doorway and the door closed.

Taking a deep breath and skirting the bushes, Kate moved swiftly toward the dark apartment, found the wooden entry door, put her ear against it. There was no sound from within. She had no reason to think anyone would be inside, but there was no reason to believe Sod's Law was not fully functional in Morocco.

She set to work with the lock picks and shrugged off a ballooning list of what if's: – *What if Tariq slipped past Maurice and returned early and found her hacking into his computer? What if, in the kurtu and kaffiyya, he took her for an intruder and shot her? What if she shot him?*

CHAPTER 45

Avenue des Orange, Marrakesh

Two miles away, a small taxi halted in front of Chez Madeleine beneath the street light. The back door of the taxi opened, a tall, bearded man in western dress exited. He carried a small package, climbed the steps of the brothel. The man moved to the side of the door and bent toward a small light next to the intercom. A few seconds later the door opened, briefly revealing Madeleine's elegantly dressed security guard.

Inside Chez Madeleine's cool and elegant foyer, the bearded man was greeted by a raven-haired woman wearing a white long-sleeved silk tunic designed with a cut out on each shoulder. Her long skirt was of graphic print in tones of dark blue and orange. "Noor, how wonderful to see you."

"And you, Hussein. It's been too long. Let me pour you some refreshment."

He followed her into the small bar in an alcove off the foyer, watched her add ice to a crystal tumbler, pour the pomegranate juice. She poured a flute of champagne for herself. "Şerefe, Hussein."

"And to yours, Noor. Is everything arranged?"

She nodded. "The Pasha's Room is yours for as long as you need it. Gingerman has already arrived.

There's no one else booked there this evening. Up-stairs, last door on the right."

Chapter 46

The lock on the door to the apartment took twice as long as the main entry gate. Sweat began seeping into Kate's eyes. She paused, wiped her forehead with her sleeve. Just as she began considering that the best plan would be to abort the whole idea, the pins settled into place with a reassuring click. She took three long, slow breaths, felt her heart beat slowing, and stepped inside.

Nothing moved. The room was still with the emptiness of a space that has no living creature. She closed the door, stood with her back to the wall and inhaled the acrid scent of Tariq's cologne. Her pen-light scanned the four walls of what appeared to be a one-room studio with a tiny kitchen, illuminating the narrow bed with the striped coverlet, the rough stone floor with three small dark rugs. Two rough wooden tables flanked the bed. A black carry-on bag sat on a rattan luggage rack. The luminous face of the clock on the table beside the open closet said 10:18. Across from the door stood a dark wooden desk with a silver laptop computer on it. A leather bound book lay on top of the computer. To the right of the desk was a partially open door.

She pushed the door all the way open, scanned

the small bathroom with a pedestal sink, a western toilet, a bidet and a tiled walk-in shower. The mirror over the sink was faintly damp, the room fragrant with sage and cardamon. The wood-encased bottle with the *1903* label stood on one edge of the white sink.

A large white towel hung over one wall of the shower. Impulsively, Kate reached for the towel and brought it to her face, inhaled. Swallowing, she replaced the towel and walked quickly toward the desk.

She moved the leather-bound book aside and settled into the wooden chair. It gave a small squeak as she sat down. The cover of the computer opened with a small click that seemed loud in the dark silence. She found the power button. A 3-D image of a mist-covered mountain lake appeared on the screen. Tentatively she touched the finger pad, moved the cursor. An empty box appeared and she was prompted for a password. Damn! She stared at the blinking cursor. She had watched Tariq check his email numerous times and had deliberately kept herself from trying to scope the password. So much for being a considerate lover.

The password could be in English, French or Arabic. Or a combination of languages. Probably an alpha numeric. She shook her head hopelessly. It was now 10:27. Tapping her fingers lightly on the touch pad in nervous frustration, her eyes settled on the small leather-covered book. She picked it up and riffled through the pages. It was a diary. Some of the entries were in Arabic, some in French and English. She flipped to the front of the book. The first entry was dated six months before they met. The first few entries were banal. Comments about a personnel problem at the bank. A rambling entry about his grandmother, followed by a cryptic comment about "the ninja." She leafed ahead to December, found the entry for the day they met, began reading with the by-now familiar sense of curiosity mixed with self-disgust.

Tonight I met a beautiful woman. She has long hair and dark eyes. I cannot wait to see her unclothed, to taste her . . . She riffled nervously through the pages to the current year and read the March 16 entry: *Tonight I have lost myself . . .*

March 16. Tariq's birthday. She'd left Thames House after lunch. Taken a circuitous route to the Tate where she'd met Sheherazade. She'd only been running the informant a few weeks. The young woman was deeply frightened, but fiercely determined to continue bringing what small bits of information she could about what was happening in the women's groups at the mosque, her husband's email correspondence with the Syrians who she suspected were planning a cyber attack on the U.K., about the fights she was having with him. She had brought three documents from his briefcase that she copied. Standing that day in the Blake Gallery beside the woman in the dark burka, pretending to stare at *Nebuchadnezzar*, Kate had murmured assurances about her safety, listened to the recited fragments of a phone conversation overheard between the husband and someone at the Syrian Embassy.

Leaving the Tate fifteen minutes after Sheherazade, she'd scurried to the Turkish deli for dolmas and stuffed roasted eggplant, then back to Canterbury Mews to set the table with her grandmother's embroidered tablecloth and the tall white candles. Tariq had been late arriving, almost an hour. Something about a delayed call to a bank client in Tokyo, a detail that faded to insignificance as the evening wore on and they'd found their way to the wide bed in the darkening bedroom, caressed their way into a vast timeless dimension that erased all other realities.

She returned to the March 16 entry: . . . *Must find some way to deal with the poisoned dwarf.*

Kate paused over the *poisoned dwarf*, then quickly leafed ahead to the date the bomb exploded. There was no entry for that day, nor for any day for the next two months. The entries resumed in July. All in Arabic now. Cryptic notes about a conversation with someone named The Fox, a reminder to check flights to Jo'Burg, some unpleasantness with his servant Ali, a brief notation about someone named Yasmin.

From outside the shuttered window, footsteps grated on concrete. *The sentry.* She sat motionless, fearful that the light from the monitor could be seen through the wooden shutters. The footsteps faded into silence. She turned to Tariq's most recent entry, the previous day. *I have returned from Chez Madeleine. The arak was perfect. The piano player is excellent. Noor is astonishingly beautiful. The night was most gratifying. S. Will be pleased.*

Jaw clenched, Kate threw the book on the desk as if it burned her fingers, turned back to the laptop with its indefatigable blinking curser awaiting the password.

She had not come to Marakesh to read her ex-lover's diary like some bloody neurotic heroine of a gothic romance. She had come to discover who killed her parents.

She frowned, thinking of her own cache of personal passwords required to navigate in cyberspace, whether to pay the utility bill or buy a pair of shoes online. A cache she stored in a small book that said *Favorite Recipes*. She glanced at Tariq's diary, picked it up and quickly leafed through to the end. On the last page she found a handwritten list titled "software." *MoneyBeirut003. Excell Jerusalem004. UBCMeknes3005. FenetresDamascus5007* . . . She typed the alphanumeric and smiled. The computer was hers.

The icon in the bottom right corner of the monitor indicated the wireless connection was active. Marcel, one of Interpol's resident geeks, said he would talk her through the instructions that would give him remote access to the computer. To call at any hour. Marcel's number was programmed on her mobile. He answered on the first ring.

"What's the IP address?" he asked immediately.

"Where do I find it?"

"Go to the website www.whatismyIP.com? You should get a group of four numbers between 0 and 255."

"I'm there. I have it."

"Read it to me."

Chapter 47

Avenue des Oranges, Marrakesh

Maurice shifted from one foot to another in the dark doorway and watched the dimly lighted entrance of the brothel across the tree-lined street. He craved a cigarette. He craved the taste of Scotch that the evening's work had denied him. He longed to be snuggled against Colette's plump backside. But these were minor annoyances. Given the anonymous monthly retainer deposited into his bank account, he had no right to complain. He didn't want to know the details, but Rousseau wouldn't have sent an MI5 officer for trivia.

Maurice lied when he told Kate he'd never been inside Chez Madeleine. Or partially lied. It had been the occasion of his nephew's sixteenth birthday. The boy was bookish, seemingly interested only in European history, raised as an only child by Maurice's dull brother and his equally dull wife in Angouleme. In the afternoon he and Colette had taken the boy sightseeing and then to dinner. Colette returned to the Riad while Maurice brought the boy to meet Madeleine, and waited in the tastefully appointed lounge, sipping absinthe like some ghostly blue figure in a Picasso drawing, while the young man learned about love in the Tsar's Palace room. Maurice smiled,

198

remembered the slightly more confident set of the young man's shoulders when he'd joined his uncle afterwards.

A light cool breeze channeled down the street. Maurice longed for the heat to be past, for the rainy season to begin. The petit taxi he'd arranged motored slowly past, idled in front of Chez Madeleine. It was 10:43. He glanced toward the house. As if on schedule, the door opened and a male figure emerged, pulled a mobile from his pocket, thumbed the screen, walked briskly down the steps. Maurice quickly verified the face against the image in his mobile's gallery. It was Tariq Kassar. The taxi paused in front of the house. Kassar hesitated, looked up at the clouds beginning to obscure the moon, and waived the taxi on. Watching the wiry figure striding away and disappearing around the corner, Maurice clicked Send on the already prepared text.

CHAPTER 48

Kate stared at the computer screen. For the past ten minutes it had been black. She tapped the desk with one index finger. Suddenly the mobile vibrated. Kate started and tore her gaze from the screen to read Maurice's text: *Il est parti a pied*. Tariq was on the way back. On foot. It was 10:45. She had fifteen minutes, maybe twenty. Staring at the black monitor, she listened for any sound of the security guard. Jean Pierre and Interpol were getting what they wanted, but she had learned nothing. Nothing to tell her why he disappeared, why he never contacted her. Nothing about his wife. Or was she the *poisoned dwarf?*

Suddenly the desktop window was back. Whatever Marcel had done to or taken from Tariq's computer was done. He had probably gotten copies of everything on the hard disk. She clicked up the Start menu, found the email program and the Inbox. Tariq was better at managing his incoming mail than she was: there were only four unread messages. The senders were H. Solo, English Sister, and Abu Dhabi Enterprises. The message from H. Solo was a forwarded excerpt of a poem by Rumi, the 13th century Sufi mystic whose poetry Tariq had shared with Kate during rainy evenings of their first winter together. Another love interest?

She checked the time again. 11:01. She clicked on the forward icon, sent the unread messages to her own e-address. She would read them later. Hurriedly, she clicked up the Sent Mail box, deleted the same three messages from the Sent log, did the same in the Deleted Messages box. Frustrated, she stared at the list of folders in the sidebar, found one that said *ninja*. Fingers shaking, she inserted the thumb drive, clicked on the copy button, watched as the light on the drive came on.

From outside in the street she heard the sound of a vehicle accelerating, then the sound of a key searching for a lock. Bloody hell! Someone was coming in the back gate. Best case scenario was that Pedro Salazar had been out and was returning. Worst case was that Tariq had picked up a taxi after leaving Chez Madeleine on foot. She jerked the thumb drive out of the slot. Trying not to fumble, she powered off the laptop, closed the cover, moved swiftly to the door, adjusting the *kaffiyya* over her hair. Barely breathing, opening the door only wide enough for her body, she thumbed the small lock on the inside of the door, heard the soft whine of gate hinges, and slipped through into the shadows behind the fountain at the very instant that the garden gate opened.

CHAPTER 49

Menara Airport, Marrakesh

From beneath the brim of her straw hat, Kate glanced around the Ryanair departure area. There was only one flight per day from Marrakesh to London Heathrow, and it appeared that all 189 seats would be filled. Refusing to make eye contact with the hirsute and obese man in a safari jacket who was staring at her breasts, Kate wished she'd held onto the abaya until she got to London.

She glanced around the lounge in exasperation. The air was thick with the scent of too many bodies. Her right ankle ached. Her left shoulder muscle was so tight it was making her left arm ache as well. She prayed for the flight departure to be announced.

Her mobile vibrated. She stared at the text message on the screen. *Security system breached. Proceed with caution.*

Someone was in her parents' flat in Knightsbridge.

About to dial the number of the porter, another text arrived. *Alarm aborted. All secure.*

The abort function only worked when the correct code was put in and the only other person who had the code was Gwen. She found the security system app on her mobile, logged in, checked the real time video. The camera was located in the salon and faced the entry door. She watched the video for several minutes; nothing moved. It had to be a system malfunction, nothing to bother Gwen with. And then, yet another text popped up on the screen. It was from Andrew Cameron, the solicitor in Dartmouth. *Neighbors brought the magistrate today. When do you return? We need a face to face. Ring me back as convenient.*

Bloody hell. She'd have to go down to Devon and that would mean putting Deborah off one more time. If Deborah found out about the unauthorized assignment for Interpol, at the very least she'd be suspended. If she tried to fit in a trip to Devon, she'd probably be sacked.

The station agents behind the counter had their heads together and a minute later, without surprise, she listened to the announcement that the flight was overbooked and that seven hundred Euros were available to anyone amenable to taking a flight the following day. When, she guessed, the same offer would be made again.

As the passengers milled about, she fought off the claustrophobia that was making her nauseous and tried to make sense of the past week.

The file on Tariq Kassar that Officer Johar had shared with her in London.

The conversation with Jean Pierre that confirmed Tariq's connection to Nadia Sultan, meaning that for all the time they'd been together he had lied, explicitly or by omission.

The late-night break-in of Tariq's apartment in

the Salazar compound that concluded with the close encounter in the garden in Rue du Moulin Rouge where she'd crouched behind the fountain watching the tall burnoose-clad figure amble across the garden and let himself into the main house. Expecting Tariq to follow, she'd remained beside the fountain for what seemed hours, psyching herself up for a confrontation.

But it didn't happen. Tariq did not return and at midnight she silently let herself out the gate and hurried back through quiet dark streets to the Riad du Maroc.

After listening to Maurice's profuse apologies for miscalculating Tariq's return to the apartment, she'd stumbled up to her room and read the messages she downloaded from Tariq's computer. One was from Yasmin who, from the provocative tone of the message, was Tariq's new squeeze.

The second one, from Nadia Sultan, was vintage Abandoned Wife: *I will never forget you. We are still married. Do not think because you have chosen to leave London that I cannot find you. Our friends ask often about you. They cannot believe you have turned your back on all we worked so hard for. I know one morning you will awaken and remember who you are. I wait for that day. Always your loving wife Nadia.*

The *ninja* file contained more messages from Nadia of the same sort, as well as a recent message from Raja'a, Nadia's sister who had worked with Tariq at the bank. *She still considers herself your wife. She will never let you go. Be careful. Warm regards, Raja'a.*

When she finally opened the last of the messages

she'd copied from Tariq's Inbox, she found the perfect bromide for the travails of the past week, a communication that provoked her to hysterical laughter. It was from a client of Tariq's who was requesting that stock be redeemed so he could spend 2.5 million dollars for a female camel that he wanted to enter in a camel beauty pageant in Abu Dhabi.

Part Three

Who overcomes by force, hath overcome
but half his foe.

-*John Milton*

CHAPTER 50

Feeling every fall she'd made in the dojo in the morning workout with Sensei Nakano, Kate St. Claire straightened her back in a vain attempt to lesson the pain in her right hip and control her bad attitude. Deborah MacKenzie was speaking.

"I covered for you with Hamish, St. Claire. He wants the Black Irish problem to disappear. I told him you were on it." Deborah leaned back in her chair, one arm propped on the arm. She smoothed a nonexistent strand of hair into her French twist. Her starched white shirt was immaculate. "I expected you would follow up your report last week with more surveillance," she continued. "More on Umarova. Then you disappeared. What was that about?"

Resisting the inclination to actually reveal what she discovered at Interpol and Marrakesh – and ask why the hell Deborah hadn't shared the intel Five had on Tariq Kassar – Kate replied, "A family issue I had to take care of. Have there been any more threats?"

"No specific threats. If he made any, of course, he could be arrested for extorting a member of the Security Services."

"What exactly does O'Connor have on Hamish?"

"There are incriminating photos," Deborah said

vaguely. "I haven't been privy, but I'm told they're quite specific."

"More pink bras and cocaine? Or pink boxers and cocaine?"

"Something of that sort. Hamish needs leverage and quickly."

"What do you mean by leverage, exactly?"

"Get more intel on his Chinese girlfriend. Find out if she knows about his escort sideline. Anything Hamish can use as leverage."

"Her name is Jenny Wen," Kate said. "She's the niece of the Chinese commercial attaché and daughter of a Chinese scientist in Shanghai. She's reading political science at Oxford, came in on a student visa."

"We already know that. What's the nature of her relationship with O'Connor? Girl friend? Mistress? Fiancée? Have you been back to the Southmoor house?"

"Girl friend, apparently. Respectfully, Deborah, Connor O'Connor is a security expert. Umarova appears to be a hacker. Given my less than friendly encounter with her last week, I doubt I'd get very far trying to do more surveillance. It's a semi-rural area. No place to hide. Are you suggesting I bug his house? Tap his phones? I'm not an IT expert. Doesn't Five have people for that?"

"Make a date with Black Irish."

"A date? Seriously?"

"Seriously, St. Claire. The sooner the better. I want access to every electronic device he owns. Hamish wants the photos destroyed."

"Easier said than done. The age of photographic negatives is over."

"Specifically Hamish wants O'Connor's mobile."

"And I'm supposed to get all this how? By drugging him? By overpowering him? O'Connor's no dummy. Why not have E-13 hack into his phone? Whatever happened to The Watchers?"

"We've already discussed why we can't do that."

Kate let the silence grow until Deborah broke it. "You're an attractive woman, St. Claire. You're smart. Set up a date with O'Connor. Get the phone or find a way to clone it while his attention is elsewhere. I think all you need is 30 seconds to clone it." Deborah opened a side drawer on her desk, pulled out a white mobile phone, slid it across the desk to Kate. "Don't put any personal information on this. Use it for all communications, including to me." From an envelope on the desktop she withdrew a credit card. "Use this to pay for the date and any ancillary expenses. Do whatever it takes to get what we need."

"Whatever?"

"Don't underestimate this bloke. Don't get caught or it will be your image on the front page of the *Mail.*"

Kate stood, reached for her leather jacket. "Any new information on Fakhouri's murder? Or my parents?"

"Not that I'm aware of. Your brief is Black Irish."

CHAPTER 51

Chagrined that Deborah MacKenzie had tasked her with an assignment better handed off to the tracking and bugging invisibles of "A" Branch, Kate St. Claire stared at the white mobile and the credit card in the name of Amanda Fox. The so-called Tinkerbell Squad were the phone tapping experts. What the hell did she know about cloning a mobile in 30 seconds? It was fucking unbelievable that Hamish McTeague was so indiscreet that neither GCHQ nor E-13 could be called on to protect the national security. If it was so bloody important, Hamish could jolly well send in a MAV for surveillance.

She turned the phone on, wrote down the number, found the Black Irish page on the *5 Star Companions* website. She clicked on the link to book an escort, was requested to acknowledge that "This site may not be used for the advertising of sexual services or to engage in activities requiring the payment of money for sex or other illegal activities." She checked the Agree box, then rang the agency.

"Thank you for calling Five Star. This is Brooke. How may I assist you?"

"I would like to book an engagement with escort #9842 for Wednesday this week."

"Your name, please."

"Amanda Fox."

"For how many hours, Ms. Fox?"

Kate considered the question. "Two hours."

"Will this be for a private or a public event, Ms. Fox?"

Kate hesitated, then said, "For drinks and dinner. At a restaurant."

"That will be £200, Ms. Fox. I'm ready for your credit card number and a text contact number."

Kate supplied the requested information, wondering who Amanda Fox's credit card was billed to.

"You are, of course, responsible for any and all expenses, Ms. Fox. Drinks, dinner, taxi, that sort of thing. We suggest you advise the restaurant beforehand so the bill can be handled discreetly. Your credit card has been approved and you may now text Black Irish directly with the details of your engagement."

It took Kate fifteen minutes to draft the text. *I would like to use your escort services at my sister's upcoming wedding next month. Could we meet to discuss this week on Wednesday?* She stared at the words. It sounded like she was recruiting for a bartender. She deleted and started over. *Your web page is impressive. You sound like a real gentleman. Would you be available to accompany me to my sister's wedding next month?* Insipid. Another delete. I need a companion for my sister's upcoming wedding. *Could we meet this week on Wednesday to discuss it?* Less than deathless prose, but what the hell. She added Amanda's name, pressed the Send button. Would he require a photograph? Would he trace the burner Deborah gave her or be able to access her GPS location? How did he keep his escorting life from Jenny Wen?

Either he would be available or he wouldn't. Now she had to learn how to clone a phone. Gianni Taramelli could tell her, but that would be pushing her luck if it got back to Deborah. As much as she hated Five at the moment, getting sacked wasn't a great idea.

There was one other person who could help.

She found Peter Szabo's business card in the inner pocket of her small leather clutch. There were phone numbers for London and Nairobi and a hand-written number on the top of the card with the notation, "My mobile." This time the text was easy. *I need cyber help with my investigation. Could we meet? Kate St. Claire.*

The reply came back fifteen minutes later. *My office tomorrow at 10. Mtg. With Zeke.*

CHAPTER 52

Malvern, Worcestershire

Connor O'Connor sat in his cubicle on the sixth floor of 5th Domaine Security and swivelled to look out the broad window overlooking the sprawling facilities. The sky was a cobalt blue dome above the Malvern Hills surrounding the town Connor often thought was more conducive to inhabitants of Narnia or a legion of hobbits than a high-tech security firm.

Turning back to his computer, he read one more time the description of the house in Shiplake that, along with the Ardnamurchan engineering drawings and now the "one more little thing" request for personnel records at Ardnamurchan, constituted Jenny Wen's escalating bride price. *Secluded setting approached by a long private drive . . . master bedroom with en suite, guest suite, 3 further bedrooms . . . And then the price, exactly the same as it was one week earlier. £1,450,000.*

If he told Jenny he couldn't afford it, she would be gone. Or that while he'd been able to access the contractor's engineering specs, he hadn't yet been able to breach Ardnamurchan's firewall and he bloody well didn't have any more money to pay Zulema to do it. Since he hadn't been able to breach it, he could only wonder if "Z"'s previous hack had been discovered.

He hadn't heard a word from Emma Whyte since the last meeting that ended with his request for a compassionate loan for his long-deceased mother. He considered the possibility Emma was calling his bluff, counting on the fact that if he did actually publish the photos he would be risking arrest for extortion. It all depended on her risk level. The wife of the French Cabinet Minister was totally risk averse, which had made that one easy. The married Spanish lawyer had balked, but ultimately ended up paying.

His private mobile announced a text from 5 Star Companions. *Request for drinks and dinner on Wednesday in London with Amanda Fox. 2 hrs. Client wants to arrange future wedding consult. Client will text details. Please confirm ASAP.*

Amanda Fox. Another lonely sex-starved female. Connor checked his diary. Jenny had an evening class on Wednesdays. He could leave Malvern early if necessary. It would take him an hour each way of commute time, but a wedding could be an all-day affair, a possible £1000 or more. If she needed an escort for a wedding, if she was single *and* wealthy, that could mean the possibility of holidays and cruises. Perhaps as much as £25,000. A bit of a challenge to keep it from Jenny, but doable under the cover of the wide-ranging 5th Dimension assignments.

The text from Amanda appeared twenty minutes later. He smiled and thumbed in a response. *Amanda, I'm definitely available for London drinks and dinner Wednesday evening at 7. Where shall we meet? Looking forward to it. Dylan*

Chapter 53

"You need to clone a mobile phone?" Peter Szabo appeared semi-amused at the idea and reached for his white coffee cup. "Not something that Five included in your trade craft curriculum along with legends and self-defense?"

"Unfortunately, no." Seated beside Peter Szabo's humongous glass-topped rosewood desk in front of the wide windows overlooking the docks and the River Thames, Kate held her cup in both hands.

"And you need to do this in aid of your investigation of your parents' murder?"

Kate nodded. "I can't go through Five's regular channels, because I'm not supposed to be involved because it's a family matter."

"Is Koslov of any help?"

"Possibly. I talked to him briefly."

"I haven't the foggiest notion of how you might clone a mobile phone, Kate, but I have someone who does. He's just finished an op in Cairo. Finish your coffee and I will introduce you."

Ten minutes later Kate found herself scanning the semi-circle of high-tech work stations and HDTV monitors that comprised Juno Capital Management's Section 10, wondering whether she'd stumbled into a

Tom Clancy novel or if Szabo was running a shadow government from the eighth floor of the Black Raven Tower. Or a shadow intelligence agency.

JCM's Section 10 included a staff of fifty, Szabo told her while they descended in the whisper-quiet lift. Handpicked tacticians, intelligence analysts, psychologists, cyber security geeks, hostage recovery experts, several former network TV anchor names. And Zeke Jacobs, former security analyst with the NSA, a bespectacled 40-something genius with pale blue eyes behind tinted wire frame glasses and militarily disciplined red hair whose sartorial taste appeared more Armani than geek. After the introduction and a brief, "Please find a way to help her, Zeke, she's family," Szabo had disappeared.

Leaning back in the chrome and leather chair, Kate studied the cut of Zeke's black silk jacket that he wore over a *Dark Knight* T-shirt.

"Do you want to clone a mobile or just extract the data?"

Kate considered the question. "I need to see all the data that's on the phone and to be able to delete data from it."

"That used to be two different tasks. Last month a U.K. security firm came out with a high-end data extraction device that will do both. The Met sent it to all their kiosks. It's driving the thugs crazy. It will circumvent the password, and extract all the phone data –– texts, call history, everything including photos, calendars, and geo-tags. Even data that's been deleted." He smiled. "And then you can take over the phone."

"And all this takes how long?"

"Two minutes, tops. As long as the phone doesn't have a fingerprint reader." He tilted his head to one side. "How well do you know the user of this mobile? Is it a family member?"

Kate shook her head. "I don't know the person. No idea what kind of device it is."

"Man or woman?"

"Man."

Zeke removed his glasses, rubbed his eyes, replaced the glasses. "Will you have, um, legitimate access, or does this have to be done . . . um, surreptitiously?"

"The latter. In his presence. And he's reportedly a security consultant."

Zeke smiled. "That might be a challenge. Are you planning to return the phone after you extract the data?"

"In the best of all possible worlds, yes. Without letting him know the phone has been hacked."

He gave her a once-over. "Do you have . . . experience with this sort of 'mission'?"

"Truthfully, no. That's why I'm here."

"When are you planning to carry out this mission?"

"Wednesday evening."

"Where will this take place? Restaurant? Club? Private home?"

"In a restaurant."

"You need a partner."

Kate sighed. "Indeed."

"I have an idea." Zeke said, rolling a pen in his

hand, swivelling in his chair as Peter Szabo stepped into the office.

Chapter 54

The Royal Docks, East London

The train had been late, stopping for a prolonged time with no explanation, and Kate rang the restaurant to say the Amanda Fox party would be delayed. The 12-minute walk from the tube station gave her ample time to fret over the improbability of uncovering any of the intel Deborah was demanding. Impossible to just blurt out to a male escort, oh, by the way, may I borrow your mobile for 30 seconds so I can clone it?

Sod all!

Black Irish was waiting by the entrance to the Royal Dockside that Zeke had assured her was London's most trendy bistro. It was also where Zeke Jacob's girlfriend worked as sous chef. The photos on the 5 Star website had not done justice to this man's looks. Kate watched her way-too-handsome date intermittently checking his mobile and searching the faces of the pedestrians milling about in front of the restaurant. In the designer jeans, charcoal suede shoes that were probably trainers in disguise, white shirt and dark jacket with a gentleman's scarf draped about his neck, he could have walked into a high fashion photo shoot.

"Dylan? Sorry I'm late." Kate mustered what

hopefully would pass for a sincere smile and extended her hand, amused at the look of relief that spread
across his face. What had he been expecting?

"*Amanda*? So nice to meet you. You look . .
. *amazing*." He slid the mobile into his right jacket
pocket.

"Thank you, Dylan." He held her hand a second
or two longer than necessary. Nice touch. Was it her
face? The low cut crimson satin top? Or what Gwen
referred to as her "statement necklace" that he found
amazing? Or perhaps the £150 Versace skinny jeans.
"Shall we go in?"

The shopping spree on Amanda's credit card
was prompted by the realization that if Zeke Jacob's
game plan was going to be effective, it was on her to
keep Dylan Chandler mesmerized. That would mean
more than sparkling repartee. Ergo, she had to ooze
the promise of carnal delights beyond cocktails and
dinner. Even if she was paying for the carnal delights.

Their table was located beside the window with
a view over the Millennium 02 concert venue. "Fab-
ulous view," he said softly, holding her chair for her.
"Do you come here often?"

Kate shook her head, settled into her chair.
Unfolding the white napkin into her lap, she leaned
forward slightly, letting the satin top do its work. "A
good friend recommended it. Supposedly great food
and great service. I hope you won't be disappointed."

Dylan's smile made his eyes sparkle. "I could
never be disappointed dining with such a beautiful
woman. Tell me about yourself. Are you a London
native?"

"Just a country girl, Dylan," she said, watching the tall blond waiter approach the table.

Two large leather menus were placed in front of them. "Good evening, I'm Jerome, I'll be your waiter tonight. Our chef's specials are bouillabaisse with saffron and orange zest served with our own crusty bread and pan-fried sea bass. May I bring you something to drink?"

Kate ordered a Macallan and water. "I'll have what my lady is having," Dylan ordered. The waiter departed. Kate scanned the dining room, glanced toward the swinging doors at the back, took a deep breath. "Our family is from the Cotswolds," she lied. "And you, do I hear some Irish in your history?"

"Spot on. Bit of a linguist, are you? Born and raised in Dublin."

"What brought you to our fair isle?" She tried not to wince as she said it.

"An aunt who thought I had potential," he said seriously. "So I got one year at Cambridge before she made a bad investment and the funds ran out."

"That must have been difficult."

"It was difficult leaving Cambridge, but I like to think it pushed me in the right direction to work I really love."

Jerome placed the drinks on the white tablecloth, glanced at the closed menus. "May I interest you in a starter while you look over the menus? Some grilled black tiger prawns? Salmon carpaccio?"

Dylan nodded. "One of each, Jerome." He lifted his glass. "It's unusual to find a woman who prefers Scotch to champagne," he said, his eyes watching hers. "Sláinte."

She took a sip of the Scotch, watching Jerome's departing back. "A taste acquired from my father. So tell me, what is the work you love?"

"Anything dealing with the cybersphere. Specifically, anything that involves helping companies keep their information safe. Energy firms, defense contractors, electronics makers. They're all at risk. I test their firewalls, try to breach their systems, make recommendations to fix any holes."

"You're one of the good guys. Are you a free-lancer? Have motherboard, will travel?"

Another dazzling smile. "I'm fortunate to work for a company that sends me to romantic places. Paris, Barcelona, Rome. Perhaps you'd like to accompany me sometime. Does your work allow you to do that?"

"Sounds intriguing, Dylan." She opened her menu, hearing the soft chime of a mobile. Her own? His? His right hand reached for his pocket, then stopped.

"It's okay if you want to answer it, Dylan. Might be someone whose firewall has been breached."

He shook his head. "Whatever it is can wait. Have you decided?" He nodded toward the menu.

"I have. The sea bass and caesar salad are calling to me."

"Excellent choice. And I can't get past the bouillabaisse. I'm a seafood fanatic." He closed his menu and leaned toward her. "Now you have my undivided attention. I want to hear about you, Amanda. What do you do when you're not charming a poor nerdy geek? What are your fantasies?"

Oh, my God. Kate reached for her drinks glass,

took a long sip, risked a glance toward the back of the restaurant where the Teutonic Jerome was exiting the kitchen with a large tray and a second waiter with red-hair was exiting the bar with a tray of drinks.

"I work for an Indie publishing company," she said, realizing her jaw was aching from nonstop smiling. "A book editor. Nothing as exciting as what you do. Just now I'm editing the memoir of a politician whose name you would recognize if I was allowed to tell you."

"And if you did, you'd have to kill me, I suppose."

Kate giggled, something she hadn't done in years, wondering if she'd uttered even one statement in the past two weeks that wasn't a lie. Or in the past ten years. Wondering if she knew the difference anymore.

"And your fantasies, Amanda?" he said softly, eyes locked on hers. "What are your fantasies?"

"My immediate fantasy, Dylan," she said, "Is that you will be my Plus One at my sister's wedding. Can you make that a –?"

Dylan's phone rang again. He frowned, pulled the mobile from his pocket. "So sorry, Amanda. This might be an emergency." He thumbed a button. "Hello?"

And then Jerome was beside the table to serve the starters and the red-haired waiter, whose attention appeared to have been diverted to an altercation outside the window, crashed into Jerome and the black tiger prawns in white wine cascaded over Dylan's tailored dark jacket, followed by four tall iced drinks that spilled over both of them, drenching Dylan's trousers, Kate screaming as the ice cubes made their way into her decolletage, both waiters attempting to mop up the two dinner guests, the maitre'd racing from the serving station.

A scene of perfect bedlam.

CHAPTER 55

Black Raven Wharf, London

On Thursday morning Kate waited for Zeke at the round glass table in Janus Capital Management's Section 10 where half a dozen of the staff clustered in front of a huge TV monitor showing a flotilla of inflatables overflowing with orange-jacketed refugees arriving on the Greek island of Lesbos. The focus of the newscast was not Europe's crisis in receiving a million immigrants from war-ravaged Syria, but rather that this scenario was merely a preview of the wave of refugees that would be moving westward as seas continued to rise and farm land became deserts.

"The boss's latest enterprise," Zeke said, eyes on the TV screen. "Establishing a worldwide fund for the resettlement of climate refugees." He pulled a black mobile and a thumb drive from his jacket pocket. "Mission accomplished. Everything from your gentleman friend's mobile is on this drive. Call logs, texts, phone numbers, photo gallery." A small smile crept across his mouth. "Even data that's been deleted. You can view it or transmit it or print out a report. You can access anything on his phone."

"So nothing was encrypted?"

"Only thing I couldn't get to was his bank account. That requires a thumb print."

Kate touched the black mobile. "And this one is now a clone?"

"It's *paired* to his phone. It's an identical twin. Receives the same calls and texts and whatever that his phone does. What you delete on this phone gets deleted on his." He produced a small smile. "I enabled the app that vocalizes incoming texts. I also activated his GPS tracker. By the by, you departed before things got interesting last night."

"I was marinating in wine and prawns. Seemed like the right exit cue. What happened?"

"One of the diners at a nearby table apparently videoed the little drama. Your friend took umbrage and a few blows were exchanged."

Kate took a deep breath. "Did he get his phone back?"

"Yes, ma'am. It was discovered in a nearby potted Ficus tree. But not before threats were made to bring legal action against the restaurant. Oh, yes, the manager will be happy to comp you and the gentleman should you decide to return. Last night's aborted service being on the house, of course."

Kate stood, gathered the new mobile and the thumb drive and tucked them into her bag. "Many thanks for your help."

To her surprise, he gave her a quick hug. "Quite fun, actually, Lady Kathryn. Ring me if I can help with any other, um, missions."

Descending in the lift, Kate allowed herself a moment of self-congratulation. She wondered what Hamish would do with the evidence of his sexual indiscretions and if he'd considered that even when

the incriminating photos on the phone were deleted, there was no guarantee Black Irish hadn't made
a back-up copy. Sexual indiscretions were so much
more complicated in an age of technology. Then for
several minutes she allowed herself to consider all
she might have discovered if she had cloned Tariq
Kassar's phone and what she might have done with
what she found.

Chapter 56

The porter at David Chaucer's apartment building motioned Kate to the private lift.

"Sir David is expecting you, Lady Kathryn."

Less than a minute later, she stepped out into the carpeted foyer of the penthouse. The handsome wooden door opened and Sir David was there with a smile. He was wearing a soft tan jumper and brown flannel trousers. He drew her inside the apartment and held her in a long embrace. "My dear Kathryn, I was delighted to hear from you."

"Thank you for making time for me."

"I will *always* have time for my godchild. Fortuitous that you found me in town. I'm heading back to Dartmoor next week for some sailing. How do you like my bridge?"

Kate stared across the spacious reception area with its red Oriental carpet on polished hardwood and beyond the outer deck to the dramatic span of the Albert Bridge, its suspension cables luminous under the darkening afternoon sky. "I think divine might describe it. I can't imagine how you could have spent all those years away."

"I shouldn't have and thereby turns a tale. But no mind, my dear, come and sit. Kemal is preparing

228

tea. The furnishings are a bit sparse, but it keeps my mind uncluttered."

Kate sank into the pale blue velvet sofa. Sir David took a seat at the opposite end, one arm along the back.

"Has Koslov been able to help you?"

"We spoke. It seems there are still no suspects. But that's not what I need to talk about."

"It's work, isn't it? Filthy Five shit. I told you to stay at Six."

"I couldn't. After Kinaid's plane was lost, my mother nearly had a breakdown."

"Tell me what's happening."

Kate sighed. "I'll probably end up hanged if I tell you about it, but it might be a national security thing, so I might get hanged if I don't." Kate glanced around the room. "I assume you have this place debugged often," she said with sly smile.

"My security system is state of the art counter-surveillance. Or so I've been assured. Unless there's an anti-countersurveillance drone lurking outside my windows." He shook his head. "Good Lord, Kathryn, what a world we've created. Now forget about the Official Secrets Act and tell me your problem."

"Deborah MacKenzie has tasked me to do background and surveillance on a person who is ostensibly blackmailing the D.G."

"Politics or some sort of sexual indiscretion?"

"The latter."

"What is the nature of this intel?"

"A cloned cell phone. Text messages, phone logs, photos."

"Who does the master phone belong to?"

"The POI. A cybersecurity geek."

"Incriminating photos?"

"Very."

"Well, there have been rumors over the years, my dear, about Hamish's proclivities, shall we say."

"No. Not of Hamish. The photos are of my superior."

"Photos of Deborah McKenzie?"

"Yes. With the POI."

"You were lied to."

"Yes."

"Good Lord. How incriminating are the photos?"

"Nude. And in compromising positions."

"Oh, my. Does the POI know the phone has been cloned?"

"Hopefully not."

"But you're not sure."

Kate shook her head.

"Does MacKenzie know you have this intel?"

"Not yet. I have to see her tomorrow."

Sir David gazed out toward the bridge for several seconds, ruffled the fringe of hair over his right ear, smoothed it down. "Your dilemma is that when you hand over the intel she will know you know she lied to you. And that you have evidence she has been behaving inappropriately. She's not going to like either of those little bits."

Kate nodded.

"What sort of relationship do you have with her?"

"She doesn't like me. And it gets worse. The POI is a cybersecurity consultant at Fifth Dimension."

"Malvern?"

Kate nodded. "Deborah thinks he might be able to hack into a top secret project in Scotland. Ardnamurchan. Or has already done it."

"The space landing port. A Friends of the Prince project."

"Is it more than just a fantasy?"

He nodded. "Yes, and you didn't hear it from me. Does your intel indicate that this POI is capable of pulling off such a hack?"

"If not him, then his housemate. A Chechen cypher punk."

"*Cypher punk.*" Sir David snorted and beckoned to the short, slightly balding, dark-haired man hovering in the dining room with a large tray. "Kathryn, this is Kemal. He saved my life. He is henceforth responsible for the remainder of it."

Kemal nodded to Kate and placed the large wooden tray on the sofa table. "Shall I pour, Sir David?"

"I will do the honors, Kemal. The borek look marvelous. Thank you."

Kemal arranged the tray of pastries and quietly left the room.

"I nearly bought the farm one night in Istanbul," Sir David said, pouring into one of the white bone china cups. "Taking a shortcut back to the hotel through an alley behind a shish kebab joint. Must have been daft. I realized I was being followed by at least two thugs, maybe more. Started to pull my weapon when an arm came out of the doorway and pulled me inside. Kemal was the cook. He'd stepped outside for a smoke, saw what was happening. Apparently a number of foreigners had come to a bad end in the area." He added a slice of lemon, handed her the cup and saucer.

"So he's Turkish?"

"Kurdish. Had his own restaurant in Damascus. After the war started, his wife left and took the youngster. He doesn't know where they are. He finally gave up on saving the restaurant and made his way to Istanbul. After Ann left I didn't feel like doing everything for myself. Seemed like I needed a gentleman's gentleman. So I brought him back. I'd like to help him find his family. May have to ask for your help. Do try the borek. Not very British, but delicious. Tell me more about your POI. And the *cypher punk* housemate. I have a suggestion that might keep you out of the Tower."

CHAPTER 57

Deborah MacKenzie ignored the buzz on the intercom. She'd been scrolling through the report on her computer monitor for over half an hour. With a data synch program Gillian had downloaded, it hadn't been terribly difficult to copy the data from what St. Claire called the "paired" mobile.

It was all there. All the nude photos Black Irish had been taunting her with plus some she hadn't seen. Shots of the two of them, coupled. How the hell had he done it?

The gallery also included shots of a big bird and of a petite Asian woman with the bird on her arm. A dozen or so recent texts with Jenny. Cryptic texts with "Z." Fifteen pages of a deleted phone call log that included the number of Deborah's personal mobile and the burner she'd supplied to St. Claire. Endless pages of 'deleted' texts, including ones to Deborah when she'd first started the trysts.

The fact that she'd allowed all this to happen made her a gormless idiot. In addition, St. Claire now knew she'd been lying. Instead of confiscating Irish's mobile and handing it over as she'd been instructed, she'd copied the entire bloody memory. What a dog's dinner.

The only inaccessible data was the contents of Irish's bank account which was secured with a biometric password.

Her fury mounting, eyes narrowed, Deborah scrolled back through the entire download. The one piece of intel she was hoping for was missing: evidence that Connor O'Connor had hacked into the top secret files at the space cargo project. Therefore, she had no evidence that would give MI5 the wherewithal to have him arrested and to permanently forestall any further requests for hush money.

Except to state that she'd used none of Five's resources in the operation, St. Claire had been obtusely evasive about how she'd cloned or paired the mobile, which left Deborah with no choice except to believe she had merely cloned the device and hadn't created her own copy of the data. St. Claire's only comment was that she didn't think there would be a second date with Black Irish, but Deborah couldn't avoid considering the nasty possibility that St. Claire could come out with the nude photos from the cloned mobile and Five would come off looking like a soap opera.

There was something else nagging her. The Chinese girl friend who was the niece of the commercial attaché and Dylan's questions about helium-3. She scrolled back through the printout of O'Connor's texts with Jenny Wen. Hundreds of them. Then she found it, text from a week ago. *Do we have a date for the wedding Jenny?* And the response, two hours later. *December? My parents will come up of course and my uncle is asking about the Shiplake house and if we will live there. He also asks about Ardnamurchan.*

"Ms. MacKenzie, everything okay? Anything I can do before I leave?"

"There is one thing, Gilly. Reach out to your contact at the Foreign Office. See what you can find out about Jenny Wen or Wen Hulan, niece of Wen Yutan, the Chinese commercial attache. She's a student at Oxford. I want to be notified if she attempts to leave the country."

She deleted all the incriminating photos from the paired mobile but who was to say Irish didn't have backups on another device? Even if she had the fifty thousand he requested for his "mum," there was nothing to prevent him for going public with any of the photos at a later date. She propped both elbows on her desk and covered her eyes, processing the implications of her dilemma. The one avenue left was to threaten O'Connor with exposing his escort service to his girlfriend. But what if she didn't care? What if she was also a paid client? Or if he called her bluff and released all the photos to the press anyway? What could be done to remove the threat?

The answer came several hours later, when she was back in the kitchen at home. The house was quiet, Cat napping on the window seat, a note from Ian on the kitchen counter. "*See you about 11. Don't wait dinner for me.*" She found the blue bottle of Bombay gin in the long cupboard, poured two shots into the glass, added a splash of chilled vermouth. As she dropped in the gin-infused olive, her personal mobile chimed for a text. *Emma darling important we meet soonest. Mum's condition deteriorating.*

She carried the cocktail over to the bar area where Ian had left the opened box intended for their neighbor. Taking small sips of the martini, her brain searched for a way out of the predicament. She idly studied the packing slip and the small packages of cellophane wrapped seeds. Two packages of Burgundy Bunny Grass. Two packages of lavender seeds (*lavandula angustifolia*). Two packages of purslane (*portulaca oleracea*). Three packages of cowbane (*cicuta virosa*). Below the lavender and the cowbane were notes for growing the seeds and special instructions.

The lavender seeds were to be started in a seed tray in fine vermiculite. Seedlings to germinate in two weeks. Adverse reactions: None indicated.

Cowbane: Plant at room temperature. Grow in full sun in moist soil. Germination in two weeks. Adverse reactions: All parts of the plant contain a toxin that is poisonous to horses and cattle. Highly toxic to humans; may cause seizures, convulsions and death.

Deborah finished the martini, fixed another, reread the instructions for the seedlings.

Dinner was a steak, broiled to a perfect shade of pink, a baked potato with Irish butter, French green beans with Celtic sea salt, two glasses of Saint-Gervais cote du Rhone.

At 10 p.m. she picked up her personal mobile, texted a response to Dylan with narrowed eyes. *Sorry about your mum. Tomorrow same place? Bring acct info for trnsfr.*

The second text she sent from her encrypted mobile to Gianni Taramelli. *My office tomorrow 9 a.m.*

CHAPTER 58

Connor O'Connor downloaded the day's activity on his special bank account and allowed himself a smug smile. There it was, Emma Whyte's first payment.

The low point of the week had been the fiasco on Wednesday night with the Amanda bird. He'd thought he was enjoying the proverbial Luck of the Irish until the idiotic scene with the waiters. The worst part wasn't the drenched jacket, it was the god-awful ten minutes or so before his mobile was located. Amanda had decamped when things got really tense. He'd texted her three times and hadn't heard a word since about her sister's wedding, an escort engagement that could have been lucrative. He considered taking legal action against the restaurant, but the week had improved considerably.

First it was the text from Emma Whyte agreeing to meet again. He thought the evening had gone extremely well. She'd brought the expensive cote du Rhone Saint-Gervais and the crystal glasses. She'd been more flirtatious than usual and the time in bed had been singular. Almost deviant.

"So very sorry about your mum," she'd murmured later, tucked back against the pillow. Ten thousand a month was all she could manage, she said. And she'd need a payback plan. When she left, she'd handed him a small foil-lined box. "For your chocolate habit, luv."

Studying the computer screen one more time, he lifted one of the fudge biscuits from the box. It was annoying not to be able to trace Emma's deposit to its source, but the important thing was now he could pay "Z" to get the Ardnamurchan personnel data Jenny's father demanded.

The biscuit was rich and dark, with a lot of vanilla and something slightly bitter. Connor smiled, reaching for another, glancing one more time at the balance on the bank account. What was the quote from the Bible? *Wine maketh merry, but money answereth all things.*

CHAPTER 59

Lying between the Bristol and English Channels, Devonshire covers over two thousand square miles. The north coast is rocky, wooded cliffs, the south coast softer and warmer. Inland the granite peaks of Dartmoor dominate the countryside where gorse and heather cover the wild uplands, the locale where the fictitious Sir Hugo Baskerville had his fatal encounter with a phantom hound.

Kate's grandfather, Angus St. Claire, created Millview, originally almost five hundred acres of rolling hills and grazing black-faced Suffolk sheep on the banks of a small river across from an 18th century mill house. Millview comprised a large house, a smaller cottage, and a stable, all constructed from native stone and surrounded by a cluster of cottonwood, poplars and boxwood trees. When the 5th Earl of Axmoorland brought Carmela Aragon to Millview as his bride, Angus St. Claire began construction of the smaller stone house, into which he and Kate's grandmother, a former Bletchley code breaker, moved when the twins were born.

Holding a large black furled umbrella, wearing an old Macintosh and Wellingtons, Emerson James was standing on the platform when the train pulled in. Kate waved through the window and gathered up her bag and computer case. The first class car had been nearly full and she waited impatiently behind a group of women in colorful knit pantsuits, some sort of mystery book club outing from the States.

The weather was warm and humid. Swollen grey clouds hung over the station. Emerson's hug was strong and extended. "Thank you for coming down, m'lady." He picked up her bags and she followed his stooped figure through the throng of arriving and departing passengers. Prior to her parents' death he had addressed her as 'lass.' It was only when she'd returned to Millview for the memorial that he'd begun addressing her in the prescribed form for an earl's daughter. She wished it hadn't changed.

More gray hairs had appeared at his temples. He'd developed a limp on his left side. What would she do if he were to become disabled or to die? Lorna could never handle the farm alone. Millview was the last remnant of family. Could she ever bear to sell it?

Emerson had brought the silver Bentley, the one that had been in for repairs when her father asked to borrow the Alfa Romeo. She watched him stow the bags in the boot and climbed into the soft upholstered bucket seat, reflecting on how major life passages hung on tiny things. If the Bentley's carburetor hadn't malfunctioned on that particular Friday, it would have been Kate herself who was vaporized at the turn of the Spider's ignition.

Thunder rumbled overhead. A light rain began to fall. Emerson maneuvered the vehicle out of the car park and waved at the traffic. "Lots of visitors this week," he muttered. "Some kind of Christie doings."

The rain grew heavier, pounding the roof of the Bentley. Emerson turned on the windscreen wiper and scowled, swerving around a lorry that was pulled half way off the roadway, its hazard lights blinking. The windscreen began to fog up. Kate pressed the de-fog button and blower, gazed out the side windows at the wet fields. A small herd of Black Angus huddled around a feed stand.

"Filthy weather," Emerson muttered. "Hot and humid. Been like this all week. Big storm up from the Azores. Should blow through tonight, maybe cool things off." Half an hour later, Emerson pulled into the semicircular drive and stopped in front of the main house. "I'll bring yer bags. Get ye inside and get dry. Lorna's most likely in the kitchen."

Kate raced through the rain to the heavy wooden door and stepped into the tiled entryway. The house smelled of apples and old books and wood smoke, and all the memories came rushing back of endless summers and fresh popped corn and mah jongg games with her mother and Kincaid on nights when her father was up in London.

She headed down the long hallway to what in earlier times was the servants quarters, now a warm and fragrant kitchen with an Australian shepherd curled on the braided rug beside the Aga. The shepherd's name was Hawkeye. Kate's mother had rescued him five years ago; she had been his Person ever since. The dog came to put his nose in Kate's hand and Lorna struggled getting out of the big leather chair. "Kate, sweetheart. Come and dry yerself."

Lorna James' long auburn hair, streaked with grey and white, was twisted into an intricate knot on the back of her head. "We thought ye might never come back," she whispered, holding Kate away to look at her. She gave a rueful glance at the kitchen window where rain sheeted against the pane. "Another big storm headed this way. Third one this summer. Flooding up north, I hear. Come and sit and have a cuppa. And some of the little san'wiches."

The tea was Lorna's proprietary blend of chamomile and passion flower. Hawkeye sat on his haunches beside Kate at the chipped enameled table. An hour later the blue porcelain pot was empty, the egg salad sandwiches had disappeared. After answering Lorna's questions about how was little cousin Gwennie and did Madison like St. Andrews, Lorna shared that she and Emerson were soon to become grandparents again. Ten minutes later Kate left the kitchen and made her way along the passage to the bedroom wing her father had added to the first floor when she and Kincaid outgrew the nursery.

The door to her room was open, the red bag just inside on the old Aubusson, her laptop computer reposing on the table beside the bed. She closed the door softly, went to the padded window seat and stared out at the river rushing past beyond the tall primrose bushes. The mill wheel turned slowly in the gusty wind. The other side of the room faced onto the courtyard with the pool and spa.

She drew the heavy wine-colored drapes, turned on the overhead light, and stared around the room. At the bed covered with the blue and white quilted coverlet and pillow shams her grandmother had embroidered, at the dark oak bureau and armoire and the antique mirrored dressing table.

The door to the adjoining bathroom was open from where a second door led to Kincaid's room. She washed her hands and shook out her hair, arranged her toilet articles. After hanging her meager travel attire in the armoire, she took the small thumb drive from the zippered compartment in her toiletries bag, gathered up the laptop, and walked down the corridor to her father's study. Lord Jonathan had often brought work home from his chambers and had high speed Internet installed. Fond of working on the veranda in sight of the rose garden, he subsequently added a wireless router. Kate turned on the computer, but could not get a connection. She searched for and found the small black router under a stack of files on the desk. It was unplugged. Four green lights began blinking when she connected it. She found the security key taped to the underside of the router.

While she waited for the connection her mobile chirped for a text. It was from D.I. Koslov. *May have identified Madame X.*

Kate called the North End station, got Koslov's VM. *I'm away from my desk until Monday. If this is an emergency, call 999.* Did he just send texts and disappear? Run out to catalog a passing cloud?

There was a knock on the library door. It was Emerson James, wet hair slicked down, his feet in a pair of scuffed leather slippers. He held a large white envelope. "Sorry to bother ye, m'lady. Here are the papers the solicitor left about the property misunderstanding." He laid the envelope on the desk. "And Lorna says, would ye prefer to have yer supper in yer room, the dining room being so empty and all?"

"I'd like that, Emerson," she said. "Perhaps around half six? I thought I'd like to get some fresh air first, maybe tramp around the grounds a bit."

Emerson smiled and glanced at the window. "You're daft, m'lady, in all this rain. But yer Mack and Wellies are in the mud room. Mind you, be careful. Might be slippery. Take Hawk with you."

Hawkeye flew out of the mud room door paying no mind to the rain falling in sheets on the bluestone path. The stable where Gwennie had kept her big Arabian all those summers ago smelled of old leather and harness oil and manure. Now two Shetland ponies with white manes and tails stood in adjoining stalls munching on meadow hay. Castor nudged her hand with a velvet muzzle.

Hawkeye eyed the ladder to the shadowy hayloft and whined softly. Kate opened the door to the tack room where the saddles and harnesses were stored. Hawkeye followed her inside, nosing about in the bits of straw on the wooden plank floor. Two bridles hung from hooks, two pairs of leather riding boots stood beneath the saddles. There was no dust on the harnesses. Emerson and Lorna's grandchildren were taking good care. After a long while she turned, followed the dog outside, and pulled the stable door shut. The hard rain had diminished somewhat, the wind had fallen.

Early darkness was settling over the grounds as

the two of them picked their way up the path past the limestone garden wall that had been built adjacent to the pool. The wall, with its Roman style arches, was more Italian than English. An apple and pear orchard lay beyond the stables. Kate's father had built a gazebo by the river, later enclosed it, added a small wood-burning stove. The structure became a holiday hangout for Kate and Kincaid and a few friends from the village.

Kate hesitated before returning to the house, staring back at the gazebo, recalling an event that occurred, it was the summer when Gwen was visiting while her parents were traveling. The still, hot afternoon in late August when she'd been reading upstairs. *Jane Erye,* she remembered. Overcome by the stifling heat, she'd stumbled down in search of some small cool breeze off the water.

The gazebo that became the river house was a spartan structure of raw wood plank floors and casement windows and chairs whose stuffing was bursting out. Kate hadn't heard their voices as she approached the house, and had shopped short in the doorway, seeing the two heads bent close together. Gwen and Kincaid. The windows were open to the river. Gwen was speaking softly, a small smile on her red lipsticked mouth. She wore a pleated linen sun dress of a pale yellow. As she leaned forward, one strap of the dress slid down her shoulder and the dress opened to disclose a clear view of her two small breasts. Kincaid was sitting on the arm of the old leather chair, leaning forward, mesmerized. Neither saw her standing in the doorway. Kincaid extended an arm and with his long fingers caressed Gwen's pale shoulder. Kate, holding her breath, had turned away to run madly along the tree-shaded riverbank, to fling herself weeping into the cool damp grass.

Hawkeye whined, standing on the path in front of the door to the main house. The reverie broken, she hurried up the path and opened the door to the scent of something freshly baked. Thirty minutes later, her damp clothing replaced by the cotton pajamas she found in the bottom bureau drawer, Lorna's soft knock on the door announced the supper tray. "I fixed some chicken noodle soup, lass. The bread's just out of the oven. Remembering how you and them used to like a glass o'wine, I went to the cellar. And there's trifle for dessert."

After golfing, collecting fine wines was Lord Jonathan's second passion. There must be five hundred bottles in the cellar, Kate thought, taking the tray from the housekeeper and placing it on the cushioned window seat. All carefully arranged by vintage and type. What would she do with it all?

Mr. Cameron, the young one, had rung while Kate was in the stable, Lorna reported. He could meet with her at eleven the following morning. And did Kate know that Mr. Cameron's wife, Chantelle her name was, had died the previous winter? A terrible accident with her drunken brother. Kate didn't, but she did remember the Cameron seniors hadn't been overjoyed with the match.

When the last crumb of the trifle was gone, Kate placed the tray and the dishes on the table in the hallway. After pouring another glass of the wine, a Chateau Simone Pallette Rouge, she opened the drapes and stared down into the rain-washed garden. The rain had ceased and high clouds roiled the sky. High above the mill stream, a creamy quarter moon attempted an appearance. She'd once spent a night in this room with Tariq. It was an early summer weekend. Her parents were in Spain, Emerson and Lorna up in Scotland. After a midnight swim and soak in the spa, they had lain in bed under the peaked ceiling with its massive wooden beams and stared through the window at the rising moon while the scent of primroses drifted through the open windows. It seemed a million years ago.

Coming back to Millview, sitting here in this familiar window seat, there was the eerie sensation of rewinding time. The sense that if she stepped out into the corridor and tiptoed down the west wing, she could open the door to her mother's room and find her seated at the dressing table. Perhaps brushing out her long dark hair. Or snuggled up in the big four-poster reading the latest Maeve Binchy novel. And everything that had happened since that Friday afternoon phone conversation with her father would turn out to be an obscene dream.

She went into the bathroom, washed her face and brushed her teeth, turned out the lights, stood again at the window. The half moon cast long shadows over the garden. Leaving the drapes open, she turned out the light, slid between the smooth sheets, covered herself with the thick quilt. If all went well, she would spend one more day at Millview, place the messy problem of the boundary dispute in Andy

Cameron's capable hands, then go over the accounts with Emerson.

Whatever Dom Koslov had discovered about Sheherazade's murder, and whatever she might face at Thames House, could wait until Monday.

CHAPTER 60

Tower Hamlets, East London

To: Sister Miryam
From: Ishtar
Date: Thursday, 8-26. 5:09 p.m.
Thank you for the lists you sent. Thank you for helping with the tickets. Zara and I are excited to join the Brigade. We are ready to leave this weekend. Can you please make reservations for us? A copy of our passports is attached. Zara's brother works at Gatwick and he will give us a ride. Please let us know what time.

To: Sister Miryam
From: Ishtar
Date: Friday, 8-27. 5:28 a.m.
Zara thinks her father called the police. We don't know what to do. We have £1545. Do you have tickets for us? How soon can we leave?

To: Whitechapel Travel
From: Sister Miryammailto
Date: Friday, 8-27, 8:14
Please book the passengers shown on attachment on soonest flight from Gatwick to Istanbul. Charge to the Sisters account.

To: Sister Miryam

From: Whitechapel Travelmailto:Snazari@whitechapeltravel.co.uk

Date: Saturday, 8-27 10:06 a.m.

Passengers Darzi and Boulos confirmed on Turkish Flt 123 to Istanbul via Madrid. Itinerary and ticket receipt attached.

Fwd to: Ishtarmailto:Ishtar@lockandkey.com

From: Sister Miryammailto:Sistermiryam@lockandkey.com

Your itinerary and ticket receipt are attached. I have also attached directions on what to do when you get to Gatwick and when you arrive in Istanbul. Read it carefully. Do not miss the flight from Madrid. Good luck with your hegira.

To: Fatimamailto:Fatima@lockandkey.com

From: Dervishmailto:Dervish@lockandkey.com

Date: Friday, 8-27 11:05 a.m.

Subject 1 arrived Exeter station Friday 4:55. CCTV tracking: Bentley license tag, registration certificate attached. Presumed destination Postbridge. No return reservation.

Subject 2 contact: Mehmet Celik, Dubai. See link to Googleearth for presumed current location. Pls. Transfer 2000 per previous instructions.

Chapter 61

On Saturday morning Kate found the table in the dining room set for one and the makings for blueberry waffles on the sideboard. She loved the room with its big window and long cushioned window seat overlooking the mill stream. Dark skies still prevailed, but no rain was falling. As she poured the batter into the heated waffle maker, Lorna bustled through the door. She was wearing what Kate recognized as her Sunday Best, carrying a Mackintosh.

"Ah, lass, yer up. I cut fresh melon and the coffee's yer favorite dark roast. I'm so sorry, Emerson and I have to leave. Liz's baby's comin' today. We're takin' the train to Edinburgh to be with the boys for the weekend. So sorry, lass."

"Not a problem, Lorna. Can I give you a lift to the station?"

"Our other daughter – that's Maggie – is on her way. The thing is, Maggie's mother-in-law is visitin' and she can't take Hawkeye . . . 'd'ye think . . . ?"

"Of course. I'll be glad for the company." Kate lifted the top of the waffle iron, extricated the golden disc. "I'm headed into town to see Andy Cameron. Then Hawk and I will go for a run."

"He'll be in heaven. I left food for ye in the

fridge. Hawk's food's in the long cupboard. He likes it both mornin' and night." She nodded toward the sideboard. "That's yer favorite honey, lass, and Emerson says the winds will be strong today. More rain tonight."

"What about the ponies? Shall I throw some hay in for them?"

"Emerson took care of them this morning. Maggie'll come over with the girls late today and tomorrow. And there's one other thing, lass. It's this article in the *Journal*." She placed a newspaper on the table. "I think they've already invaded the garret."

Kate looked at the large photograph on the front page. A winsome masked grey creature peering through a weathered wooden fence. "Raccoons?"

Lorna nodded. "There's a big invasion of 'em in the county. If ye have time, check out the garret. There's a stack of yer mum's boxes up there and some furniture and stuff. I'd hate to have the little pests destroy somethin' valuable. This is the key to the upper door. Be careful, lass. There might be loose boards up there. Best take a torch with ye."

"I'll take a look." Kate returned Lorna's embrace. The kitchen door closed. She reached for the pitcher of honey as her mobile announced an incoming call. The caller was Dominic Koslov, but by the time she found the phone under the window seat cushion the connection was gone. She returned the call, was directed to VM. Half an hour later, lingering over the dark roast coffee and watching the big wooden wheel of the mill turn in the wind, she read an incoming text from Koslov. *ID'd Madame X in the park. Call me 2nite. Watch your 6. BTW report of altocumulus lenticularis over Exeter.*

Kate peered out the window and saw only heavy grey clouds and she had no idea if any of them were *altocumulus* whatever. She had a bit more than an hour before her appointment in Dartmouth, perhaps time to check out the garret. Kate couldn't remember when she'd last been in the upper regions of the house. The access was via a narrow stairway with many creaking boards at the end of the second-level corridor. The wooden door at the top of the stairs gave way to the large black key. Inside was generic attic: dust, spider webs, and the smell of something she couldn't quite identify. There didn't appear to be any mold on the slanted wooden ceiling nor was it an animal smell. Perhaps just the smell of dust and memories. A hanging chain with a string attached turned on a dim sidewall light. There was a large black trunk of the sort that women of a certain class once packed for a long ocean voyage, a dark wood bureau with four drawers, an ancient secretary that Kate remembered used to sit in the salon, a stack of cardboard boxes with chewed corners. Apparently the cute masked pests had made it into the attic. A quick investigation of the boxes turned up many items that should have long ago been donated to a local jumble sale: a set of alphabet blocks, a faded barn jacket, an obsolete computer, two ancient mobile phones each the size of a large brick, a tangled mess of power cords, probably of the same vintage as the computer.

The black trunk appeared to be intact, as did the wooden bureau. The lower door on the oak secretary was hanging askew and the wavy beveled mirror was cracked, held in place with large chunks of grey duct tape. Kate straightened the door and pulled down the top opening that became a shelf-type writing desk. Behind the pull-down were half a dozen pigeonholes that had fascinated Kate as a child. She ran her hand over the knob on the small center drawer and the entire drawer slid out into her hand. She stooped down to replace it, then stopped. Behind the drawer, where there had always been a wooden divider, she glimpsed an opening. She reached into the opening and the entire arrangement of small wooden pigeonholes fell off into her hand and she stood staring into a stack of moldering envelopes wrapped in faded blue ribbon.

There were two stacks of envelopes, cream-colored, hand addressed in black ink. Kate leafed through them, noting the postmarks. The first stack, around twenty in all, addressed to Mrs Carmela Aragon at a PO Box in Dartmouth, carried postmarks from Sofia, Bulgaria and Nairobi, Kenya. The posted dates corresponded to the first three years Kate had been away at school in Oxford. The second stack of envelopes, eight in all, were postmarked from Istanbul and Kate was unable to decipher the dates. None of the envelopes carried a return address.

Kate extricated the top envelope from the Istanbul group, pulled out the single page of cream-colored stationery with its distinct crest at the top of the page. The sheet was covered in the black backward-slanted handwriting that Kate knew well.

My dearest,

I am just returned from what should have been, at the least, a fascinating evening. I dined with four friends, all CD personnel, at the Four Seasons on the Bosphorus, amazing setting, Italian chef. It was nearly more than I could manage to keep up my part of the conversation when all I could think was how deeply I miss you and what a different sort of evening it would be were you sitting across the table from me. We would have ordered your favorite red wine and shared the eggplant begendi and ended with a baklava and a cafecito. I would have stared into your wonderful dark eyes the entire evening, knowing that the night would go on and on, wrapped about your beautiful body. I cannot stop thinking of your velvety skin, and that delightful mole below your right breast.

I most enjoyed your last epistle, and I share your concern for Kate. I'm not sure Lyon was the best choice and I know she's been troubled by Kincaid's growing infatuation – I don't think it deserves any other term – for the woman in Jo'Burg. I had a background done on her and found some suspicious blanks in her vitae. I am debating whether to share them with him. What do you think, my love? I wouldn't offend him for the world. My devotion to the twins began with the drops of holy water at the fount in Dartmouth and continues to this day. I will always regard them as partly mine.

Sleep is overtaking me. If only you were here to share it with me. Sueña con los angelitos, amor de mi vida.

Always, David.

CHAPTER 62

The Quay, Dartmouth, County Devon

"The problem is, the Austins insist on following the old survey, laid out in metes and bounds, which differs by three feet from your father's survey last winter using GPS coordinates. The area of contention is behind the stables. They claim about 50 feet of the new fence is on their land."

With a large part of her brain still focused on the letters she'd found in the old secretary –love letters from David Chaucer to her mother --, Kate slipped out of her leather jacket and tried to focus on what Andy Cameron was saying. Sturdier than the last time she'd seen him, a bit pudgier around the jaw. His attire was Saturday casual, plaid shirt untucked over jeans. The blue eyes that peered over the rimless glasses were as kind as when he'd rescued her from the school bully when she was eight. The large window behind his desk gave out onto the wharf area where a small crowd of people were milling about.

"Are they just being berks?" she asked. "Do they want money? How can we make them go away?"

Andy laughed. "Austin is a bit of a berk. A 'principled' berk, so I've heard. But here's something he doesn't know: I spoke with your father's surveyor, who told me that there's a much larger discrepancy where their sheep pen is actually built on your land at the bottom of the hill."

"So, a little quid pro quo?"

"Exactly. I also know he's applied for membership at the yacht club. I could make that go either way."

"And if you offered to put in a word . . ."

"Precisely. I'll ring him this afternoon." Andy swivelled his chair to face the wharf. Whitecaps whipped across the bay. "Big turn out today for the regatta."

"I'm surprised you're not out there."

Andy grimaced and rubbed his right hand. "I got stupid in a race last month. Got my thumb wrapped in a spinnaker line. Lucky I didn't lose it."

"I'm very sorry about Chantelle, Andy. I just learned about it yesterday."

"Yeah. Shouldn't have happened. I told her to stay away from him." He removed the glasses, rubbed his eyes and replaced the glasses. "You've had your own losses. Way beyond mine. Any idea who the car bomber was? I haven't seen anything in the press."

Kate shook her head, thinking about the morning text from Koslov. "The Yard is working on it."

"Whatever that means." He stood up, put both hands in his back pockets. "Katie, it's been too long. I'd like to hear about your plans for Millview. Are you free to have dinner with me tonight?"

Kate smiled. "Not free, but available. I'm off for a run with Mum's dog, should be back at the house by three."

"Perfect. Pick you up at half five. "

CHAPTER 63

Postbridge, County Devon

After a five-mile run under heavily overcast skies and no glimpses of any spectacular cloud formations, Kate and Hawkeye arrived back at Millview at half past three, minutes before the new weather front moved in. Traffic was light, rain beginning to fall beneath a rapidly darkening sky. On the river road, half a mile from the house, she spied a blue Ford Focus parked in a layby, then a bit farther on, a man walking a black dog. The man waved and Kate wondered if it was the troublesome neighbor.

She left Hawkeye in the mud room to dry out his paws, grabbed a piece of cheese in the kitchen, hurried down the hall to the bedroom. She turned on the bedside lamp, peered out the window to the pool where small waves were sloshing about. Fatigued in every muscle, Kate lifted her arms over her head, pulled off the sweat-soaked black jersey and shook out her hair. Peeling off the black leggings, she heard Hawkeye whimper, then a sharp bark.

She padded down the hall in her underwear, opened the door to the mud room. She knelt down and gave the dog an effusive hug and scratched his ears. "We had a good run, Hawk. Now settle down. You're too wet and muddy to come inside just yet."

Back in the bedroom, she peeled off her underwear and stuffed it in the rattan hamper outside the bathroom door.

The water in the big marble shower was hot and strong. It was good to be home, away from the frantic pace of the city, away from all the ugly truths she'd discovered in France and Marrakesh. Away from the constant need to look over her shoulder, to dissemble, to disguise. She rinsed the shampoo from her hair and lathered her body in Tahitian body wash. About to rinse off, she heard a sharp bark that sounded like Hawkeye was inside the house.

Had Maggie come to feed the ponies? Was Andy early? Another bark, louder, the challenging bark Hawkeye used for strangers. Kate turned off the water and frowned, listening. Were the French doors to the pool area locked? She stepped out of the shower and wrapped a towel around her. "Maggie? Is that you? Andy?" There was no reply. Instead, she heard another bark from Hawkeye that broke off and ended in a whimper.

There was someone in the house. It wasn't a friend.

She'd left her mobile in the kitchen. She peered through the half-open bathroom door toward the bedroom door beyond, uselessly recalling Koslov's query: Do you have a gun?

Sod all!

She padded into the bedroom, thought for a moment, reached for the land line on the bedside table. She dialed 999, heard Hawkeye whimper again. The call was answered on the first ring. "What is your emergency?" Before she could reply, the line went dead. She heard a hard thud and another loud whimper, both sounds coming from the salon. She dropped the phone, jerked open the door, and moved quickly down the hall.

Hawkeye was crumpled against the wall, licking one hind leg. A dark-haired woman with hard dark eyes stood in the middle of the room. She was tall, nearly as tall as Kate, and wore a long-sleeved dark cotton shirt and long dark denim pants. Her hair was gathered into some kind of a knot at the back of her head. Her black footwear was low black boots. The land line phone that had been sitting on the grand piano lay on the floor among the wires that had been jerked out of the wall. One of the French doors leading to the pool was open. Had the woman already been inside before they got home? *Bloody hell.*

"Shut your dog up, or I'll shut him up permanently," the woman ordered. Apparently unarmed, she stared at Kate, arms akimbo, a mocking smile on her face.

The same face that Kate had seen on Jean Pierre Rousseau's computer screen at Interpol.

Nadia Sultan. The poison dwarf.

"Get out of my house," Kate yelled with a glance at Hawkeye, who was still curled into a silent ball against the wall.

The woman continued staring, looking her up and down, then smiled a mirthless smile. "So," she said slowly. "We meet. Kathryn St. Claire. *Sharmuta.* Filthy thief." She walked toward Kate and halted, four feet or so away.

"Get out before I call the police."

"You're not calling anyone, slut." Sultan squared her shoulders, arms hanging easily at her sides, continuing to examine Kate from head to toe with narrowed eyes. "I will destroy you, *Inshallah*." The woman gave a hoarse laugh. "*Kelbeh*! You escaped me once when your racy little car went up in smoke. This time you will not escape."

Kate struggled to breathe. This was the fiend who set in motion the events of the entire last ugly year. The car bomb. The death of her parents. Her own injuries and surgeries. All the empty, sad days of mourning and despair. All thanks to this one deranged woman.

Sultan chuckled. "You stupid bitch. You thought you could get away with it? Stealing my husband?" She gave another ugly laugh. "Let us see how your spook training measures up against the best that Sudan has to offer, eh, *koos*? I will crush your bones and tear your eyes out. Then we will see how much he likes you."

Sultan had the wherewithal to build a bomb. She'd been in Pakistan. This was no ordinary abandoned housewife. If Sultan had a bomb with her, it was not immediately visible. This was about bare-handed vengeance.

Since the night of the bombing Kate's will to survive had been in semi-hibernation. Now it was back, sharp and defiant, along with a profound, raging intent to avenge the deaths of the two people closest to her.

Afterwards, Kate was never able to remember

the details of the ugly struggle. What she did recall was the sudden lunge Sultan made for Kate's towel and the vulnerability of her nakedness. Then the weaving and closing and the striking hand and the sinking realization that the woman was better trained and that she, Kate, was way out of condition. She'd been stupid to ignore Kovlov's warning, stupid to think the bomber wouldn't try again.

She knew her own bare feet lashed out, that she tried a leaping kick and nearly lost balance on take off and twisted away from a whiplash counter with Sultan's foot. Then the circling back, gliding and turning. She felt a searing pain in her right rib cage and knew that Sultan's kick had torn her flesh. She knew also the Tahitian bath oil she hadn't had time to rinse off had helped her deflection. Twice Sultan caught her briefly, once by the shoulder, once by her ankle as she evaded Kate's kick. Each time Kate's slick skin allowed her to twist away. Then Sultan gave a loud shout and made a move Kate thought was a feint, and suddenly both of them were moving out the open French door into the wind, into a dense grey curtain of rain. With a great effort Kate twisted away, off balance, realizing that here, outside, any fall would be on hard stone.

Crouching slightly, arms spread, Sultan edged toward Kate. "I will crush you into little bits," she hissed. With an amazing rush of adrenalin, at a speed she didn't know she possessed, Kate moved forward, straight into Sultan's arms. Her face was against Sultan's wet clothing, against her breast, her arms around her waist. Then Sultan was an inch off the ground, then she was laughing, knowing there was no way

Kate could throw her. Sultan hooked her hands together behind Kate's back, preparing to crush her, but Kate was moving, carrying her mad opponent back, back, into the pool, and then with a scream, Sultan lost her, Kate's slippery body writhing from her grasp, both bodies hitting the surface of the pool with a tremendous splash.

As Sultan thrashed and kicked, Kate was immediately behind her, a forearm under her chin, clamping tightly against her throat. Using every remaining ounce of strength, she evaded Sultan's flailing limbs, increasing the pressure against her opponent's throat. Sultan was out of control, as if she had suddenly forgotten her training, feet kicking wildly, her hands scratching at Kate's arms, unintelligible gasps coming from her throat. She screamed something in Arabic. About to inflict the final squeeze that would extinguish her parents' murderer, Kate stared at the contorted body in her control, the wet black hair in strings over her face.

Stalking me. Planning my murder. Setting the bombs that killed two people.

Tightening her fingers around Sultan's throat she heard the words of one of her martial arts instructors, a Chinese woman. *To kill without being killed is an illusion.*

Inhaling a deep breath before the final crushing squeeze, Kate heard a shout. She raised her head and stared through the pouring rain into the barrel of a firearm held by a man wearing the custodian helmet of the Devon and Cornwall Constabulary.

CHAPTER 64

Whitehall, London

Deborah MacKenzie turned away from her computer and checked the time on the small ormolu clock on her desk. Only 2:35. Driving rain obscured the River. She stretched her arms and shrugged her shoulders nearly up to her ears, trying to loosen the shoulder muscles that had tightened while she'd worked on the report for next morning's meeting of the Joint Task Force. The report contained the updated names and bios on all the Russian and Chinese intelligence agents operating in the U.K. The list was far longer than she'd anticipated.

Her private phone line rang. Less than a dozen or so people had the number. She stared at the caller ID.

"Yes."

"Leopard here."

"What do you want?"

"I have a situation. I'm not on a secure line."

"Where are you?"

"In Devon. The mujaidaat, Nadia Sultan, tracked me down, tried to kill me. She confessed to bombing my car. She also killed Sheherazade."

Deborah sucked in a long breath. "Nadia Sultan? Fatima? She's in Devon?"

"She's at the Constabulary in Exeter. "

"Call me back on a secure line."

Deborah cut the connection and massaged her right shoulder muscle. She considered what St. Claire had said. The bombing of her car, the murder of her parents. The murder of the Syrian informant. What the hell was Sultan doing in Devon? How had she found St. Claire down there? When they got her back to London, she would recant whatever confession she might have made. A long shot at best. Even if they did build a case for any of the murders, it would be her word against St. Claire's and then the personal stuff between St. Claire and Kassar would come out. The press would have a field day with it. She could see the headlines in the *Standard: MI5 Operative Embroiled in Terrorist Love Triangle.*

Why the hell hadn't St. Claire just eliminated her?

CHAPTER 65

Devon and Cornwall Constabulary

Accompanied by Andy Cameron who had arrived at Millview only minutes after the constable, it was well after seven p.m. before Kate completed her report on the afternoon B & E and bodily assault by one Nadia Sultan. Cameron had not so much as raised an eyebrow as Kate provided a synopsis of her assailant's history, ending with the suggestion that the superintendent confirm with Scotland Yard and/ or MI5.

Now, en route to Cameron's office in Dartmouth with the promise of a semi-secure phone line and then supper, Kate rubbed her sore neck and checked her mobile. Three text messages: two from Dom Koslov requesting she ring him; one from Lorna's daughter Maggie reporting Hawkeye, with a severely bruised hind leg but no broken bones, would be overnighting with the local veterinary.

Leaning back against the smooth leather of the Fiat's seat, Kate brushed her still damp hair away from her face and watched the windscreen wipers trying to keep up with the hard rain. A sharp pain shot through her lower ribs. She gingerly touched the bandage. The gash from Sultan's vicious kick was deep and had most likely fractured several ribs. The bleeding had finally been stanched. After she rang Deborah back from Andy's office, she would get some stitches put in. Reflecting that she had probably left a trail of blood on the carpet, she replayed the sequence of events that began with Hawkeye's first warning bark while she was in the shower and ended with the mortal struggle in the swimming pool.

Thanks to the efficiency of the Constabulary's enhanced 999 tracking capabilities, the gun barrel Kate faced as she pondered the ramifications of terminating her vanquished assailant belonged to a Force Contact officer who happened to be in the Exeter office when Kate's aborted call came in. It had taken the better part of an hour, and Maggie's fortuitous arrival, to convince the officer that the struggle he witnessed in the pool, despite Kate's bloody ribs and total lack of clothing, had nothing to do with domestic violence, lesbian or otherwise.

Along with a dark blue abaya and face-covering niqab, the police had discovered a passport in the carry-on bag in the trunk of the blue Ford Focus issued to Salima Mansour, age 39, eyes brown, hair brown, height 5'6", with an address in east London. Neither the name nor the photograph matched those on the U.K. driver's license in Sultan's wallet.

Kate was only partially successful in convincing the officer taking her statement that prior to finding Sultan in her living room, she'd never laid eyes on her before, confining her statement to saying she believed Sultan was a person of interest to Scotland Yard.

The officer frowned and turned away from his computer. "You're Jonathan St. Claire's daughter. For

God's sakes, woman. Why didn't you say? Was that Sultan's work?"

"She confessed to it. The bombs were meant for me."

"If at first you don't succeed . . ." He shook his head, pressed a button on his mobile. "Jackson, get ahold of the Met. Looks like we've got a bloody terrorist on our hands."

CHAPTER 66

Postbridge, County Devon
to Hacking Wick, East London

On Sunday morning Kate awoke in her bedroom to a silent house and sullen skies. The storm front had passed through. After the conversation with Deborah MacKenzie, who'd already taken steps to put Sultan and her aliases on the Home Office's version of a no-fly list, there was a brief stop at the urgent care center in Dartmouth and a late, late supper on the wharf. Andy had deposited her back at Millview around midnight. She'd declined his offer to spend the night, promising to call if she needed anything.

The clock on the bedside table said 10:04. She'd been asleep for over ten hours. She attempted to rise from the bed and then fell back on the soft mattress. The pain in her ribs was excruciating. The adrenalin that sustained her through the ugly near-death struggle with Sultan was gone. She was running on empty. She lay back against the pillow, speculating on what might be expected of her on returning to London, heard her mobile chime. It was Dominic Koslov.

"You don't follow orders well, St. Claire."

"You mean Sultan? How the hell did I know she'd follow me? At any rate, she's behind bars. Or on her way to the Yard with two escorts."

"No. She isn't."

"What do you mean?"

"She escaped. Clobbered the two constables assigned to transport her, killed one of them. Broke his neck. They stopped at a layby on the M5. She took off with their vehicle. Whereabouts currently unknown. Cameras caught the whole thing. It's on the news."

Kate sat up, stifling a small moan of pain. "Koslov, you're making this up."

"Don't we wish. Where are you?"

"My parents' house in Devon."

"Who's with you?"

"No one."

"No cooks or stable people?"

"They're in Scotland."

"You're not safe. Not there, not in Knightsbridge. Can you get back to London today? My associate passed on some new evidence on Fakhouri's murder. I'd like you to see it."

Sultan was on the loose. Kate glanced around the room, at the open door, shivered, wondering if she'd locked all the exterior doors last night. "I'll get packed up. I'm driving back. Where shall we meet?"

"My flat. I'll text you the street address. St. Claire?"

"Yes."

"I know lightning never strikes twice, and all that rot, but we're dealing with a persistent killer."

"Otherwise known as a mujaidaat."

"Exactly. Text me your ETA."

It took Kate over an hour to get packed, tidy up the bedroom, compose texts to Lorna's daughter and Andy Cameron, and forage in the kitchen for fruit and croissant. She'd asked Maggie to please warn Lorna about the condition of the house.

Resisting the urge to read more of the letters she'd found in the old secretary in the garret, she tucked the packets into her suitcase. She held in her hand for several minutes the brass key she'd found beneath the letters. It was an ordinary key, attached by a tarnished silver chain to a silver medallion in the shape of a sailboat. Was that where they had met all those years? Sir David's sailboat in Dartmouth? Had her father ever found out?

She placed the key in her travel handbag and did a final walk through of the house, stood for several minutes in the salon where the fight with the ninja had started. The phone still lay on the floor with the wires that had been tripped out of the wall. Ruefully she picked it up, placed it on the piano, straightened two chairs, rearranged two cushions on the chesterfield. Thank God Lorna and Emerson were away. Heading for the bedroom, her foot crunched something small in the carpet. She picked it up. It was a plain gold band. A wedding band with an inscription inside. The initials "N" and "T" joined by a minuscule rose.

Five minutes later, carrying her coffee in a commuter cup, she wheeled the suitcase out to the old Bentley. It sat in the gravel driveway, unlocked, where she'd left it when she and Hawkeye returned from their run in the Park the day before. Not that anything would have been accomplished by leaving it in the garage with no security.

She scanned the area around the house and garden, circled the vehicle twice, checked the undercarriage with a torch. Remembering what Koslov had said about VBIEDs that were wired into the ignition –" crude and old fashioned," she opened the car door, released the hood, checked under what she thought was the fan belt. Nothing. If Sultan was smart, she'd either be fleeing the country or losing herself in the city. But vengeful jealousy didn't usually equal smart.

With a deep breath, trying not to twist her torso, Kate lowered herself onto the leather seat, closed the door, stared at the ignition key for several seconds, then turned it. The motor turned over, purred softly. She exhaled and shifted into reverse.

CHAPTER 67

Sir David Chaucer swirled the Scotch in the cut glass tumbler and carefully placed it on the oak table between the two overstuffed chairs upholstered in burgundy colored fabric. "If you can believe the bartender," he murmured, gazing around at the framed portraits on the dark wood walls, "This particular drinking establishment hasn't been closed in 200 years, Peter."

"And quite the den of decadence and depravity, I understand, while it was still a chocolate house."

"I've heard it said that there are but two things an Englishman cannot command. The first being made a Knight of the Garter . . . "

". . . and the second becoming a member of White's."

"Having attained the second, perhaps I should aspire to the first."

"Is it the blue velvet mantle you lust after?"

Peter Szabo chuckled. "No, my friend, it's the bonnet. The white ostrich and black heron feathers." Peter nodded to the hovering attendant. "Another round, Jason."

"Levity aside, Peter, I'm glad you rang today. You know I consider White Blossoms as the first step of

273

what you and I know is The Only Solution."

Szabo stared into the crystal glass and sighed. "It's the only way. To keep taking out the leaders and retake the territory in Yemen and West Africa. One sodding country at a time. A lot of wet work, David."

Sir David smiled. "The Prince is pleased with your report on White Blossoms. He became quite euphoric over the addition of the drones."

"Impossible to fight a war without drones." Szabo frowned. "Five have been delivered, but there's a delay with the second shipment."

"Of drones?"

"No, the ammo for the AK'47's and the RPG's. I'm trying to determine if Semchov is holding us up for a bigger commission or if he really can't get the export certificates from Bulgaria."

"Perhaps I can help. You remember I spent two years at the Embassy in Sofia. Mostly issuing passports."

"So you did. I recall Helene said Ann was not overjoyed at the posting."

"She referred to it as the Dark Ages of our marriage. Although the real Dark Ages were Riyadh. Not for me, but for her."

"I gather she didn't take to the ex-pat life."

"The truth? Ann didn't take to me. I don't know if she decided that before or after she met the Greek banker." The attendant arrived with the tray of drinks, retrieved the empty glasses and replaced them.

"Is that where she is now? Greece?"

Sir David chuckled. "I think the Greek banker has recently found himself in straightened circumstances. The latest postcard I received was from Corsica. Your Helene is with her. Now tell me why you rang, Peter."

"Do you still have contacts in Sofia? I could send either The Fox or Gingerman to scope out the situation, see what Semchov is really up to."

Sir David smiled. "I have a friend whose brother is Minister of something or other. I'll ring you with a name and contact number." He took a sip of the Scotch. "Kate visited me recently. Asked if Kassar had a connection to Six."

"What did you tell her?"

"I said no and she knew I lied but she didn't pursue it. What do you hear from The Fox?"

"Gingerman appears quite content in Dubai. Has a new sleeping partner. Daughter of an oil sheik or tycoon or whatever they're called there. Someone with an abundance of petrodollars or whatever's replacing petrodollars just now."

Sir David lifted his glass. "Quite a coup, my friend. Whose idea was the fatwa?"

"We can thank The Fox for that. At the end of the day your goddaughter deserves better than a quasi-reformed terrorist."

"So we've become a pair of pompous manipulating twerps."

"What else do insecure, big-bottomed bores have to do?"

CHAPTER 68

Postbridge, Devon to Hackney Wick, London

Four hours and fifty minutes after leaving Mill-view, with one pit stop, Kate exited the A106 and headed to Hackney Wick, an inner city development five miles Northeast of Charing Cross. Despite its industrial past, a number of trendy bars and bistros had recently opened, and new developments were planned, the latter already giving nightmares to the creative types who populated the area. Wherever she might have expected the Cuban Russian Detective Inspector to hang his hat, it wasn't the three-bed-room brick Georgian with a well-tended garden in the back.

Whoever had constructed or re-constructed Koslov's house had managed to create a small oasis. Inside, the house had a military neatness, from the all-white industrial style kitchen where Koslov was brewing coffee to the futuristic furniture in the reception. A rectangle of well-trimmed green grass fronted the glass box of a breakfast room.

Perhaps in sympathy with her bruised body, Kate was drained of emotion. She wondered what sins she might have committed in a former life to endure such bad karma in this one. Kincaid, her twin in body and soul, his plane lost en route to visit his girlfriend in Jo'Burg. Michael Farraday, another bad ending. Finally, her parents blown up because she unknowingly became involved with a man married to a mujaidaat. The more she thought about Sultan's confession – *Your racy little car going up in smoke* – the deeper the depression. And the mad perpetrator, still at large and likely to strike again.

Watching a large black spider swing softly on a perfect circle of silky web suspended against the wooden fence, wondering when it would be safe to return to the flat in Knightsbridge, Kate heard a phone ring in the kitchen.

Koslov answered the phone, spoke briefly, came into the breakfast room and placed two large white mugs on the table. He wore a dark red shirt open at the throat. The rolled-back sleeves exposed well-muscled brown arms lightly covered in curly dark hair. The blue jeans were faded, the brown leather sandals well worn. His bare feet were long and sturdy. Everything about the man exuded leashed power and testosterone.

The coffee was black and fragrant. Kate was far too exhausted to ask for milk. She hadn't wanted to take pain meds before driving and now the pain in her ribs was unrelenting, along with an ache in the back of her skull.

"You look like you've been run over by a truck. It would be dangerous to appear in public with you." Koslov propped his elbows on the table and scrutinized her face. "With that black eye, I'd probably get arrested. Do you feel as bad as you look?"

Kate reached for the white mug, cradling it in

both hands to steady the trembling. "Worse. I'd like to know who taught Sultan hand-to-hand combat. If she hadn't panicked when we crashed into the pool, I wouldn't be sitting here."

"You were *swimming* when she broke in?"

"Worse. I was in the shower."

"That must have been interesting. Sorry I missed it." He took a sip of the coffee. "Nudity aside, I just got a call from my superior. The vehicle Sultan stole from the constables turned up behind a warehouse in Tower Hamlets."

"Any video?"

"Fairly useless. Nearest camera shows it passing by at 2:40 a.m., then disappearing into a black corner. A warehouse security guard found the vehicle this morning."

"So she could be anywhere."

"The Met has redirected a camera on your Knightsbridge flat. She hasn't turned up there yet."

"Lucky me. I was away from the flat for three days last week. Someone breached the security system and then reset it." She lifted the white mug, drank, swallowed. "Good coffee, Koslov."

"Thank you. Did you report the breach?"

"I forgot. Nothing was disturbed or missing. Probably a malfunction. You said you found some evidence that might tie Sultan to my asset's murder? To Jamila Fakhouri?"

"It's on my laptop. Let's go look at it."

Koslov's office on the second floor faced toward the street. All the windows were frosted glass. The floor was worn wooden planking. His laptop sat on a tall table beside a tall bookcase. Kate stood behind Koslov and scanned the titles. *Crime Scene Analysis*. Chesterton's *The Blue Cross*. *The Complete Collection of Modesty Blaise*. *The Storm of War*. *Hitler: A Study in Tyranny*. *The Road to Stalingrad*. *The Hut Six Story*. More than a passing interest in World War II.

Koslov gestured toward the computer screen. "Video footage in Tavistock Square the afternoon Jamila Fakhouri was killed. Watch this." He scrolled across the screen, stopped, enlarged the shadowy shot of a black garbed figure approaching a park bench. Another dark garbed figure sat on the bench, holding a mobile phone. He scrolled further. The approaching figure blocked the view of the camera. "Look at the wrist of the figure behind the bench. He or she put their left arm around the victim." He advanced the footage, halted it, zoomed in. "Look at the bracelet."

Kate peered at what first appeared to be a woman's wrist watch. She leaned closer. "It's a bracelet on a black cord. A white horse."

"Does a white horse mean anything to you? Anything ritualistic?"

Kate frowned, trying to remember. Something from the Qur'an? Or the Bible? Something Tariq read to her. A comparison of Biblical Revelations and . . . what?

"'*I looked up and saw a white horse,*'" she recited slowly. "'*Its rider carried a bow . . .*' I can't remember the rest. It's from Revelations. The first of the four horses of the apocalypse?"

"I probably looked at that shot a dozen times, thought it was a wrist watch. I found the source in

Croatia. I called them. They've sold thousands of them online, including several hundred in the U.K."

"So?"

"Did you hear that a judge's chambers were bombed in the City on Friday night?"

"Missed it. I was on my way to Devon."

"The judge recently detained two young women from Manchester to prevent them from traveling to Turkey. They're still in custody. It's not been released to the press."

Kate rubbed her lower back and winced.

"You're in pain. Sorry, St. Claire. Let's go downstairs. I can offer wine or hydrocodone."

CHAPTER 69

Tower Hamlets, East London

The Uber cab came to a stop in front of the stone passageway on Fournier Street. The block was empty, no flashing blue lights, only a hard driving rain splattering against the sidewalk. The Ethiopian driver turned and looked back at the passenger he'd picked up at three a.m. in front of the Urgent Care entrance on Whitechapel Road. "Thirty," he said.

"I'll be right back with the fare. Don't leave, I'll need you later." Ignoring the driver's protestations, Nadia Sultan climbed out of the cab and raced through the passageway to the courtyard. The key Salima kept hidden under the giant pot of geraniums was covered in mold and grime but it opened the door. The flat was dark, empty and silent. She stumbled down the hall to Salima's bedroom, found the door open and clothes strewn on the bed. Salima was probably overnighting with Hani.

She raced back to the kitchen, turned on the small light over the range, found a torch in the drawer next to the sink. The stash of money was in the tiny safe behind the faux vent in the kitchen. She pulled out the vent, entered the combination, found the thick roll of bills tucked behind the two passports and the stack of I.D. cards and credit cards. Giving thanks yet one more time to Dervish, she peeled off forty quid and raced back to the waiting cab. "Keep the change. I'll need a ride in 30 minutes. Will you come back?"

The driver nodded, counting the bills. "I be here."

Back inside the flat, she locked the door, headed for the bathroom. She closed the door, turned on the light, peeled off the orange scrubs she'd appropriated in the supply closet at The London Hospital. It had been ridiculously easy, the intake nurse occupied with a distraught woman and two crying children. Then telling the Uber driver she'd just finished a long shift in the maternity ward.

She stripped down to her skin, shook out her still damp hair, regarded herself in the mirror. Two large cuts on her forehead, huge bruises on her neck beginning to turn purple. Pain in one wrist that was hopefully only a sprain. She took a deep breath, fighting off panic. She could still feel the water closing over her head. Never had she imagined she'd be so grateful for the arrival of the constabulary.

There were CCTV cameras all over Tower Hamlets and especially at The London Hospital. By daylight her face would be all over the news. *Female prisoner escapes constables, leaving one dead.* Within hours if not sooner, police would be pounding on the door with a warrant. She had to get her face off the streets. No time for a shower. She threw the scrubs in the laundry hamper, found clean underwear. She washed her face quickly, applied antiseptic to the abrasions, patted on moisturizer and then foundation. From the closet she pulled out the black jersey tunic and black trousers, laced up the black trainers.

Chagrined at the thought of the bag she'd packed so carefully and left locked in the boot of the blue Ford Focus, she scrabbled in the bottom of her closet for a large black leather handbag. She filled it with the essentials, unplugged the small black burner phone she kept charging on her desk. Back in the kitchen, she opened the hidden safe again, was reaching for the passports and credit cards when she heard a pounding on the front door followed by a shout. "Police, open up." She froze, kneeling on the floor.

More pounding, twice, then three times, one final shout. Then silence. From outside came the sound of a vehicle accelerating, then silence again.

Trying to control her trembling fingers, Nadia tucked the passports and credit cards into the hidden zipper space at the bottom of the bag, locked the safe, stood for several minutes at the kitchen door. When she went to the front door, she peered out the sidelights. The street was beginning to lighten, rain tapering off. There was nothing forensic to link her to the judge's chamber, but the trip to Devon had been a mistake. Nearly a fatal mistake. How had she so underestimated the whore? She was still having a hard time shaking off the deep, deep depression that had descended when she'd been chucked into the backseat of the police vehicle.

She started to hyperventilate. She took a long, slow breath, then another, pressed one fist against her mouth. The original plan would have eliminated both the whore and the traitorous flatmate. Now it was ancient history. No point in striking cold iron.

She needed access to a computer. Her own laptop she'd left stashed in the boot of the hire car. She moved into Salima's bedroom, found the white laptop on the bureau. She pressed the power button, waited for what seemed an eternity, then smiled as the Start Up screen appeared. No lock, no password. So trusting, her flatmate.

On the Internet, she logged into her own email. Trying desperately to steady her wildly beating heart, she found her itinerary. The flight was leaving from Heathrow in four hours. She had to be on it. She sent one brief and one longer message, erased the sent messages, shut down the computer. Back in the entry foyer she peered out the sidelight one last time. The Uber driver had returned. She belted the Burberry and wrapped the black scarf closely around her head. As if by reflex, one hand went to her chest, feeling for the ring. It was gone. She must have lost it in the pool. Locking the door behind her and heading out into the rain, she prayed that Saffaya's shop would be open.

CHAPTER 70

Hackney Wick, East London

Kate opted for the wine, a three-year-old Montepulciano that Koslov poured into two crystal glasses. "I'm not going to let you go home until Sultan is behind bars, but I'm not a bad cook. Take it slow on the wine. It's going to be a long evening." Before Kate could retort that she was perfectly capable of taking care of herself, he disappeared into the kitchen.

A disk snicked into place on the CD player. Kate took a slow sip of the wine and leaned back gingerly in the dark leather chair. The guitar chords of an Afro-Cuban piece drifted from the four speakers. From the kitchen came the sound of a refrigerator opening and closing, the muted clatter of pots and pans. A telephone rang and rang again.

Kate reflected on her aborted visit to Millview and the discovery in the attic. How long had her mother and Sir David been involved? Years? Decades? Both he and Ann had been frequent visitors to the farm. There had been family picnics, beach expeditions. When had it become something more?

Koslov came to stand in the doorway, wineglass in hand. "Police went to Sultan's flat. All dark, no one answered. For some reason no one can explain, the nitwits didn't have a warrant with them. By the way,

I should have warned you. Dinner will be leftovers. Bouillabaisse. I made it last night for my sister."

"Does she live in London?" Kate asked, almost certain that Sultan wouldn't leave the country until she'd finished what she set out to do in Devon.

"Alicia's a dancer with the Miami ballet. She's in town for a special exchange performance of *Romeo and Juliet.*"

"Will you see her perform?" *If Sultan knew how to find her in Devon, then the woman would have intel on where Kate lived in London.*

"Nope. Don't like the way it ends. Never thought it was necessary to kill the two lovers."

"Your critique may be a tad late. I believe Shakespeare based the play on a 16th century tale."

"True. However, Prokofiev's original ballet score included a reunion of the two lovers. The purists made him change it."

"I didn't know that."

"Most people don't."

Another CD slipped into place. Tango, with a percussive beat. Kate smiled.

"Gotan Project. You like it?"

"Very much. Who are they?"

"Three talented dudes in Paris who play neo-tango. Eduardo, Phillipe and Cristof. I saw you checking out the poster in my office. Do you tango?"

Kate nodded. "Before she met my father, my mother was a dancer with the group that became the Compañia Nacional in Madrid. She taught me and my friends to tango. Our neighbors called it dirty dancing. Did you learn in Cuba?"

"Yes, and in B.A. and a few other places at the end of the world."

CHAPTER 71

Dubai

Early morning here is my favorite time, just after sunrise and morning prayer, before the desert heat descends. I love sitting here as the sun rises, clothed only in this caftan Yazmin gave me – a color she calls Spanish red. The sliding doors are wide open, with nothing between myself and the air and the water. The villa was designed in the elegantly simple style of the Swiss architect Le Corbusier, similar in style to the Villa Savoye, outside of Paris. Like the Villa Savoye, it is of unrelenting white with horizontal windows.

Tariq Kassar aka Gingerman aka Mehmet Celik paused in his journal writing, reread the page, gratified he could still write in the literary form of Arabic. Briefly he considered the conundrum that despite the language being spoken by more than 300 million people – and that the greatest challenge to Western hegemony was currently from these same 300 million souls –- it was a language incomprehensible to the remainder of the world. Yasmin, the sister of a petrobillionaire client, was a designer who was educated at Sarah Lawrence and then Parsons School of Design in New York.

He thought about the sexy designer and sighed. He wanted to be able to tell her the truth about his marital status, but given the situation with the poison dwarf, such a discussion would not only put a swift end to their relationship but probably also a swift termination from the petrobillionaire client. Just as it would have with *l'anglaise*. But at least here, *inshallah*, he and Yasmin were out of Nadia's orbit of evil. Almost diabolically, as he thought about his "ninja wife," he glanced at the list of morning emails that had finished loading into the Inbox. One of the senders was Nadia. He considered deleting it without reading, and returned to his journal.

I will have to make one more trip for White Blossoms, perhaps two. S. is unhappy, he thinks it is my fault. My take on the delay is that the Russian wants more money and is holding the second package hostage and blaming it on the Algerians. I shared this with the Fox. He says it cannot be solved from here.

He glanced across the waters of the infinity pool rippling in the soft breeze.

Yazmin mentions often how lovely is the house. I know she is waiting for me to speak.

The last sentence, with its unsolvable dilemma, sapped his creative juices. No matter how he approached Nadia, it would be a deadly Catch-22. He shrugged, closed the journal, turned back to the email Inbox and opened Nadia's message. He girded himself for either protestations of eternal love or the vitriol of hatred. In the event, he found neither.

My dear husband: I know the past two years have been difficult and sad for both of us. After much thought, I have decided it is time to end this union which it does not appear will ever improve. I would like to visit you and discuss the documents we will need to void our marriage contract. I will be arriving in Dubai tomorrow. Your loving wife, Nadia.

CHAPTER 72

Tower Hamlets, East London

The Nigerian dropped her near the Liverpool Station. Rain poured off the roof tops and raced down the gutters in torrents. Two errands to complete, then she would be on her way, *inshallah*. She paid the driver, watched him drive away, then tucked a stray lock of hair under the head scarf and headed for the Batik Shoppe.

Tucked away in an alley, the boutique provided a viable outlet in East London for women's Indonesian attire. But Saffaya had diversified beyond the colorful sarongs and harem pants and sequined vests that were in great demand by western tourists wandering about after a Brick Lane curry dinner. It was this diversification, a handmade article from Sri Lanka available only on very special order for special customers, that was the object of Nadia's errand.

Nadia had spoken to Saffaya on the phone the day before she left for Devon. Saffaya's English was poor and she frequently lapsed into French. Nadia's French was limited.

There was a light on inside the shop, but the "Closed" sign was displayed in the front window. Nadia peered through the window and knocked on the wooden door with the peeling green paint. A small woman with smooth tan skin and long straight dark hair stood behind the glass counter, folding a stack of brilliantly colored silk shirts. She looked up and came to open the door. "Yes, madame?"

"I am Fatima. We spoke on Thursday about a special order." Nadia handed Saffaya the small angel pin. Saffaya glanced at the pin and handed it back, then looked pointedly at her watch. "You said tomorrow, *non*?"

"I'm sorry. There was a small change of plans. Is the order ready? I only need one this morning."

"Please to come in." A string of brass bells accompanied Nadia's entrance through the door. Muted Egyptian music filled the shop.

"You want only one? Not ten? You not want me to come to the meeting next week?"

"I need one now. We still want you to bring the rest to the meeting."

Saffaya gave her customer a long look and moved toward the door behind the counter, hesitated. "It is for an *event private* . . . ?" another hesitation. "Or a public event?"

Nadia bit her lip. "A private event."

"*Bien, madame.*" Saffaya disappeared through the swinging door. Nadia glanced around, her gaze drawn to a rack of what appeared to be satin harem pants. She had owned a similar pair in a shade of ice blue when she was eighteen. Her grandmother had made them. Nadia wondered what had become of the garment. The music changed from instrumental to vocal. Um Kaltoum and her famous *Enta Onri*. You are My Life.

The swinging door opened and Saffaya placed a blue and white piece of batik on the glass counter top. The vest was tailored to fit a woman's body. Bright sequins decorated the front. Nadia smiled, staring at the sparkling decorations. It looked almost . . . bridal.

"It is perfect."

Saffaya opened the vest. "Seven pockets," she said. She tapped one of the pockets. "Instruction page inside. You travel out of the U.K.?"

Nadia nodded.

"May one ask, where you travel to?"

Nadia tore her gaze from the vest and looked at Saffaya. She hesitated, then shrugged. At the end of the day, what did it matter? "I am going to Dubai."

"Ah, you must see my cousin when you arrive, so you can fill the pockets."

"Where will I find your cousin?"

"*Dans le souk d'or.*" She removed a business card from the carved wooden box on the counter, wrote several words on the back, handed it to Nadia. "I advise her you are arriving. She have a package for you. Give her the card. Say you come for the silver bracelet."

Saffaya touched the detonator. "It is sensitive, madame. Just a small, what do say? A small press, yes? *Et voilá.*" She folded the batik garment and put it in a silver bag with woven red handles. "*Bon voyage, madame. Et bonne chance.*"

CHAPTER 73

Dubai

On Tuesday morning, in an attempt at normalcy, Tariq Kassar made the usual morning entry in his journal. *The second package has been released. Turkey has given permission for the flyover of humanitarian aid to Damascus. The Noor connection was a good one. The white blossoms will bloom again.*

Nadia arrives momentarily. I deeply dread any contact with her, but I will tolerate it, knowing that once we have signed the papers, I can begin to think about a real existence. A life with Yasmin, inshallah. Selim has drawn up the dissolution of marriage documents to include a generous financial settlement. It is so generous, it should keep the ninja from changing her mind, which is my greatest fear. Or, dissuade her from playing some twisted game.

His handwriting was distorted from nervousness. He stared at it in disgust, twisting the gold pen between his fingers. He checked his watch, tapping one foot on the tile floor. He glanced out the wide window to the garden where two stonemasons were constructing a hardscape around the pool. His mobile buzzed. He stared at the LCD, fearful it would be Nadia saying she had changed her mind. That she missed her plane. That she did not want the divorce.

He flipped the phone open. The caller was Yasmin, full of the details of her shopping expedition. She had returned from Abu Dabi two days ago. Because of internecine family matters revolving around her sister's upcoming wedding to a doctor in Alexandria, they had not seen each other, and Tariq longed for a night with her silken, perfumed body and lascivious tongue.

He stared out at the edge of the infinity pool and tried to focus on what she was saying. "I have cancelled my client appointments for the afternoon," she purred. "I will be finished about one o'clock. Will you be working at home this afternoon, *mon amour*?"

He shook his head in frustration, cursing Nadia's bad timing, cursing the day he met her, cursing life in general.

"Mehmet, are you still there? Is everything all right?"

He inhaled a deep breath. "Yasmin, *habibi*, unfortunately I have a commitment this afternoon," he said carefully.

"Is it something you could cancel?" she asked coquettishly. "For me?"

If only. With trembling fingers he moved the file of divorce papers into the center of the desktop. "Unfortunately, my love, I cannot, however much I might wish to. I will call you when I am finished. Will that be okay?"

Now there was silence on Yasmin's side. When she spoke, the warmth in her voice had dropped about twenty degrees. "Of course. I will wait for your call."

Tariq watched the mobile connection disappear, heard the front doorbell chime. He heard Ali's footsteps in the corridor, then the door opening. He stood, smoothed his hair, and walked into the hall as his wife, wearing a pale blue abaya and white hijab, came into the house, an elegant silver shopping bag in her hand. The letters on the bag said *Bijoux de Henri, Souk d'Or*. Ali closed the door and stood to one side, studying the pattern in the wooden floor. Tariq was the first to break the awkward silence. "*Salaam aleikum*, Nadia."

To his consternation, she moved to his side with a smile, kissed him gently on one cheek. *She had changed her mind.*

"*Aleikum salaam*, my husband. Thank you for meeting with me."

"Ali, bring tea to the salon." He turned to his wife. "Perhaps you would like to freshen up from your trip," he suggested awkwardly. "You could use the guest room." He gestured down the hall. She stared at him for a long minute, then she smiled, nodded, and moved softly away, carrying the silver bag.

Ali delivered the tea and Tariq dismissed him on an errand to the market. Ten minutes passed, then fifteen. Tariq brought the folder of papers from his office and placed them on a small table in front of the sofa. More time passed. Hands clasped behind his back, he began to pace the elegant room, a cacophony of memories flooding his brain. *The day Nadia's sister Raja'a introduced them. The training camp in Peshawar. The clandestine Hizb meetings in London, the trips to South Africa. Their wedding in Damascus. The*

Seven-Seven Bombings, his disgust with the lone wolf attacks on innocents, disgust with Nadia, the encounter with Hussein aka The Fox and the recruitment. The night he met l'anglaise. The last night he spent with her. He sighed deeply. It would soon be over, *inshallah.*

He heard the guest room door open, then the tap-tap of high heels on the parquet floor. As Nadia came into the salon, he stared at her in confusion.

Her dark eyes were highlighted in kohl. Her lips were rouged an iridescent pink. Gone was the all-enveloping abaya, replaced by a white gauze skirt, a white silk blouse under a white and blue batik vest with sequins. The white hijab partially covered her dark hair. Against her olive skin the white fabric was dazzling. He stared at the deep cleavage of her full breasts in the low-cut blouse. There was a sheen of sweat on her olive skin, a faint scent of orange blossoms. The overall effect was one of dense sexuality. Speechless, he felt himself become aroused and watched with astonishment as she moved toward him, saw her right hand reach under the vest, heard her murmur, "*Habibi.* Paradise awaits us."

Chapter 74

Whitehall, London

Deborah MacKenzie contemplated the stack of folders overflowing her inbox in order of priority and reached for the cup of Dragonwell tea. The tea was superior to the dreadful Japanese gunpowder brew, yesterday's selection from Gillian's sampler box. Vaguely nostalgic for a simple cup of Earl Grey, she delayed opening the first folder, turning instead to gaze out the big window to the River, nearly invisible in the pouring rain. Her computer chimed for an incoming message. It was from Gianni Taramelli in E-13 and consisted of five words. *Transfer reversed per your request.*

Deborah deleted the message, drained the cup and reached for the first folder in the stack. The file label read *Wen, Hulan.* Inside she found a short memo from Gillian: *According to my contact at the Home Office, Wen Hulan, aka Jenny Wen, a student at Oxford University admitted to the U.K. the previous September, passed through Heathrow Airport yesterday. Ms. Wen held a one-way ticket on Air China to Shanghai. Ms. Wen was accompanied by her uncle, Wen Yutan, Chinese Commerical Attache. Security photo attached.*

Deborah clicked up the photo showing a man and woman leaving the airport security area. The man carried an attache case. The female carried a bird cage. Deborah shredded the memo and photo and three hours later, as she prepared yet another report for the next day's Joint Task Force meeting, her stomach clamored for sustenance. She glanced at her watch, then at the next file in her inbox, hoping for something simple.

It was a report from Sara Johar, the operative who had been assigned to the Sisters surveillance. Along with the report was a brown package with a Marks and Spencer label. While the report was short, only a page and a half, it was far from simple. Deborah scanned it with mounting alarm.

. . .*went with a "friend" from the Mosque to a Sisters meeting in Leeds, address and directions shown below. There were eight women, including my companion, all were fully veiled, including niqab. I believe the woman known as Fatima was not present. The agenda for the meeting was the presentation by one Saffaya (surname unknown), a female of approximately 40 years (judging by her voice and her hands), nationality unknown (Sri Lankan? Egyptian? Syrian?), on the use of suicide vests specifically designed for women (see attached package). Vests are available in various batik patterns, with straps that go over the shoulders, and inside pockets for shrapnel and explosive. Saffaya modeled a vest and helped the other attendees try a vest on, and demonstrated how to add the shrapnel and plastique. She advised that the vest always be worn under an abaya and full face covering for maximum disguise. Each vest costs £50. Five of the women plus myself purchased one each. The meeting lasted approximate-*

ly an hour. I followed the other attendees outside as the meeting broke up. It was raining heavily and very windy. As Saffaya opened her car door, a late model Mini (plate # below), the wind whipped a bundle of papers out of her car. She tried to retrieve everything, but a small card was whipped out of sight behind a debris can. After she left I retrieved the card (see attached). Respectfully submitted.

As Deborah reached to open the Marks and Spenser package, her intercom buzzed. It was Gillian. "A priority delivery from Six, Ms. MacKenzie."

Deborah buzzed Gillian in, glanced at the Eyes Only red stamp on the front above her name. She ripped off the sealing tape, pulled out a single typewritten sheet of paper. It was a copy of a report from MI6's asset in Dubai. Attached to the report was a handwritten note from her counterpart at Six: *Tariq Kassar's wife, Nadia Sultan, left the U.K. Monday, destination Dubai.* Deborah lifted the note and read the report. Despite her best efforts, the corners of her mouth tilted up at the corners.

"Good news, Ms. MacKenzie?"

"Yes, Gilly, exceedingly good news. Please forward a copy of the Dubai report to Officer St. Claire."

"Will do. May I bring you some tea?"

"Do we have any Earl Grey?"

"I'll brew a cup just now. By the by, Ms. MacKenzie, you remember the, um- special guest we had at the hen party last year?"

Deborah frowned, stacking the loose papers on her desk. "Can't say that I do, Gillie. Should I?"

Gillian blushed. "The stripper. Black Irish he called himself."

"Ah, yes." Deborah continued organizing the papers. "Quite a stud, wasn't he?"

"I found a piece in the *Sentinel* this morning." She handed Deborah a news clipping. "Rather sad actually. I'll bring the tea in just now."

Deborah examined the clipping. **Malvern security consultant found dead in suspicious circumstances.** *Connor O'Connor, an IT specialist employed at 5th Dimension Security, Malvern, was reported dead on arrival at the Urgent Care Clinic in Southmoor yesterday morning. Police were called by O'Connor's housemate who declined to give her name and who was unable to rouse Connor. Cause of death is being attributed to poisoning, according to D. I. McIntyre of the Thames Valley Police who is investigating the matter.*

Deborah smiled, recalling a fragment from a Shaw play. *What use are cartridges in battle? . . . I always carry chocolate instead.*

CHAPTER 75

Covent Gardens, London

Late on Thursday evening, Kate St. Claire watched her barrister cousin and the CEO of Juno Capital Management execute a series of nearly perfect *molinetes* on the crowded dance floor of the Café Buenos Aires. Her thoughts, however, were on the two messages received from Deborah MacKenzie just before leaving Knightsbridge.

The first was a brief text: *Black Irish green file cleared. See me Monday for new assignment.* The second message was forwarded from an unidentified MI6 asset in Dubai. Even now, as the *tanda* ended and dancers began returning to their tables, Kate could see the image of the amazing words on the screen.

At 3:18 p.m. yesterday, an explosion was reported at the residence of Dubai investment banker Mehmet Celik. The residence was destroyed, as was a portion of a neighboring house. It is believed two people were in the house at the time of the explosion. No identifications have yet been confirmed. A taxi driver reported transporting a woman from the Gold Souk to the Celik residence thirty minutes before the explosion. According to public records, the property is owned by Talal Enterprises of London, U.K.

The Romeo solution. Who could have known?

Lost in thought, Kate touched the damp petals of the two red roses in the vase on the white table covering. The Argentinian owner of Café Buenos Aires circulated among the tables, greeting, encouraging, complimenting. Across the room his wife chatted with Gwen and Szabo at the wine bar. The musical piece that separated the *tanda* – the three-piece tango set -- ended. The opening chords of the *bandoneón* began a new set. Carlos Gardel was the singer, she thought, the legendary Argentinian baritone.

A tall dark-haired man came through the main door. White shirt against tan skin, faded jeans. His eyes searched the room, found her. He gave a small nod toward the dance floor. She nodded and stood up. Moving toward him, she felt a lightness of being.

"White becomes you," he said. She met his eyes, moved her left arm around his shoulder, felt his arm come around her tightly, completing the embrace.

"The lyrics of this song were written in the 40's by an Italian named Bigeschi," he said. "It's called *Caresses*."

There was the brief back and forth and they moved into the opening steps. Two steps backward, three quick ones, the cross, a long pause, the resolution.

She closed her eyes, absorbing the lyrics of lost love. Following Koslov's lead into a back *ocho*, she ceased to think. She felt the skin of his face touching hers, felt the silkiness of his shirt under her bare forearm, felt the clasp of their two hands. She inhaled his cologne, a soft musk.

There was a pause as they moved into silence.

His embrace tightened, boundaries fell away. Gardel finished another verse.

"One must dance the silences," she heard Koslov murmur. "One must dance the violins, even though they don't exist."

Wending their way back to the table at the edge of the dance floor, Kate heard Koslov's mobile chime. He read the text, smiled. "We'll have to miss the next *tanda*. Notilucent mesopheric clouds over the Eye. Let's go, St. Claire."

The End

Author's Note

In the interests of protection of the Security Services, let me assure my readers that MI5 is not the place I have described. I have never been inside Thames House and I have neither met nor spoken to any MI5 or MI6 personnel. The current Director and Deputy Director of MI5 bear no resemblance to my Hamish McTeague and Deborah MacKenzie. I have never met the chief of MI6; Sir David Chaucer is completely a fiction of my imagination, as are all the characters in the novel. There is no Ebony 13.

I have never been inside the offices of Scotland Yard. There is no Black Raven Wharf in London. Pablo and Alicia Repun, *tangueros extraordinarios*, who contributed over several years to my tango education in Florida and Buenos Aires, served as the inspiration for Café Buenos Aires, and introduced me to Gotan Project, but they do not live in London.

While London has numerous billionaires, oligarchs and clandestine entities, Peter Szabo and Juno Capital Management do not exist. I should most enjoy an invitation to White's, but I doubt that will occur in this lifetime. No person in this novel is based upon an actual person in the real world and any actual places are used fictitiously.

The mining of helium-3 on the moon may sound fantastical, however, if one can believe the press, an agreement to share such a project has already been made by China and Russia. Hence, docking stations for space cargo craft are most likely on the drawing boards.

Acknowledgments

The author wishes to thank the following individuals for their input to *Going Dark*, as well as expressing gratitude once again to the First Readers who perused, commented, and inspired various iterations of this novel: Barbara Angel, Linda Cassens, Donna Donahoo, Nan Droz, Sandy Eldred, Wayne Eldred, Rosalie McCreary, Eleanora Peluchiwski, Ann Ponzi, Don Thompson, and Louise Wells.

SHARON DUNCAN is a recognized linguistic scholar, former university lecturer, a tango dancer, and accomplished saltwater sailor. She is the author of the Friday Harbor (Wa.)-based Scotia MacKinnon mysteries and the Officer St. Claire novels. She divides her time between the Pacific Northwest and a hideaway on the Gulf of Mexico.

Also by Sharon Duncan

Death on a Casual Friday

A Deep Blue Farewell

The Dead Wives Society

The Lavender Butterfly Murders

Our Agent in Mayfair